Indigo Incite

Jacinda Buchmann

Many thanks to

my mother, Claudia, for without your help, this book may never have reached completion.

and to

my grandma, Carrol, for your inspiration,

and to

my husband, Travis, for believing in me.

CONTENTS

1 TYLER AND TOBY

Their foster mother's shrill voice hollered up to them, "Dinner!"

Tyler replaced the toilet bowl brush in its holster and turned to his identical twin brother. "I think that's good enough. Thanks for helping. I guess we should go down."

"Yeah, I guess so. We're having Brussels sprouts."

"Ugh, are you sure?"

Toby closed his eyes. "Yep, positive. I see a blue bowl on the counter, and that's definitely not broccoli in it. Please don't get in trouble tonight, okay?" The last time Tyler had refused to eat the dreaded green vegetables, he had been forced to scrub the kitchen floor with a toothbrush and then had been sent to bed without dinner.

"Don't worry. I learned my lesson last time. I won't refuse to eat them." He winked at his brother then bolted down the hall.

Tyler, Toby mentally called, from behind, *don't do anything stupid.*

Tyler ignored his brother and darted down the stairs.

Cybil stood with hands on her hips when he entered the kitchen. "Chores all done?"

"Yep."

"Homework?"

"Uh, no. Not yet. I've been doing chores since I got home. I'll have to do it after dinner."

"How hard could eighth grade homework possibly be? It shouldn't take that long."

He wanted to say that he was faced with at least four hours of homework, to include studying for an algebra test and writing a history report, but didn't want to get into an argument. The last time he had dared speak against her, he had been grounded for two weeks; so instead, he changed the subject. "What's for dinner?"

"Tuna casserole, French bread, and Brussels sprouts." She

stared him down as though she dared him to complain.

Tyler glanced at the blue bowl of vegetables. The smell made him want to gag, but instead he said, "Mmm, I like French bread." Apparently unaffected by the dinner selection, he grabbed a pitcher out of the fridge and poured a glass of juice.

Toby entered the kitchen a moment later and glanced from the blue bowl to Tyler. *You seem too happy. What are you up to?*

Tyler smiled at his brother. "Would you like a glass of juice while it's out of the fridge?"

"Sure," Toby said, as he sat at the table. "Thanks."

Tyler poured juice for his brother and then grabbed both glasses and sat beside him. He glanced from Toby to the blue bowl and smiled.

No, Toby thought to him. *I knew you were up to something. Don't do it. Cybil will be pissed.* Having a telepathic connection with his brother definitely made conversations around their overbearing, foster parents, Kirby and Cybil Smith, more convenient.

Who cares? She can't be mad at me; I'm nowhere near the counter. He glanced at Cybil; her back was to them as she took plates out of the cupboard. Then he looked at the bowl. It sat about four inches from the edge of the counter. *Easy,* he thought. He focused his energy on the blue shape. It took only a few moments, and then it slowly shifted.

Tyler. Don't.

Shh...I'm concentrating.

He focused harder and before he had time to blink, the bowl lurched forward and crashed to the floor. A few Brussels sprouts rolled under the table; the remainder lay in a pile, amidst blue shards of glass.

Cybil swirled and stared open-mouthed at her ill-fated vegetables then she glared at him. "What happened?"

"It looks like the bowl fell." Tyler tried to hide all signs of amusement from his face. "That's too bad."

"You think this is funny?"

"No, Ma'am. I'm not laughing."

She continued to glare. *If looks could kill*, he thought. He could hear her thoughts. She wanted to say something. She wanted to blame him but knew that it couldn't have been his fault.

"Clean it up!" she snapped.

"Yes, Ma'am." He cleaned without complaint, and after he had dumped the last of the round, green balls into the garbage, he returned to the table and ate in silent glee.

*****

Wickenburg, Arizona was a small town, and so, without a lot to do, the dollar store had become a popular hangout. One day, after school, Tyler decided to tag along with three boys who were in search of hot girls and book report supplies. One of the boys, Carlos, split off from the group to talk to a group of girls, and the other two boys, Jake and Max, went in search of poster paper and markers.

Tyler decided to buy a bag of chips to munch on, for the walk home, and headed for the snack aisle. After he rounded the corner, he spied his two missing buddies. Obviously not in search of book report supplies, Max appeared to be on the lookout while Jake stashed a load of candy into his open backpack. Unwilling to be caught and associated with them, he decided that it would be best to leave the store before any trouble brewed, lest the boys get caught in the act.

He turned, in hope that his friends hadn't noticed his presence. Then he paused and returned to the head of the candy aisle. He took inventory of the scene and noticed a tall display of Cracker Jacks, positioned directly behind the boys. *Hmm...should I?* he wondered. He smiled. The opportunity was too good to resist.

Tyler focused on a box at the bottom of the stack. It slowly began to wiggle. He imagined it slide out and forward, and then it happened. Before he had time to reconsider, the box slid out and fell to the floor; it was promptly followed by the entire display which cascaded down onto the unsuspecting boys.

Tyler had hoped to escape, unnoticed, but a group of onlookers, Carlos included, rushed up from behind to check out the scene. He tried to retreat but was pushed forward with the crowd. When they reached the mess, Max and Jake stood to brush off flakes of the caramel popcorn that had sprung from some of the boxes.

They turned when the voice of the gruff, store manager shouted, "What is going on here?"

Jake looked at Max and hollered, "Dude, we've gotta get out of here!" Then, he rushed to Tyler and said, "Here, take this. Come meet us later!" He tossed Tyler the backpack, and the two hooligans ran out the front door before they could be incriminated in any wrongdoings.

"Who's responsible for this mess?" the manager demanded.

"They were." Tyler pointed to the two boys who ran out the door.

"Alright, I want all you kids out of here!"

More than happy to follow this command, Tyler was shocked and scared that he still held the backpack filled with Jake's loot, and he wanted nothing more than to be rid of it. First he would have to escape from the crowd; then he would find a place to stash it.

He turned to leave the scene but stopped when a girl shouted, "Wait, Mr. Gregory! Stop that boy with the backpack. I saw it all on the cameras from the back office. He's stealing candy!"

"Wait a minute, Boy," said Mr. Gregory, the manager. He placed a hand on Tyler's arm, and then turned to the employee who had viewed the security camera. "What's this all about, Lindsay? You say this boy is stealing?"

"Yes, Sir. Well, that is, those other boys were. I saw them stuff a bunch of candy in there." She pointed to the backpack.

Mr. Gregory glared at him. "What do you have to say, Young Man? Would you care to open your backpack and show me what's inside, or do I need to call the police and have them take a look? There's no point in running. Everyone knows you and your twin brother, whichever one you are. You live up at the Smith's place. If you take off, we'll just send the police after you."

Tyler's hands trembled, and his heart thudded like a drum. *How am I ever going to get out of this mess?* he wondered.

"It's not my backpack, Sir. Max and Jake tossed it to me when they ran away."

"And why would they do something like that?"

Tyler gulped. "I don't know, Sir. Honest."

"Well then, I guess if it's not your backpack, you won't have a problem opening it up, so we can have a look."

He was in a no-win situation. If he refused, Mr. Gregory would call the police, who would arrive to find him with the stolen merchandise. They would assume that he was equally guilty. However, if he complied and opened the backpack, they would assume that he was an accomplice.

When Mr. Gregory realized that a crowd of onlookers had formed he said, "Why don't we take this up in the back office. Lindsay, would you lead the way, please?"

There seemed to be no other choice. Followed close behind by the manager, Tyler reluctantly followed Lindsay to the back of the store. He could feel the eyes of the customers follow his every step and could hear their incriminating thoughts. *I knew that boy was no good from the moment he arrived. Wait til his mother hears about this.* He didn't have to look to know that particular thought came from Cybil's friend, Georgia. *She's not my mother!* He wanted to shout back but kept his eyes forward and continued to walk.

In the end, charges were filed against Tyler, Jake, and Max. The judge let all of the boys go with a few hours of community service, but that wasn't enough for Cybil. After his community service hours were complete, she made arrangements with a military school, in southeastern Arizona, where he would be sent to "shape up and learn how to behave".

The news of military school didn't upset Tyler; after all, nothing could be worse than the treatment he'd received from the Smith's. It was the news that he would be separated from

Toby, for the first time in his life, which he found to be unbearable.

2 CONTACT

Tyler ran a hand through his tousled, floppy, brown hair, disarrayed from the wind and took a deep breath. He had decided to spend the day communing with the horses. Outside, the wind pounded against the side of the barn and fought a nearby gate as the latch reverberated in squeaky rhythm, but inside, he found peaceful sanctuary. Most of the other boys avoided the close confines of the barn, claiming that it stunk. Tyler couldn't have disagreed more. He found the slight odor of manure mixed with horses and hay to be peaceful and comforting.

He couldn't believe that he had been at BRATS for almost two and a half years. No one was certain if the founders had tried to be intentional in their creativity, when they had ironically named their facility, 'The Boys Rehabilitation and Treatment School'. The title had been shortened to B.R.A.T.S.; and so, it followed that the students of the school came to be referred to as a 'Brat'.

His favorite aspect of BRATS was the fact that it offered equine therapy. The boys were encouraged to befriend the resident horses. His counselor had explained that time with the horses was supposed to be healing or something like that; he really hadn't paid attention. He did like horses though and was happy to escape to the barn whenever he had the opportunity.

When he picked up a handful of hay, MacGuyver stamped, impatiently, for his friend to feed him. The horse eagerly accepted the proffered hay and after the snack had been disposed of, he once again stamped his foot.

"You still hungry, my friend?"

In response, the black gelding sent an image of an apple to Tyler's mind. "I love ya, old buddy, but it's freezing outside. There's no way I'm going back up to the kitchen to fetch you an apple."

Another image popped into his head; this time, he envisioned a small bucket of apples in the corner of the barn. "Oh, yeah? Someone must have brought that in since yesterday. Let me see if

I can find it."

It took only a minute to locate the metal bucket of red apples. He found it in the back corner, beside a shovel. He selected the largest McIntosh off the top and took it back to his friend, who promptly gobbled it up.

When the gelding's appetite had been satisfied, Tyler selected a brush and opened the stall door. He gently caressed the horse with the brush, and then took extra care to lightly massage each leg. Spoken words were unnecessary as the two settled in to their comfortable, weekly routine.

After some time had passed, Tyler's thoughts drifted to the horse. *I'm worried about my brother. He usually chats with me every night, and I haven't heard from him in three days. I've tried to contact him, but he hasn't responded.*

The horse seemed to sense Tyler's concern and gently nudged his arm with his head.

I know I shouldn't worry; it's just frustrating not knowing what's going on. Toby's always been the one to have a sense of what's going to happen. I wish I could see the future like he can.

His thought was answered, not by the horse, but by Toby. *Who's your friend?* his brother mentally asked. Even with the distance that separated them, they still possessed the ability to telepathically communicate.

Tyler smiled. *Hey, Brother! I was just talking about you. This is MacGuyver. Since you haven't been in touch lately, I had to have someone to talk to. Where have you been? I've been worried.*

It's a long, weird story. These people came to the house a few days ago to talk to Cybil. They told her that I had a full ride scholarship to attend a residential, gifted school, in Scottsdale. Of course, she immediately took them up on their offer, and I was told to pack a bag then they whisked me away.

You're going to a gifted school?...Really?

Toby laughed. *Hardly! I wish that were the truth!*

So, where did they take you? Where are you?

I don't know. We drove a couple of hours, south, but after that I don't know what happened. They gave me something to drink, and it must have been drugged. When I woke up, I was inside a building with no windows.

What? That makes no sense! Why would anyone want to kidnap you? Who are these people?

They want to track down kids with special gifts. That's what I've gathered from one of my captors. At first, I tried to read his thoughts so I could find out what he was up to, but he caught on and started to block me out of his mind. It turns out, he's just like us, and he could hear my thoughts, too.

He gave me a list of names, Toby continued. He explained that they were the names of other kids, under surveillance, who potentially had unique gifts. He asked me to look at the list and use my ability to "sense" if any of them should be brought in, like I was.

You didn't help him, did you?

I did. Toby sounded ashamed. I didn't want to. I held the list in my hands and looked at it. There must have been about fifty names on the list. I kept telling myself that I wasn't going to tell him. I wasn't going to help him, but as I looked at the list, there were certain names that popped out. I found myself saying the names out loud before I could stop myself.

So, what happens now?

You've got to figure out how to get me out of here, before they come after you.

They're coming after me, too?

Yeah and soon. They know that you're just like me, and they want you.

Tyler was speechless. Toby's story made no sense. How am I supposed to rescue you if you don't have a clue where you are? I want to help, but I don't know where to begin.

I know; that's the tricky part, and the problem is, you can't go to the police. Whoever these people are, they're powerful and they have connections. They've covered all of the bases. They have a gifted school, in Scottsdale, with real students. It's totally legit. And right now, someone is on their way to the Smith's house to inform them that I have run away.

Oh...so, where does that leave us?

Let me think on it. I've seen the future; as soon as Cybil and Kirby get the news that I ran away, they're going to pick you up and bring you home.

Ugh! No!

No, it's okay. It's a good thing. If you're at their house, it will be easier for you to get away.

Where am I supposed to go?

I'm not sure yet, but I'm working on it. You have to get away before these guys come for you. You have to find the other people who I identified on that list. I think they're the only ones who will be able to help.

How many others are we talking about? Do you know where they are? Do you remember their names?

I remember. There were four, four others. I don't want you to write the names down, though. If they find you, they'll find the list, and they'll know that I was able to contact you. I'll give you the first name so that you can meet him. Hang in there; if I'm able to contact him, I'll arrange a meeting for you.

Tyler couldn't believe that this was real. It seemed like some bizarre dream that he expected to wake up from, any minute. But somehow, it was real, and he was prepared to do whatever it took, to get his brother back. *Alright*, Tyler thought, *what's his name?*

Eddie, Toby replied. *Eddie Espinoza.*

3 EDDIE

The snow covered the top of Eddie's boots when he stepped out of his Jeep. It was light and fluffy and floated in swirls as he walked toward the Northern Arizona University science building. He was only eighteen but already a sophomore in college. He had graduated from high school a year early and had received a four-year scholarship to the university, where he was preparing to go to graduate school, to study quantum physics. There wasn't a whole lot that Eddie could learn from his classes that he didn't already know, and so he had convinced his physics professor to sponsor him in an independent research project of quantum physics. He had written a proposal for his study, and other than an occasional check-in with his professor he was basically left on his own to continue his research.

A small Volkswagen, parked near the entrance of the building, belonged to his friend Jenna, who no doubt, already waited for him in the physics lab. In her junior year, she was also working on an independent research project. They often made plans to meet at the lab, so they could toss ideas back and forth. Eddie suspected that her interest in meeting him went beyond academic. The way she looked at him and "accidentally" brushed her hand across his, left little doubt of her interest.

Her back was turned to the door when he entered. She wore tight, curve flattering jeans, and he couldn't help but notice the shapeliness of her figure, as she wiggled slightly back and forth with a mirror in hand. Two other mirrors were propped on a table and faced each other, about six inches apart. A lamp was angled to shine down on a small object between the two mirrors.

With a smile in his voice, he said, "Are we having fun, yet?"

She turned to him with a grin. "Hey, *Buuudy*! I was hoping you'd show up. I could use a hand for a few minutes, if you've got time."

Her gorgeous smile was contagious, and even though he was anxious to start his own project, so that he could make it home in time for Abby's party, he couldn't say no. "Sure, just for a little bit, though. Today's my baby sister's birthday, so I have to get out of here a little early."

"Oh yeah? How old is she?"

"Eleven."

"I don't know how to break it to you, my friend, but your little sister isn't exactly a baby anymore."

"Tell me about it."

He took off his winter jacket and hat and ran a hand through his short, tousled, black hair. "So, where do we begin?" He mischievously rubbed his hands together in preparation.

"I'm working to prove the theory of parallel universes, by using the reflection of photons. I've been working on it for a week; I'm just trying to figure out where to go from here."

Eddie wondered if a girl so beautiful was actually interested in him or if it was his imagination. Other than the black rimmed eye glasses he always wore, he didn't fit the stereotypical appearance of a quantum physics major. He supposed that he could be considered good looking. His broad forehead, high cheekbones, and large, crystal brown eyes were a combination of his Native American and Mexican heritage.

She had laid out several research books, and while she flipped through the pages of one, she unconsciously twirled a strand of long, blonde hair that had escaped its ponytail.

"Well, you're on the right track with the mirrors," he said, "that helps to prove the theory of infinity. The next step you need to work on is to prove that the electron can be in two separate universes at the same time. Once you get that figured out, you'll be on the right track."

Jenna looked at him with raised eyebrows and tucked the strand of loose hair behind her ear. "It sounds like you've done this before."

"Oh, I have. I was fourteen."

"*Fourteen*? You certainly didn't waste any time, did you? All of the fourteen-year-old boys that I knew were busy figuring out the theory of the best way to score with a girl. You probably had that figured out by the time you were eight, right?"

"Not exactly. I definitely chased after a girl or two when I was in high school, but I wasn't exactly head of the football team or anything. Most girls weren't too interested in the president of the physics club."

She smiled. "Well, I don't know why. Those girls didn't know what they were missing."

"Oh, yeah? You dated a lot of science nerds, did you?"

Jenna paused for a moment. "Well, not exactly; though deep down, I was a science nerd, myself. I just didn't announce it to the world. I had two older brothers who were both varsity quarterbacks. By the time I got to high school, my brothers had graduated, but my name was already known because of them. It didn't take much to become the cheerleading captain. I was very talented at cheerleading; don't get me wrong, but popularity will get you a long way in high school."

"And so naturally you dated the quarterback, you were probably the prom queen, and no doubt the class president, as well."

"Well, yes...and yes, but I wasn't the class president."

He laughed. "Oh, well in that case, forgive me for assuming."

"I was the vice president," she added, with a meek smile.

He chuckled. "How silly of me to assume. How did you ever end up here?" He indicated the science lab, around them. "Not exactly a place one would expect to find the cheerleading captain. Forgive me for being presumptuous."

"Don't worry about it. I know what you mean. Like I said, deep down I was a science geek. While I was busy going to cheerleading practice after school, during school I was acing all of the science and math classes I could take. I just didn't advertise it.

"Looking back on it now, I would have done things differently," she continued. "I had nothing in common with my quarterback boyfriend, and my lab partner in chemistry was one of my best friends. He was pretty cute, too, but I never gave him the time of day, even though I'm pretty sure he had a crush on me. If I could go back and do things differently, I would. These days I know exactly what I want and I'm not afraid to say so." She looked at him with a twinkle in her eyes.

Eddie caught the slight innuendo, and even though she presented the perfect opportunity to advance their friendship to the next level, he didn't pursue it. A relationship would only get in the way of his research. He would have plenty of time for dating, in the future. Perhaps after the semester was over, he would ask her out. Instead, he turned the subject back to her parallel universe study.

Time flew by easily as they laughed and chatted and occasionally remembered to work. Jenna's laugh made him smile. *Yeah, when this semester is over*, he thought, *I really need to ask her out*. He glanced at the clock and was shocked to realize the time. "We've been here for two hours? I need to get going, pretty soon."

Jenna followed his gaze to the clock on the wall. "We haven't accomplished much today, have we?"

"No, not really." He picked up his gray and black, knit hat and casually played with the dangling tassel. "It's all good. Sometimes the best work comes from just formulating thoughts. The next time I come to the lab, I'll be ready to rock and roll."

"Oh? You formulated a lot of thoughts today, did you?"

He tapped his head. "There's a lot more that goes on in here than you'd ever believe. Sometimes, it's scary."

At this, Jenna laughed out loud. "Scary, huh?"

"Mmm...unbelievably. I should get going. I don't want to be late for my sister's party. According to the forecast, the snow's supposed to continue to fall, and the roads are probably going to get nasty. You might want to get home before the roads get too bad. Can I walk you out?"

Jenna hopped down from the table and looked at the mirrors and other objects scattered about. "Sure, I don't think I'll be getting much more done here today, anyway. Like you said, I need to formulate my thoughts." She smiled sweetly. "Just give me a minute to put this away and I'll walk out with you."

*****

"Come on Eddie! Give it a swing!" his father called. "I can't stand here all day. My arm's going to fall off and I'm freezing. Get this thing open so we can get inside! One good swing, that's all we need."

"Yeah! Come on Eddie, you can do it!" his sister encouraged.

As a crowd of giggling girls gathered around, Abby handed him the bat.

"Alright, stand back, girls." He pushed his black glasses firmly in place and swung the bat a few times in preparation.

One quick, hard swing at the piñata was all it took; and suddenly, the girls swarmed his feet. They laughed as they dug through the snow in search of lost candy. His dad stood by to watch over the clean-up, and Eddie turned to his grandmother, who was huddled and shivering, in a snow parka.

"Hey, Grandma, want to go inside? I'll make you a cup of tea." He held the door open for her.

She smiled and patted his arm. "What a treat, thank you."

With a warm cup of tea in hand, his grandmother sat at the rustic, wood table, in the kitchen, and observed him. "You seem tired. Is everything alright?"

"Yeah, I'm fine. I just haven't gotten a lot of sleep the last few nights. I've had these dreams, really vivid dreams. Each night it's the same, and as soon as it's over, I wake up and can't stop thinking about it."

His grandmother sat in silent contemplation and sipped her tea. "You know, our people have always accredited vivid dreams to prophecy. The elders, your great-grandmother included, used to say that if we listen to our dreams, we will meet our destinies."

"And if we don't listen to our dreams? Then what happens?"

"Well, it is said that if we fail to receive the message that is brought to us, we will either continue to receive the message through other aspects of our life, or we may miss the opportunity to learn, altogether."

"Learn what?"

"That all depends. What is your dream telling you?"

"It's about a boy, a teenage boy, who I've never met. He keeps telling me that I need to meet him somewhere, that I need to help him."

"And where does he want you to meet him?"

"I don't know. I never asked. I keep waking up before I can get that far. It just seems so real; I don't know how to explain it. I've had vivid dreams before, but never anything like this. When I wake up, I can't stop thinking about the kid. It's like, if I don't help him, something bad is going to happen, and I can't stop thinking about it. Silly, huh?"

His grandmother slowly sipped her tea. "My boy, nothing you have ever said or done has ever been for nothing. I have no doubt that if this dream seems serious to you, then it probably is. If you have the same dream again, I would suggest you focus on it, instead of push it away."

"But, how can I have control over what I do in my dreams?"

"Even when you are asleep, you are always aware. Dreaming is just another state of alertness, of consciousness. Stay with your dream, remember who you are and why you are, and you'll learn what you need to learn." She smiled and patted his hand. Her own hand was weathered and wrinkled, strong and warm. It held kindness and years of wisdom, and as she touched him, he felt assured that if he had the same dream again, he would pay attention.

*****

A family of wild turkeys startled him when they squawked and thundered out from behind a tree. Large wings flapped, and they half ran, half flew across the path and were gone from sight, just as quickly as they had appeared.

"A little jumpy, aren't you?" came a familiar voice, off to his right.

The sun had almost set below the horizon, and it took a moment for Eddie to focus on the dark forest. Then he spotted him. He was tall and lanky, with shaggy brown hair that hung below his eyebrows and over his ears.

"I've been waiting for you to return," the familiar stranger said. "I hoped you'd be here. Did you think about what I said, last time?"

"Um...you're going to have to remind me. My memory's a little foggy. You wanted me to help you with something?"

"Not just me. You'd be helping yourself, my brother, and the others."

"Others? What others?"

"The others like us, with special abilities. If you don't help, we'll all be in trouble, including you."

They walked side-by-side, along the path. The snow continued to fall in hushed whispers, around them.

This was where Eddie's dream had always ended, but from somewhere deep inside, he heard his grandmother's voice tell him to stay with it and hear the message. "What do you want me to do?"

The stranger stopped and turned to him.

"I need you to find my brother. Find him and then the two of you need to find the others, before it's too late. They're going to come after you. You don't have a lot of time."

"Who's going to come after me?"

"The same people who took me."

Eddie was thoroughly confused. "Someone took you? What do you mean? You're right here."

"No...I'm not. It appears that I'm here with you, but it's just a dream. I came here to warn you, to get your help. They've captured me and they're going to capture you, too, if you don't help."

"Who are *they*? And where are you?"

"I don't know. I don't know who they are and I don't know where I am."

"Well, that's not a whole lot of helpful information, is it? How am I supposed to help you?"

"The first step is to find my brother. If you find him and then find the others, you'll find a way. You need to hurry before it's too late. I told my brother that you would meet him at the rodeo, in

Wickenburg, tomorrow."

"*Tomorrow*?"

"You have to. That's the only day that he'll be there and be able to get away."

"How will I know him when I find him? What does he look like?"

"He looks exactly like me. He'll be waiting for you."

"What am I supposed to do, once I find him?"

"Fly to Seattle."

"Seattle? As in, *Washington*? What are we supposed to do there?"

"You'll need to look for a girl. Along with you and my brother, they're also after her.

"So, we fly to Seattle, and then what? How do we find her? Do you know where she is?"

"Not exactly, but I'm working on it. I'll contact my brother once I know where she is. You need to get to her before they do. She'll be able to help. Once you find her and the others, you'll have to figure out a way to find me."

"What others?" Eddie asked, not for the first time.

"The people who took me are looking for others like me, like you. They know who you are, and they're going to come after you."

"But why?"

"You're powerful. They need you."

"*Powerful*?" This dream seemed crazier by the minute. It made no sense.

"Think about it and you'll know what I'm talking about. Now, can I count on you to meet my brother, tomorrow?"

"He's just supposed to come with me? What if I get charged with kidnapping, or harboring a runaway, or something? How old is he?"

"He's sixteen, and kidnapping is going to be the least of your worries if you don't help. Can I count on you?"

Eddie couldn't believe that he was ready to give serious consideration to this crazy scheme. But before he could consider the wisdom behind his words, he said, "Well, I guess it couldn't hurt to at least go and meet him. You said he looks like you? What's his name? What's your name for that matter?"

"I'm Toby. His name is Tyler."

4 THE RODEO

Tyler found Cybil in front of an open pantry, a bag of potato chips clutched in one arm. From the doorway he silently read her thoughts and attempted to gauge her mood. He hoped to find something in her head that he could use to his advantage.

I need to add dish soap to the shopping list, she thought. Then, she ran her fingers through her hair. *My roots are starting to show; I should see if I can get an appointment to get my hair done, before the dance, tomorrow night. I wonder if I should get a new dress, too? While I'm at it, I should buy Kirby a bigger shirt. I don't want his fat belly to be hanging out, as he swings me around the dance floor.*

Tyler chuckled under his breath as he imagined Kirby on the dance floor with his fat belly jiggling and exposed to the world. It was true though, Kirby had put on a few extra pounds since Tyler had been sent to BRATS.

With a game plan set, he took a deep breath and entered the kitchen. "Hey, Cybil, would you like me to finish the dishes?"

She bit into a potato chip and turned to him with glaring suspicion. He never offered to help around the house, and she undoubtedly wondered what he was up to. With a mouth full of chips, she said, "Sure, Kid, have at it."

He said nothing while he loaded the dishwasher but continued to listen to her thoughts, waiting for the perfect moment to make his pitch. With his back to her, he listened to her open the fridge and take out a beer. He waited until she had popped the top and took the first sip. It was now or never.

"So, the rodeo's tomorrow. I'll bet Kirby would like to take you to the dance. You two should get out and have some fun." He hoped this was the right thing to say. When it came to Cybil, nothing he said was ever certain to be safe.

"Oh, I was thinking about it." She reached up to stroke the dark roots of her hair.

"Oh, yeah, by the way, I got an offer to work, tomorrow, at

the fairgrounds. They need someone to pick up trash and stuff, for the rodeo."

The rodeo would be an ideal location to get lost in the crowds and meet Eddie. He had talked to his brother the night before, and everything had been arranged.

You've been back for less than a week, and you're already a pain in my ass. I don't have time for this, Kid, he heard her think. *I have to get my hair done and go shopping and—*

Before she could think of another reason why he couldn't go, Tyler said, "It's okay if you can't drive me; I'm sure I can get a ride from a friend."

He could hear her try to think of another reason why he couldn't go, when Kirby walked in the back door.

"Hi, Honey." He brushed past his wife, gave her a brief kiss on the cheek, and then made a beeline for the fridge, in search of beer. With his prize in hand, he plopped down in a chair, leaned back, and propped his dirty, work boots on top of the kitchen table.

"Sorry I missed dinner, but with all these extra people in town this week, everyone's calling me to come fix somethin'. The motel, out on the highway, had plumbing problems, and that new diner in town already had a broken toilet, and it's not even a month old yet. Tomorrow I need to head out to the fairgrounds to fix a few things I didn't have a chance to get to today."

"Oh," Cybil began, "I thought maybe you'd like to take me to the dance, tomorrow night."

"Hey, that sounds like fun. I won't be working all day; it'll just be few hours in the morning, then I'll have time to come home and pick you up."

"And *shower* and get *cleaned* up."

Kirby grinned. "Of course."

Tyler saw his opportunity. "I got a job offer to work at the rodeo, for a few hours, tomorrow morning. Do you think I could go with you?"

From the corner of his eye, he noticed Cybil shake her head and silently mouth the word "no", but it appeared that Kirby either didn't notice or simply didn't care.

"Sure, Kid, I can take you; but just keep in mind, you're only there to work. You won't be there to have fun and hang out with friends. Got it?"

"Yup. Yes, Sir. Thank you." Hopefully, Eddie would be at the rodeo, as promised, and Tyler would be able to meet him, away from the watchful eyes of his guardian.

*****

When lunchtime rolled around, Tyler had just finished up trash duty. He leaned against a hotdog stand and surveyed the crowd. Between the hot dog stand and parking lot was a corral where the bulls were penned, left to anxiously await their admittance into the arena. Tyler watched a group of cowboys work to get a struggling bull out of the back of a trailer and into the pen.

He took a bite of hot dog and looked beyond the corrals to the parking lot. A few vehicles drove in, stirring up dust in their wake. Among them was a Jeep that caught his attention. His eyes remained glued to the vehicle as it parked and the door opened. From a distance, the driver seemed to match Eddie's description. He was still too far away to be certain. *It has to be him*, he thought. His stomach tightened. The hotdog that had tasted so good going down, now felt like an unwelcome intruder. He needed this man to be Eddie. *What if it is him?* he wondered. *What if it's not him? Only one way to find out.*

As he headed for the parking lot, he tried to contemplate an introduction. What would he say to the guy? Halfway there, he spotted two small kids, about five-years-old. They had climbed the fencing to peer over the side of a bull corral. *Dumb kids*, he thought. *I wonder where their parents are?* He was about ten yards away, when one of the boys must have decided that he needed a closer look. He climbed to the top, placed one foot on the highest rail, and leaned over.

Tyler didn't have his brother's precognition ability, but it didn't take a psychic to foresee what was about to happen. He took off at a run toward the corral just as the boy's grip slipped, and he toppled forward, out of sight, behind the fencing.

His heart began to race as adrenaline kicked in, and he ran faster. He prayed he would get there before it was too late. The second boy remained perched on the fence and began to scream for his father, who was still nowhere in sight.

Without pause to rationalize a plan, Tyler leapt onto the fencing and scaled it to the top. He later thought that it, perhaps, would have been wise to appraise the situation first, before he entered the lion's den, or in this case, the bull's pen. He didn't pause though, and before he had time to reconsider, he had landed in the soft manure and dirt, beside the boy.

The child sat motionless. Tyler followed his transfixed gaze, to the massive bull, who had equally massive horns, aimed in their direction. He had seen it before in the movies; the bull snorts and stomps his foot a few times in preparation to charge. He could now safely say that this didn't just happen in the movies. Bulls did in fact snort and stomp, when angered. And angered he certainly must have been, for the bull lowered his head, shook it, and grunted.

Given the short distance between the fence and the animal, he estimated it to be about ten feet, he guessed that he might have time to get the boy hoisted to safety in time, but by then, he knew that the bull would be upon him and he wouldn't have a hope of escape. One slight move and it would charge. No time to reason, he needed to get the boy and himself to safety, before the bull decided that he had shared his pen long enough.

Tyler grabbed the boy's hand and helped him to stand. He placed a hand on the boy's chest and pushed him closer to the fence. He then took a slow step in front of him. Thankfully, the boy's state of shock had rendered him speechless; any sudden noise would further agitate the creature.

He kept his eyes trained on their probable tormentor, while he reached a hand behind his back and grabbed the boy's wrist. In a calm, hushed voice, he whispered, "When I say 'go', I want you to climb back up to the top, just like you did when you got in here. Do you understand?"

The boy whimpered but managed to whisper, "Uh, huh."

"Good. Not yet, you understand. Wait until I say 'go'."

"Okay."

Tyler wanted to ensure that the bull was calm before the boy made a move. He began to send calm thoughts and positive energy to the animal. He was answered with a snort and a stomp. *Oh, God, please let this work*, Tyler thought.

He continued to hold his focus. *It's okay*, he thought, *we aren't here to hurt you. My little friend, here, made a mistake. All we want to do is go and leave you alone*. He doubted the bull understood but hoped that he caught the meaning.

The bull retreated a step, and Tyler knew that it was now or never. With his eyes still on the creature, he squeezed the boy's wrist once, released it, and whispered, "Go!" Thankfully obedient, the boy quickly clambered up the side.

A moment later, a man's voice shouted, "Timothy! What were you thinking?"

Tyler tuned out the commotion, from the other side, and continued to emit calm, relaxing thoughts and energy. He was fairly confident that he could climb safely to the top, without getting speared with horns, but was still hesitant to turn his back.

And then, an image entered his mind. He saw *himself* climbing up the fence. The bull was telling him that he could go.

"Thanks, Buddy," Tyler whispered. Assured of his safety, he turned to climb. He was two rails up, when he turned back to the massive, horned creature and said, "Good luck out there". Tyler wondered if it was his imagination but could have sworn that the bull winked.

A man stood to greet him as he landed back to safety, on the other side. He wore a cowboy hat and boots and sported a thick, black mustache. "That was very brave of you. I owe you my thanks for saving my nephew. He could have gotten real hurt if you hadn't come along."

"I'm just glad that I was able to help." Tyler brushed the dirt from his hands, onto his jeans, and accepted the man's outstretched hand, in a firm shake.

The boy was snuggled in a giant bear hug, in the arms of a woman whom he assumed to be his mother, while a man, whom he assumed to be his father, stood by and scolded the boy. "Don't you ever do anything so stupid, ever again! Do you hear me? Do you have any idea how lucky you are?" The boy burst into tears and buried his head in his mother's neck.

Tyler realized that a small group had gathered around the commotion. At the front of the crowd stood a tall, Hispanic guy, about eighteen-years-old, with thick, black rimmed glasses. This had to be Eddie. They made eye contact and then he smiled and stepped out of the crowd, toward him.

Tyler turned to the boy's uncle. "I'm sorry; could you excuse me for just a minute?"

"Of course, I'll be right over there." He touched the brim of his cowboy hat and gave a nod, then wandered over to check on his nephew.

Tyler turned to the newcomer who extended a hand in greeting. "Hi, I'm Eddie."

"I'm Tyler."

Eddie accepted the handshake and said, "Your brother wasn't kidding; you do look exactly alike."

Up to that point, the entire situation with Toby and the kidnappers had seemed surreal, but now that Eddie stood before him, in person, his reality suddenly seemed to take on a new countenance, and he found himself momentarily speechless. When he finally found words to speak, he said, "Um, yeah...we are identical...I was worried that you wouldn't show up. I'm so glad that you're here."

"Well, to be honest, I wasn't sure if I was going to come. I'm still not convinced that I'm going to go through with this insane plan."

Tyler was overcome with panic. He needed Eddie's help to find his brother. He looked around to make sure he wouldn't be overheard and then said, "You have to help. We need you."

"I saw you jump into that bull pen. I don't know if you're brave or stupid."

Eddie's attempt to avoid the subject was obvious, but Tyler couldn't help but laugh. "I was kinda wondering that myself, after I jumped in there. No one else was around though, and somebody had to save the kid."

"How did you manage to get the two of you out of there, in one piece?"

"Um...I guess you could say I have a way with animals."

"Whatever you did, it was pretty cool."

"Can we go somewhere else to talk?" Tyler hoped to convene their meeting elsewhere, preferably somewhere far away from the rodeo grounds. "Kirby, my...guardian, is going to be looking for me soon. If he finds me, we're done."

Just then, the boy's father walked over. He also sported a thick mustache and wore a cowboy hat and boots. "I don't know how I can ever thank you. You saved my son. If there is anything that I can do for you, anything at all..."

Tyler was ready to say that he didn't need anything. He was just happy that he had been in the right place at the right time, but then he looked over the man's shoulder and spotted Kirby. He was near the food vendors and headed their way.

He turned his attention back to the boy's father. "Actually, Sir, this may sound strange, but there is something that you could do for me...if you wouldn't mind. Do you see that man over there, in the green overalls, walking this direction?" Tyler nodded his head toward Kirby.

The boy's father glanced over his shoulder. "I do."

"Well, you see, I was supposed to be working and picking up trash. If he finds out that I was over here and not doing my job, I might get fired. Do you think that you could, maybe, forget that you saw me and distract him for a minute or two, so that I have time to get back to where I'm supposed to be?"

The man smiled and gave him a friendly slap on the shoulder. "I was young once, too. No boy wants to be stuck picking up trash at a rodeo, while there are pretty girls to see and excitement going on. I understand. Don't you worry about it. I've got you covered. You go on that way and get outta here. I'll keep your boss talking for a few minutes.

Tyler grinned, thankful for his good luck. "Thank you so much!"

"No thanks is needed, Young Man; it's the least I can do. Now, go on that way, behind the trailers, and get outta here."

"Thank you, Sir!" Tyler turned to Eddie, with a smile. "Come on. Let's go."

They escaped between two horse trailers and made a beeline for the parking lot.

It wasn't until they had reached Eddie's Jeep that Tyler spoke. "I need to get my bag. I left it in Kirby's car." He had stowed the duffle bag, filled with clothing, on the floor of the backseat of the car, the night before. The floor was riddled with old McDonald's sacks, work boots, receipts, coats, and water bottles. It seemed the rubble had taken up permanent residence, and Tyler knew it was unlikely that it would be cleaned up, anytime soon. He had been confident that his bag would remain safely hidden.

"Where's the car?"

"It's parked on the other side of the lot."

"Hop in. We'll drive."

Halfway across the parking lot, Tyler realized that he held his breath and had a death-grip on the edge of the seat, as Eddie careened down one dusty lane and up another. He prayed that no children ran out from behind a car as they left a trail of blooming dust in their tracks.

Tyler didn't want to be a backseat driver to someone he had just met, but at the same time, he felt compelled to speak. "I, uh...know we're in a hurry and all, but you might want to slow down a bit so you don't draw attention."

Eddie glanced at the speedometer and immediately released pressure from the gas pedal. "Sorry, I'm usually a cautious driver. I just..." He shook his head and kept his eyes trained on the parking lot, as he now drove at the designated speed limit. Then, he glanced at Tyler. "I just had my priorities all laid out. You know? College. My future. I had it all figured out. And then your brother came along and kinda threw a kink in my plans. I'm not ready to throw everything I've worked for out the window and risk jail time for harboring a runaway.

"Before I drive any further, where's your father's car?"

"Ugh, Kirby? He's definitely not my father. His car's right over there, though." Tyler pointed straight ahead and to the right. "It's that old, red Pontiac, second from the end."

Eddie pulled up behind the car and parked. "This is it?"

"Yep, I'll just be a second. I left the bag in the backseat."

Tyler glanced at Eddie. There was an unmistakable look of concern written on his face. Eddie had said he wasn't ready to throw everything he'd worked for out the window. What was that supposed to mean? He'd come this far. Was he going to back out now? Without conscious effort, he tuned in to Eddie's thoughts.

I could just drive away, he heard Eddie think. *I could keep going, never look back, and pretend we never met.*

"You could," Tyler said. "It's definitely an option."

Eddie looked, as expected, very confused. "I could do what? What's an option?"

"You could drive away and never look back."

"How did you know...?"

Tyler shrugged. "My brother's not the only one with talent. It's true; you could drive away, pretend that you never met me, but it wouldn't put an end to all of this. My brother isn't the one who threw a kink in your plans. The people who kidnapped him did. You're damn lucky that my brother had the power to contact you. If he hadn't, you could be in the same position that he's in, right now. The people who took him want you, too. Like it or not, we have to rely on each other, if we're going to make it through this.

"Now, I need to get my bag. Can I trust that you aren't going to drive away, once I get out?"

Eddie gave him a half smile. "Go ahead. I'll wait right here."

Tyler checked on Eddie's thoughts one more time. Once he was certain that his new friend wasn't going to leave him in the dust, he jumped out of the Jeep and yanked on the door handle of Kirby's car. It was locked. It couldn't be. Kirby never locked his car.

He walked around the vehicle and tried each handle, but to no avail.

Eddie got out of the Jeep and came to stand by his side. "Car's locked I take it?"

"Yeah, he never locks the car." He slammed his hand on the roof.

Eddie sighed. "Just add breaking and entering to my police record, along with kidnapping."

Tyler glanced at him. "You're going to break in? Do you have a lot of experience with breaking into cars?"

Eddie scowled. "No, I don't. Until I met you, the idea of breaking the law never crossed my mind. Do you see anyone coming?"

Tyler peered up and down the aisle of parked vehicles. They were parked in the back of the lot, and thankfully, there was no one around. "Um, nope. Looks clear."

"Good. This should just take a moment."

"What will? What are you going to do?"

Eddie grinned. "You and your brother aren't the only ones with powers. Watch and see." He placed his right hand on the door, slightly above the handle and placed his left hand near the locking mechanism. In less than ten seconds, Tyler heard the click.

"Voila." Eddie smiled and flourished a hand toward the door. "One unlocked car, as you wished."

"That's awesome! Besides my brother, I've never met anyone else with powers like that." He touched a hand reverently to the car door and then lifted the handle. "I could have done that. I don't know why I didn't think of it." He gave Eddie a sly grin. "Of course...*I* didn't break into the car...*you* did. You know what that means, don't you?"

"Um...it means now the car's open and you should hurry up and grab your bag, before anyone sees us."

"Well, yeah. But it also means that now you're part of this crazy escapade, too. There's no turning back."

"Right...why don't you grab your bag so we can discuss this, somewhere else? We should get out of here before Kirby discovers that you're missing."

Eddie drove in focused silence until they had left the fairgrounds a few miles behind. Then, he glanced at Tyler. "Grab my phone and see if you can make us a flight reservation." He handed over his wallet. "Here ya go. You can use my credit card."

"Does that mean you're in? Where are we going?"

Eddie kept his gaze straight ahead, on the road, when he spoke, "We're going to Seattle. Crazy as this whole thing is, it looks like I'm in. Like you said, there's no turning back now."

5 LILIANA

Liliana watched the sparrows flutter about on the power line, outside the glass, balcony door of her grandfather's third floor apartment, in Chinatown. From the table, she could clearly see the apartment building across the alley. On one of the apartment's balconies, an elderly woman fed her two cats.

Her parents, both dentists, had gone to China for a month, on a goodwill mission to bring dental care to needy children. Her grandmother, who hadn't returned to China for thirty years, had eagerly gone with them. Liliana had begged her parents for the chance to go along, but they insisted that it was more important for her to stay in school. So, it had been arranged that she stay with her grandfather, until their return.

She glanced at the clock. It was early still, and she had half an hour before she would need to walk to the corner bus stop. Had she been home, she would have walked to Aimee's, and her mom would have driven them to school. Her grandfather's apartment, however, was miles away, in the opposite direction, near Elliott Bay. The city bus was, unfortunately, her only option.

When the phone rang, Liliana reached over to the old wall phone, which thankfully had a cord long enough to reach the table. She smiled when she heard Aimee's voice on the other end.

"Hey, Liliana! So, I just talked to my mom, and she said that you can stay with us, while your parents are gone. What do ya think?"

"Um...I don't know." She swirled her cup of hot tea. "I'd feel bad leaving Grandfather here, all by himself, you know? If Grandmother were here I wouldn't feel so guilty, but she went to China with my parents. He doesn't speak any English, and if he needed help or something I don't know what he'd do."

"Liliana, he lives in *Chinatown*. I'm sure he'll manage, just fine. It's not like there's no one around for him to talk to."

"I know...you're right. I just feel guilty leaving him alone."

"Well, don't. If he and your grandma are anything like my

grandparents, I'm sure that he would welcome the opportunity to be alone and have a little bit of freedom, for a while.

"And besides," Aimee went on, "you don't really like riding the city bus to school every day, do you?"

"Definitely not!" Liliana agreed. "The bus is one downside to staying here."

"Will you at least think about it?"

"I will."

"Promise?"

"I promise." She looked out the window again and spotted the two cats on the neighbor's balcony. A fat, black cat, sat next to its food bowl and delicately licked a paw. The other, a skinny tabby, jumped onto the railing. Its tail swished frantically back and forth as it watched the small birds flitter about on the power line. Liliana held her breath, anxious for the cat's safety. The railing wasn't wide, and the alley was a far drop from the third floor balcony.

Just then, one of the birds caught sight of the feline and flew away. Startled by the bird's hasty escape, the rest of the flock took off as well, some flying in confused circles. There was a loud thump as one of the birds hit the glass door and bounced to the hard balcony. Liliana watched, breath held in anticipation, to see if the sparrow would fly away, but it lay motionless.

"I have to go," she told Aimee. "I'll see you at school, okay?"

Her friend sighed. "Alright...think about it, okay?"

"I will. See you in a bit."

She forcefully urged the old, sliding glass door open and was assaulted by the cold, February breeze. For once, the Seattle sky was clear; not a cloud was in sight, and the sun winked down between the rooftops. Still, the temperature was near freezing, and the damp breeze that blew in from the bay sent chills down her bare arms.

She gazed down at the motionless bird. Unsure if it was dead or simply stunned, she didn't want to stand out in the cold trying to figure it out. Regardless if it was alive or dead, she couldn't leave it on the balcony. She looked around for something to pick it up with and grabbed a kitchen towel, from a nearby counter.

Her toes curled when she stepped, barefoot, onto the frozen balcony. Quickly but gently, she scooped the bird into the towel and leapt inside. With the towel enwrapped bird held against her chest, she struggled one handed to shut the rickety, glass door.

She sat at the kitchen table and carefully opened the towel, wary of the chance that the bird might fly up at her. It didn't however, and as she laid the towel in her lap, the sparrow remained motionless. She observed it carefully for any sign of life and thought that she detected movement in its chest. Delicately, she touched a finger to the top of its head and gently stroked its back. After a few moments, its eyes opened. Startled, it stuck out a wing as though to fly. Liliana reacted quickly and cupped a hand over its back to hold it in place. She noticed that while one wing fluttered in its will to fly, the other remained crooked at its side.

Poor thing, it has a broken wing, Liliana thought. She frowned when she realized that it had stopped its attempt at escape and now lay still in her lap, breathing heavily. With one hand cupped over its back, she continued to gently stroke its head.

Her grandfather, known around the Chinese community as a healer, was well practiced in the art of ancient Chinese medicine. If he were home, he would have known exactly what to do with the poor creature, but he had stepped out to the morning marketplace.

She looked down at the bird and frowned, again. It had been over a year since she had used her healing ability. *Well, it's certainly worth a try*, she thought. Gingerly, she fingered the broken wing, and then cupped it between the palms of her hands and closed her eyes. Heat radiated from the spot that was broken. As she concentrated, heat and energy began to radiate from her own hands, and her energy began to overtake the heat that radiated from the broken wing. In her mind she saw the bones heal and fuse together, and then she imagined the bird take flight in freedom.

She opened her eyes and slowly released the wing. Unsure of how the bird would react, she took hold of the towel, prepared to cover it if it should panic. The last thing she wanted was for the bird to take flight in the apartment and reinjure itself. It remained motionless on her lap, but it was clearly more relaxed and at ease. Its breathing had slowed and it had stopped trembling.

A rustle of keys at the door caught her attention, and a moment later, her grandfather entered. His arms overflowed with brown paper packages of all shapes and sizes. When he set them on the table, Liliana's nose told her that along with the vendors that he visited for herbs and plants, he had also visited the fish market.

He peered over her shoulder. "What do you have here, my granddaughter?"

She responded in his native language. "It flew into the window. Its wing was broken, but I think I might have healed it. I was going to let it rest for a minute and then see if it's okay."

She carried the sparrow to the balcony and her grandfather followed to open the door. After she set it outside, they stood together in the doorway to watch. It sat for a moment and twisted its head sideways to look up at her. Then it stood, took flight, and landed on the power line. Two other sparrows flew in and landed beside it. The birds remained on the line for a few moments, and then Liliana and her grandfather watched as they flew away, in unison.

As they continued to look out the window, he put an arm around her shoulders. "You know, my dear child, our culture holds value and symbolism behind birds. They are seen as messengers."

Liliana looked up at her grandfather who stood just a few inches taller than her own height of five foot one. "You think the bird was sent as a messenger?"

He looked down at his granddaughter. "I would not take this event lightly. Why do you think this bird came to you? It was not a coincidence. You have given this bird a second chance at life. Remember what I have always said, what you put out into the world will come back to you. This bird could represent a life changing event. Stay aware and good things will come your way."

Liliana smiled. She had been born in America and loved the

American culture and all that it had to offer, but she also valued her Chinese culture and always took heed to what her grandfather had to say. *Good things will come your way*, he had said. She repeated his words to herself, as she headed out the door for school, and wondered at their meaning. When she stepped out to the sidewalk, the damp wind chilled her to the bone. She tightened her coat and headed to the corner to wait for the bus, optimistic and open to the day that awaited her.

*****

Liliana and Aimee shared their last class of the day, English Writing, and after the final bell, they made their way downstairs. With hats and gloves donned, they were immediately assaulted by the frigid wind when they stepped out of the double doors, onto the concrete steps, of the old, brick building. The day had become slightly overcast, and there was no doubt that the temperature had dropped to below freezing.

"Hey, I see my mom parked down there," Aimee said. "Do you want a ride home?"

"No, that's okay. It's out of the way. I don't want to inconvenience her. I'll walk down with you, though."

When her mother saw their approach, she got out of the car and walked around to the sidewalk to give Liliana a hug. "Hi, Liliana. Did Aimee tell you that you're welcome to stay with us, while your parents are gone?"

"She did. Thanks for the offer. I told her that I'd talk with my grandfather about it, when I get home. I'll give you guys a call tonight and let you know what he says."

"Great! We're having spaghetti tonight, so if you're interested, we'd love to have you! I'd be happy to stop by and pick you up."

"Thanks so much, I really appreciate the offer." Her mom got back in the car and Liliana turned to Aimee. "I'll give you call in a little bit."

Her friend opened the car door and climbed in. "Okay, ask him right when you get home, alright? See ya!" She waved and then closed the door against the cold.

Liliana waved goodbye and then turned to head for the bus stop. She stopped when a car, parked across the street, caught her attention. Just as she looked over, two guys stepped out of the vehicle. They closed their doors and seemed to stare directly at her.

At first she thought that it was her imagination. She didn't know them; they must have been waiting for another student, and so she continued on. She had only walked a few feet, however, when she stopped again. She felt as though their eyes followed her every move, as though their energy reached out to her. She casually glanced over her shoulder, and sure enough, they continued to watch her.

For a moment, she wondered if she should be scared, but then she noticed their auras. The taller of the two had an aura that glowed brilliant turquoise with a slight rim of purple; he had only good intentions. The guy who stood on the passenger side of the car was surrounded by blue with slight tinges of yellow; he was confident and at peace.

Neither posed a threat; and yet, what else could explain why they continued to watch her? She started to walk away, but curiosity got the better of her, and she wandered back to the front of the school. Again, their eyes followed her every move.

She turned when someone from behind called out to her. Cat was at the bottom of the stairs and waved to get her attention.

"Hey, Liliana!" she called out. "Are you going to the game Friday night?"

"I haven't decided yet. I'm staying with my grandfather for a few weeks while my parents are away, and I don't really want to ride the bus at night. I might go if I can get a ride with Aimee."

"Oh, okay. Well, if you decide to go, Joey and I are going out for pizza after the game. You're welcome to join us."

"Thanks! I'll keep that in mind. I should know by tomorrow. I'll let you know in the morning."

Cat grinned. "Alright, have a good evening!"

"You too. See ya!"

Cat turned for the student parking lot and then Liliana remembered the two guys across the street. She looked over to see if they were still there.

They weren't.

They were walking across the street, straight toward her.

Liliana froze, not from fright, but from curiosity. Whatever these guys wanted, they didn't intend to harm her; this she was certain of. As they got closer, their positive energy radiated out to her.

Time seemed to slow as she waited on the sidewalk. They stopped about two feet from her and smiled.

The shorter of the two caught her attention, first. *I'm so glad that we finally found you*, she heard him think.

Really? Cuz I don't have a clue who you are, Liliana thought, in return.

The shock on his face was obvious; he hadn't expected to hear her silent reply. Liliana was just as shocked, when she realized that, he too, could hear her thoughts.

You can hear me, he thought.

Yeah and you can hear me. That's a first. She was more perplexed than ever.

They continued to stare at each other. He appeared to be about her age. Thin, but muscular, he had dazzling green eyes and dimples. Knowing that he could hear her thoughts, Liliana tried her best to mask them as she thought, *Wow! He's cute!* She hoped that she had succeeded but wasn't sure. She thought that she detected a slight smile, but it quickly disappeared.

It was his companion who spoke first. He wore glasses and appeared to be Hispanic or Native American. She thought that he was probably a couple of years older than the other guy, but not by much.

"You're Liliana?"

She was hesitant to reply. "Uh...yeah...Do I know you?"

"No. I'm Eddie. This is Tyler." He indicated the guy beside him, who smiled when he was introduced. "We've traveled a long way to find you. Can we talk?"

6 SEATTLE

Tyler understood Liliana's desire to meet in public; after all, she didn't know them, and a restaurant would provide a sense of security. Few words were exchanged during the short drive to the restaurant, by the marina. While she sat in front and provided directions for Eddie, Tyler sat in the back and eyed her with curiosity.

He hadn't known what to expect. He certainly hadn't anticipated the instant attraction. Easily nine or ten inches shorter than he was, she had striking features, fascinating eyes that twinkled, lush, full lips, and long, silky, jet black hair.

She liked him, too. Even though she had attempted to block her thoughts, he had heard enough to know that she thought he was cute. He would, of course, have to resist the mutual attraction, at least for now; any flirtations might impede the search, and he couldn't afford any setbacks. He needed to maintain focus and keep his mind clear of distractions.

He hadn't heard from Toby since they had arrived to Seattle, and he tried not to worry. Now that they had located Liliana, they would need to move quickly to locate the next person on the list, and he still didn't know who that was.

In the meantime, he and Eddie would need to convince Liliana to join them on their unpredictable and perilous mission. He had remained silent, during the drive, as he contemplated various scenarios. She could laugh at them; he certainly wouldn't blame her. Their story did sound absurd. Worse yet, she could call the police and report that they had tried to abduct her. Guilt teased the edge of his conscience. He didn't want to bring her into this dangerous journey but knew that, in the end, there wasn't a choice. If she didn't go with them, she faced certain abduction, by the same people who had taken his brother.

Liliana and Eddie made small talk as they walked from the parking lot to the restaurant. Tyler followed close behind, acutely aware of the hollow thuds of his footsteps, on the wood plank walkway. He took advantage of his final moments, alone, to rehearse what he would say.

The restaurant, which sat high on a cliff and overlooked the water, boasted several tables on an outside patio. Given the cold, wintry day, however, they headed inside. The damp, frigid wind zipped off of the lapping waves and whipped around their coats. Having grown up in the desert, Tyler had never been near the ocean, and he took a deep breath of the salty, seaweed air. He found the scent to be pleasant and invigorating, in an odd sort of way, and he made a mental note, that one day, he would like to return. He hoped that Toby would be with him.

✶✶✶✶✶

"You've got to be kidding," Liliana said, after Tyler and Eddie had explained why they had flown over a thousand miles to find her. "It's a joke, right? Did Aimee put you up to this?" She took a sip of hot chocolate and looked seriously from Eddie to Tyler.

Tyler noticed that she looked slightly over his head when she spoke. She squinted in concentration, furled her eyebrows, then frowned. Then she shook her head. "You're not kidding. I can see that. If this was a joke your colors would be...," she paused and shook her head, again. "But, they're not. You're colors are pure. I don't get it." She examined the space over his head, once again. "You're for real, aren't you?"

Tyler nodded. "Um, yeah...yep, we are." He glanced at Eddie, who nodded, as well. "This is about as real as it gets," he continued. "You mentioned our colors. What colors are you talking about?"

Before she could reply, Eddie smiled and nodded his head in understanding. "You see auras, don't you?"

"Yeah, can you see them, too?"

Eddie shook his head. "No, I can't. I've read about auras though. You can see them, huh? That's cool."

"Cool? Yeah, I guess so. The older I get, the more I'm beginning to appreciate it."

"So, what does that mean? You can see if I'm lying or not, just by looking at my aura?"

"Well, yeah. For the most part, I can. It's taken some practice to learn about what I see, but I've observed auras basically my whole life, so I've had some time to figure it all out."

"And you can hear other people's thoughts, too," Tyler said. "So really, you can always know if someone is lying."

"Yeah, auras are definitely truer, though. People can try to mask their thoughts, but no one can fake an aura. Auras show what a person is truly about."

"So, you'll come with us then?" Tyler felt a wave of relief. Maybe it wouldn't be so hard to convince her, after all. She would *have* to see that their intentions were true.

She didn't answer immediately and turned to look out of the large, picture window, next to their table. Tyler looked at the view beyond and waited with patience as a few sailboats passed by, in the harbor. He watched a group of seagulls swoop out of the sky and dive into the cold, murky water, below. Finally, she turned back to them.

"I believe you. As odd as your story is, I do believe you. I just don't see why you need me. Why don't you just call the police or the FBI and let them know about your brother? Let them find him for you. I mean, really, as much as I feel for you and would like to help, we're just teenagers. What can we possibly do?"

"The people who took Toby are smart," Tyler said. "They know what they're doing, and they've covered all of the bases. As far as the police are concerned, Toby's just another runaway. Even if we did explain that he's been kidnapped, they wouldn't believe us. We don't have proof."

"Okay, so I get that. But, why do you need me? I understand that my name is on this list, but I don't know where your brother is. I may have a few unique abilities, but I'm not psychic, by any means. I wouldn't have a clue how to find him." She looked at him with wide, unblinking eyes, as though daring him to convince her.

Tyler glanced at Eddie, who shrugged and gave him a look that said, *I don't know what I'm doing here, either.*

Tyler took a deep breath and met Liliana's gaze. "We don't know how we're going to find Toby, either. I know that's not what you want to hear, but it's the truth. Right now, we're just trying to stay one step ahead of the people who have him; because the truth is, they're after us, too. The people who took Toby also want us, *all* of us. It won't be long before they track us down, and when they do, we won't be any better off than Toby is, right now.

"I don't know how we're going to find him, but we *will* find him. And honestly, as of right now, I *don't* know what you can do to help us. But, I do know that we can't leave you here, alone. If you stay, they *will* find you. They'll take you, and you'll be considered another runaway, just like Toby."

"If I go with you, my grandfather will worry about me. He's old; I can't put him through that. And my parents aren't even in the country. If they find out that I'm missing, they'll have to come home. I can't even begin to imagine how angry my father would be."

"So, you *would* consider coming with us, if your family didn't find out?"

"Well…um…I guess, but…"

Eddie looked at Tyler as though he were an idiot. "And what exactly do you have in mind? Don't you think that her family would notice her absence?"

Tyler grinned at him, but addressed Liliana. "One thing that I've learned is to never say never. There's always a way to accomplish something; sometimes you just have to think outside the box."

"I'm open for ideas," Liliana said, "but I really don't see what I can do."

Tyler sat for a moment, in silent contemplation. There had to be a way. He watched a lone seagull, with a fish in its mouth, land on a pillar in the water. Another seagull landed on a nearby pillar and eyed the fish enviously. Viewing the other bird as a threat, the seagull with the fish flew away.

Tyler turned to her. "You said that your parents are away, right now? Who are you staying with?"

"I'm staying with my grandfather, but I think I'm going to go stay with my friend…" Liliana paused for a moment and thought,

Of course, maybe, I could tell my grandfather that I'm going to stay with Aimee, but really, I could go with you.

Perfect! Tyler thought back. He smiled at her and winked when she realized that he had heard her thoughts.

This is too weird, Liliana thought. *I've never had someone else in my head. You must be used to it, having your brother and all, but it's a first for me.*

It's kind of a first for me, too. I mean, I'm used to my brother; he's been in my head since the day we were born, but I've never had anyone else hear my thoughts.

He smiled at Liliana. She really was pretty. Remembering that she could hear his thoughts, he focused to push all feelings of attraction aside and worked to keep his mind on the problem at hand. *So, what do you think?* He continued the silent conversation. *You tell your grandfather that you're going to stay with your friend and then you come with us? What about your friend? Do you think she'll say something?*

No, I trust her. Obviously, I can't tell her what I'm up to, but if I ask her not to tell anyone, she'll stay quiet.

What if your other friends call your grandfather's place and ask for you?

They won't. Aimee's the only one with his number. My other friends would call my cell phone. Liliana frowned as she thought the plan through. *I'll have Aimee tell my friends that I have laryngitis. And even if they did happen to get his number and call, my grandfather only speaks Chinese. Basically all he'd be able to say is, 'Liliana not here'.*

Tyler laughed. "It's perfect," he said, out loud, "probably the best plan we're going to be able to come up with."

Eddie looked back and forth between Tyler and Liliana, who still smiled at each other as though they shared a secret. "Excuse me? Plan? Why do I get the feeling that I just missed out on an entire conversation?"

Tyler shared a smile with Liliana and laughed. "Sorry, I guess we forgot for a moment that this is a three-way conversation."

Their waitress stepped up to the table, then, and interrupted.

"Can I get the three of you anything else?"

"Uh, no, thanks," Tyler replied. "I think we're ready for the check."

"Okay, then, I'll be right back," she said and departed.

Eddie turned to Liliana. "So, what's the plan? You coming with us?"

"It looks like I am. I must be crazy."

"Join the crowd. I've been convinced that I must be crazy since I began this escapade." He looked to Tyler. "Where are we headed next?"

"We need to go to Liliana's place so that she can pack a bag and pretend to go to her friend's house. And then...I don't know. Hopefully I'll hear from Toby, soon."

"What about my school?" Liliana interrupted. "When I don't show up, tomorrow, they'll call my house. And when they don't get ahold of anyone there, they'll call my grandfather. The school secretary *does* speak Chinese."

"Does the school know that your parents are out of the country?" Tyler asked.

"No, we never told them."

"Does your father speak English?"

"Yeah, what are you thinking?"

"I'm thinking that Eddie can call the school tomorrow morning, pretend to be your father, and tell them that you're going to be out sick for the rest of the week."

Liliana raised her eyebrows and frowned with skepticism.

"Don't worry. It'll work."

When she still looked hesitant, Tyler sent a pleading look to Eddie for assistance.

"Yeah, don't worry about it," Eddie reassured her. "It'll work." Then, he spoke in a baritone voice, "I'll call the school tomorrow and pretend to be your father."

Liliana laughed. "My father doesn't have that deep of a voice. Your own voice should do just fine. They don't know my father that well to recognize what he sounds like, anyway."

Just then, Toby's thoughts entered his mind, *Good, you found her, didn't you? Are you with Liliana?*

A wave of relief swept over him and he spoke to his brother, out loud, "You're here! I was so worried that you wouldn't be able to reach me. Yeah, I'm with Eddie and Liliana."

Eddie glanced at him with a look of curiosity. "Um, are you talking to us?"

"No, it's Toby. He's here."

Liliana looked just as confused as Eddie. "He's...*here*?"

"Yes and no. Physically he's still...somewhere else, but mentally he's here. I can hear his thoughts and he can hear mine."

Can you go outside? Toby asked. *With all of the conversations and people around, your words are broken up, like a bad cell phone connection.*

"Yeah, hold on just a second and I'll walk outside," Tyler spoke out loud, for the benefit of his companions. Then, he looked at them and said, "Can you two wait here until the waitress comes back with the check? I need to go outside to talk to Toby. I'll meet you out there?"

"Sure, go ahead," Eddie replied. "We'll be out in a minute."

So, is she cute? Toby asked, once they were outside.

You and I both know, Brother, that now isn't the time or place for romance.

Who said anything about romance? Is she hot?

Have you figured out where we need to go next? He ignored his brother's question and looked out to the water. To any passersby, it would appear as though he was simply enjoying the scenery.

Oh, so she is hot.

Um, really, Toby? Focus please.

Sorry. Her name is Sarah Hughes. She's in a little town called Granite Falls. It's just north of Seattle, not too far from where you are now, maybe a two hour drive.

Okay, we have to go back to Liliana's place so that she can pack a bag, and then we'll head up there. It's getting late, though, Tyler thought, as he watched the rare Seattle sun near the water's horizon. *It's going to be dark by the time we get up there. Do you know where we can find her?*

Yeah, she's a waitress at a diner, next to a small motel. She's not there now, but she should be there again in the morning.

Right now, a motel sounds great. It's been a long day.

Are you getting one room or two? Toby teased.

Though Tyler couldn't see him, he knew that his brother was smiling.

She's HOT, Toby reminded him.

Yeah, I know, Tyler thought. *Don't remind me. And I don't know if we're getting one room or two, so I need to stop being reminded that she's hot. She can hear my thoughts.*

She can? Really? Toby sounded fascinated. *NICE!*

No, Brother. NOT nice if I have to share a room with her, not cool at all!

Toby laughed. *Hey, so good luck with that.*

Yeah? I'm going to need some luck finding Sarah.

Um, yeah, about that...you're going to want to find her as soon as possible. I didn't tell you before, but the guys who are after you are getting closer. I overheard one of them thinking about a flight that he was going to catch to Washington. If they're not there already, they'll be there soon.

Great, I hope we're not too late. What if we're too late?

You won't be, Toby reassured him.

Do you know that for sure, or are you just trying to make me feel better?

I had a vision of you talking to Sarah. You will find her; don't worry.

I hope you're right.

His companions stepped up to the rail, beside him. "Are we ready to go?" Eddie asked.

Tell Eddie I said 'hi', and tell Liliana that she's hot, Toby thought.

"No," Tyler replied, out loud, to his brother.

Liliana looked confused. "No? We're not ready to go?"

"No, I mean, yeah, we're ready. My brother says 'hi' to the both of you."

Well, those weren't my exact words, but it'll do. Toby laughed. *Good luck, Brother. I'll catch up with you, tomorrow.*

"Alright, hang in there," Tyler said, out loud. "I'll see you soon, Brother. We're going to find you."

I know you will. See ya soon.

"So?" Eddie asked. "Where to? Did he say?"

Tyler nodded. "Yeah, we're headed north."

It was late. The quaint town seemed all but deserted as they drove down the main strip of Granite Falls, passing tourist shops, gas stations, and bars as they went. Other than a few motorcycles, parked outside of a saloon, there was no sign of inhabitants.

They didn't stop, but followed the GPS directions on Eddie's phone and continued the short drive through town. The restaurant, where Sarah worked, was next to an inn, nestled close to the mountain. They would stay there for the night, and with luck, would find her in the morning.

When they checked in, the manager informed them that the restaurant had just closed, for the night, but graciously let them in and assembled a simple meal of sandwiches, chips, cookies, and drinks to take back to their room. Apologetic that she couldn't offer more, she proclaimed that dinner was on the house.

The room, which consisted of two queen sized beds and a small sofa, was dark and cold when they entered. Eddie promptly found the lights and cranked the heater up to the red zone.

Huddled in her snow coat, Liliana sat cross-legged in the middle of one of the beds and took a bite of her sandwich. "Mmm, I don't think ham and cheese has ever tasted so good," she said.

Her companions took up similar positions around the room and ate in silence, for a few minutes, as the relief of food and the realization that the long day had finally come to an end, sank in.

"Wow, I can't believe it was only yesterday that all of this started," Eddie said.

Liliana was surprised. "This all just started yesterday?"

"Yep, I met Tyler yesterday and Toby, the night before. It's been a whirlwind ever since. Now, here we are, a thousand miles from home, and on the run from kidnappers. How did we end up here?"

"That's a good question. I've only known you guys for a few

hours, and I can't figure out how I ended up here, either."

"I called my father and told him that I went on a research trip, to Tucson. That excuse will work for a couple of days, but then what? Who knows how long it will take to find Tyler's brother."

"I know what you mean. I have a good cover story, and it should be a few days before anyone misses me, but then what?"

"Well, whatever," Tyler said, "I say we face our worries tomorrow."

Liliana turned to him. "You don't sound concerned. You're not worried about what you're going to face when you go home?"

Tyler shook his head. "No, not really."

"You don't think your family will miss you?"

"Nah, I was staying with a foster family; and really, I don't care what they think. The only real family I have to speak of is my brother. Once I find him, then I guess we'll see what happens."

"I'm sorry; I didn't know that you lived with a foster family."

"Don't worry about it. Anyways, I say for now we enjoy this gourmet, paper bag dinner and get some rest. Hopefully tomorrow we can find Sarah and get ourselves one step closer to finding my brother."

"Sounds good to me. I claim the bed," Eddie declared, to Tyler. "You can have the couch."

"Why don't we flip for it?"

"Hmm, let me think...no," Eddie said, with a smile. "The couch is short and my legs are long. I need a good night's sleep because I'm the one doing the driving. The bed is mine."

Tyler looked at Liliana, who sat comfortably on the other bed.

Don't even think about it, she thought. *I'm the girl. I get the bed.*

The idea never crossed my mind, Tyler thought, *but since we're on the subject, it would make more sense, don't you think? You're a lot shorter than I am. The couch would fit you much better.*

The bed is mine. She smiled sweetly, but her thoughts held a slight tone of glee at the idea of his discomfort.

To make his point, Tyler stretched out on the short sofa, his feet dangled over the edge of the arm rest. *You're going to feel guilty all night, as you lay in your nice, comfortable bed and think of me on this hard, lumpy couch.*

And that's supposed to convince me to give up the bed? You're going to have to do better than that. She laughed out loud.

From his own bed, Eddie looked amused at their interaction and shook his head. "I don't have a clue what you two are thinking, but I can sure guess." He turned to Tyler. "Let her have the bed. Maybe tomorrow night, wherever we are, you two can compromise, and you can have the bed."

Or, we can share the bed, Tyler rationalized. She raised her eyebrows and blushed. Tyler bit his lip and looked away. He obviously hadn't meant to share that particular thought.

Whether or not he was aware of the awkward moment that had passed, Eddie helped to ease the tension. "Hey, Tyler, do you have the remote for the TV, over there?"

"Nope, I don't see it."

After a quick search of the room, which resulted in no remote, Tyler pressed the power button on the television but discovered that the buttons to change the channel were broken off.

"Ugh, I think I would rather watch nothing than have to listen to a show on politics," Liliana said. "Did you try to push the spot where the channel buttons used to be? Are you sure it won't work?"

"Yeah, I'm sure," Tyler said. "You sure there's no remote over there?"

Liliana peeked in the nightstand drawer for a second time. "Nope, nothing but a bible."

"What do you want to watch?"

"Anything but this. Why? Are you going to make the channel magically change?"

"Maybe," Tyler said, with a sly grin.

He moved to sit on the front of her bed and situated himself in front of the television. He stared at the screen for a moment, and then suddenly, the political talk show was replaced by the news, a game show, then a homicide detective show, and then a re-run of an old sitcom.

"Will this do?" He turned to face her with a proud smile.

She was speechless as she looked back and forth between the television and Tyler. "That's so cool! How did you do that?"

Tyler grinned. "Just one of my many talents."

"Well, thanks. I don't suppose there's anything you can do about the heat? It's still freezing in here."

"Let me take a look," Eddie said. He fiddled with the dials on the heater, cranked up the fan, and held his hand over the vents, but it only blew out cold air.

Liliana peered over. "Is it broken?"

"Looks like it. Give me a minute. I should be able to do something with it."

Liliana watched with curiosity as Eddie rested both hands on top of the heater and closed his eyes. A moment later he turned to her. "You cold? Come over here and stand by the heater for a minute. It'll warm you right up."

"You fixed it?" Even though she was exhausted, the prospect of heat was enough to get her off the bed, and she hurried to the heater in anticipation. "Oh my gosh, thank you!" She rubbed her hands over the blowing air and closed her eyes, allowing the heat to warm her through.

Eddie smiled. "You're welcome. Now that we're not freezing, maybe we'll be able to get some sleep tonight."

They watched TV until Liliana could no longer keep her eyes open. "I'm exhausted," she said. "If you guys don't mind, I think I'm going to bed."

"I hear ya," Eddie said. "It's probably going to be another long day. We should get some rest."

Curled up under the blankets, Liliana felt the cusp of sleep open its arms to greet her, when Tyler's silent voice filled her head. *You asleep yet?* he thought.

She smiled to herself, as his thoughts invaded her mind. She had, in fact, been thinking of him, before she had closed her eyes. Even though it was impractical, she felt an undeniable attraction for him. *I was almost asleep.*

Oh...sorry. I just thought you might be awake, still. I'll let you go back to sleep. Night.

Wait, it's okay...really. I probably won't sleep that great, anyway. I've got too much on my mind. I'd rather talk to you.

You would? He sounded both surprised and pleased.

Well...sure. I mean, I've never met anyone who I could mentally communicate with. It's kinda cool, don't you think? But, then again, I guess you're used to it with your brother, huh? I suppose it's no big deal for you.

Well, yeah. I mean, I can mentally communicate with my brother, but this is new for me, too. I'm not sure what I think; it's fun, but I have to stay on my toes. I forget that you can hear what I'm thinking, if I let my guard down. It's one thing to have my brother in my head, but having a pretty girl in my head is a whole different ball game.

Liliana was glad that it was dark, so he couldn't see her irrepressible grin. *Pretty girl?*

Well, you know what I mean. You're a girl. I'm a guy. We think differently.

You're scared what I might discover in that mind of yours? Liliana teased.

Something like that.

She tried to suppress a giggle but failed horribly.

You think that's funny, do you? You'd better watch yourself. I might just start having thoughts that you wish you'd never heard. You'll wish that you had stayed out of my head.

She turned her face into her pillow in an attempt to stifle her laugh.

He threw a pillow from the couch. In the dark, his aim was amazingly accurate as it found its directed target and landed on her head.

"Ow!" she said, out loud. Silently she asked, *What was that for?*

Shhh..., he thought, *you're going to wake up Eddie. Can I have my pillow back?*

Why did you throw it? That hurt.

That did NOT hurt. It sounded like he tried to suppress his own laugh.

It did, she thought back. *Would you like me to smack a pillow on your head so you can see how it feels?*

If it would mean that I get my pillow back, then yes, please. Bring it on.

She smacked the pillow a few times, nice and loud, so he could hear. *Hmm, I don't think so. I kinda like this pillow. I think I'll keep it. Thanks.*

Oh, I see how it is. You're going to leave me over here, pillowless, on this small, cramped couch. Now I'll wake up in the morning with not only a sore back, but a crick in my neck, as well.

Are you whining?

Maybe. I think I deserve the right to whine a little, don't you? My brother's been kidnapped, I'm a thousand miles from home, there are people chasing us, and really, if I don't find my brother, I don't have much of a home to go back to.

Well, when you put it that way, I guess you do have a little reason to whine. Just don't make it a habit, okay?

Tyler laughed out loud. *Okay.*

Do you want to tell me about it? About your family, I mean. You mentioned that you live with a foster family. What happened to your parents? You don't have to tell me if you don't want to. I'd understand.

It's okay. I don't mind. My mother died in an accident when I was four. My dad was a workaholic, so Toby and I stayed with my grandma most of the time. One day, our dad just decided that he wasn't coming home. Personally, I think he missed my mother too much, and we reminded him too much of her. In any case, we never saw him again. A few months later, our grandma died, too. The state tried to locate our father, but they couldn't find him. So they placed us in foster care. We were bounced around from one family to another for a while, and then eventually we landed with the Smith's. I won't go into details, but basically, the only reason they kept us around was for the money from the state and for the free help around the house. It was no secret that they couldn't stand us.

I'm sorry. I imagine you must miss your brother, a lot. How was it that he was kidnapped, but you weren't?

I wasn't home at the time. A few years ago, I got into a little bit of trouble, and they sent me away to a sort of military school.

A little bit of trouble? What did you do?

I didn't do anything...really.

Liliana laughed. *Of course not, because boys who are innocent always get sent to military school.*

No, really. I haven't always been perfect, but in this case, I was just in the wrong place at the wrong time. I don't know why I care so much that you believe me, but I just do.

Liliana was silent for a moment. She sensed his sincerity and wished that it wasn't dark so that she could see his aura.

Without thinking, she grabbed his pillow and swung her legs over the side of the bed, bringing her feet to rest on the rough, threadbare, motel carpet. Then, she silently made her way to the sofa and knelt on the floor. She lifted his arm and secured the pillow beneath it. With her hand still on his arm, she gave it a gentle squeeze and whispered, "Here ya go."

"What's this for?" he whispered back.

"Maybe I felt sorry for you."

"Oh, so my trick worked? You bought my poor, poor, pitiful me story?"

"What?" She snagged the pillow from under his arm and smacked it on his head. Then, she turned toward her bed.

He laughed and caught hold of her wrist to stop her. "I'm sorry," he whispered. He tugged on her wrist to pull her down to the floor and then sat up on the sofa. He reached out for her other wrist and held both of her hands in his. The lighting was dim, but she could vaguely see that he had taken his shirt off. She could see the outline of his broad shoulders and muscular arms. His large hands held hers with a firm grip.

"I'm sorry," he whispered, again. "Everything I told you is true. Other than my brother, I have no family to speak of; and I swear, I didn't do anything wrong to get sent to military school."

"Well, if you did something wrong, or not, it doesn't matter to me."

"It matters to me, that you believe me."

"Why?"

"Because...I li...because I'd like us to be friends."

"I'd like us to be friends, too." She wondered what he had been going to say. Because I like you? She pushed the thought aside.

He squeezed her hands and then released them. "You'd better get some sleep."

"You too. Sleep good...on the *sofa*." She laughed softly and then hurried to crawl back under the warm blankets.

Sweet dreams, Tyler thought.

Same to you, she thought back. As she drifted off to sleep, visions of a shirtless Tyler, lying alone on the sofa, were the last images to float through her mind.

*****

"Toby contacted me last night while you were sleeping," Tyler informed them, in the morning. "The final name on the list is a girl named Grace. She lives in Salt Lake City."

"Salt Lake, huh?" said Eddie. "Well then, I guess we go meet Sarah, this morning, and then we'll head back to the airport."

"Well then, rise and shine, boys," Liliana said. "It sounds like we have a fun day in store." She glanced at Tyler and thought back to their conversation from the night before. In the moment, when he had held her hands, she had felt as though they had shared an emotional connection. She wondered how he would act around her, this morning. She knew that he had to focus on finding his brother. Would he pretend that last night had never happened? She sighed. Only time would tell.

*****

The sunshine that had embraced the previous day was gone;

and in return, their morning was welcomed by thick clouds and a new wave of cold which seemed to declare that snow would soon be upon them.

Liliana stepped out to the sidewalk and held her palm up to the air. She wasn't sure if it was from the fog or if it was actually starting to snow, but a few small, white flakes fell onto her outstretched hand.

She took a deep breath of the fresh, mountain air and looked around. Her senses were filled with lush evergreens and damp, foggy air. The fog that had set in overnight seemed to envelop them. It felt as though ice crystals crawled on her exposed skin, crept down her coat, and up her pant leg.

"Right now, I'm all about getting out of the cold," Tyler said. "I say we head over to the restaurant, get some food, and see if Sarah's working, yet."

Liliana turned to Tyler. "What are we going to say to her?"

"I don't know. I guess the same thing we told you. We'll just explain to her who we are and what we're doing, here."

"And what if she thinks we're a bunch of freaks and won't come with us? What then?"

Tyler was silent for a moment as he stared at the restaurant. It was kitty-corner from their motel room, on the other side of the dirt, parking lot. "I don't know. I don't want to think about that possibility. We need her. Toby was insistent that it would take all of us to find him. He also said that his kidnappers are on their way, here. If she doesn't come with us, they're sure to find her. Then what?

He stared out across the parking lot for a moment, as though in deep thought and then shook his head. "No, she has to come with us. I can't think of any other option, so let's go and get this over with." He headed down the sidewalk, toward the restaurant, and Liliana and Eddie followed behind.

They had walked only a few feet, when Liliana noticed a blue, four-door sedan in the parking lot. There was nothing particularly unusual about the car, but it seemed to stand out from the other vehicles. As she neared the car, it suddenly seemed brighter. She continued to stare and was overcome with a sense of dizziness. She grabbed on to Eddie's arm to steady herself. "Stop for a second," she said.

Eddie and Tyler halted in mid-step and turned to look at her. As they did so, they followed her gaze to the car that had attracted her attention.

"What is it?" Eddie asked.

Tyler walked back and stopped by her side. "What's up? I'm still freezing. Is this something that we can talk about once we get inside?"

"Something's wrong. That car..."

Eddie looked at the vehicle in question. "You have a bad feeling about it?"

"Not necessarily a feeling; I'm not psychic. It's just that...well, remember I said that I can see auras?"

"Yeah," Eddie said, slowly. "Do cars have auras?"

"Well, sort of...sometimes they do."

"I thought it was just people or living things that have auras," Tyler said.

"Not really," Liliana began. "Auras are just a reflection of energy fields, and everything has an energy field, including inanimate objects. Inanimate objects give off a different sort of aura, though. Their auras are more influenced by recent human contact. So, sometimes I get visions of auras from things like cars, or even jackets, or jewelry, and other times I don't. It just depends how recently someone has been attached to it and what sort of emotion is connected to the object."

"That's all fascinating," Tyler said, "but long story short, what does this have to do with that car?" His nose and ears had turned bright red, from the cold, and he tapped his foot, impatiently.

Liliana smiled, amused at his physical discomfort. Tyler came across as strong and invincible. His intolerance to the cold made him seem vulnerable. She found his weakness to be cute, in an odd sort of way, and her attraction for him grew.

She looked back and forth from Eddie to Tyler. "Long story, short? Simply put, that car has a bad aura. It stands out from all of the other cars in the parking lot. Something is definitely not right. Whoever has been in this car recently is not a good person."

Eddie looked from the car, back to her, and frowned. "You think it might be the people who took Tyler's brother?"

Liliana met his gaze and shrugged. "Could be. I don't know. Like I said, I'm not psychic; I just see energy. And this car has some bad energy around it. If we walk in there, and the kidnappers are already there..."

"We're screwed," Tyler concluded for her. "But, what choice do we have? We've come all this way to find Sarah. We don't know for sure that the car belongs to the kidnappers. It could belong to any number of bad people who happen to be here, right?"

"Yeah, it could be anyone, but what if it's not?"

"I'll go," Eddie said.

Tyler turned to him. "*You'll* go? What about us?"

"You and Liliana should go back to the room and wait. I'll find Sarah and talk to her. Then I can bring some breakfast back to the room, for you."

"Why do you get to go? Toby's *my* brother. I've come all this way to help him."

"I know," Eddie said, patiently. "And it's not going to do him or any of us any good if you get taken. The kidnappers know what you look like; you're the spitting image of your brother. Chances are, they don't know what I look like. I'm safer. If they see you, they'll be on to us. But, if I go in by myself, we might still have a chance."

"You shouldn't go alone," Liliana said. "They probably don't know what I look like, either. Let me go with you. Sarah might be more likely to listen to a girl, than some single guy. She might just think that you're trying to hit on her."

Eddie smiled. "She might, but it's not worth jeopardizing your safety. Your parents are already going to be upset enough, if they find out that you've run away with me. If you get kidnapped under my supervision—"

Liliana took a step back. "Excuse me? Your *supervision*? I am *not* a little girl!"

"No, you're not. But I am eighteen and you're under age, which means I would be held responsible if anything should happen to you."

"I see your point. I do. But, you still need me. We're all in this together, for better or worse. If we're going to succeed, we're going to have to help each other, however we can. I agree; Tyler should stay in the room so he's not recognized, but I can help. You can't hear thoughts; I can. If the kidnappers are in the restaurant, I should be able to hear their thoughts and spot them out, before it's too late."

She frowned, folded her arms, and looked up at Eddie. He was at least a foot taller, but she stood her ground and fixed her best look of determination. She knew he didn't want to put her in danger, but he had to know that she had a valid point. The kidnappers could be anyone. He could sit right next to them and wouldn't have a clue.

With obvious reluctance, Eddie said, "Alright, you can come. But, you have to promise to stay alert and pay attention."

"I will."

He reached into his pocket and handed Tyler a room key. "Here ya go. Go back to the room and wait. Put the 'Do Not Disturb' sign on the door, and don't answer it for anyone."

Tyler frowned and with a deep sigh said, "Fine, but you'd better bring me back something to eat. I could go for some pancakes or a breakfast burrito."

Eddie smiled. "I'll see what I can do. I've got my phone. Call me if anything's wrong or if you see anyone suspicious."

"Don't worry about me. I'll stay hidden in the room, with the curtains closed. Just don't take too long, okay?"

"No worries. We'll grab a quick bite to eat, talk with Sarah if she's there, and we'll be back."

"With my food," Tyler reminded him.

"With your food," Eddie said, with a chuckle. Then, he turned to her. "You ready?"

She took a deep breath. "Ready as I'll ever be. Let's go."

8 UNEXPECTED VISITORS

Designed to look like a log cabin, the restaurant boasted old, soda bottles, arranged on wooden shelves, and a butter churn, positioned in a nearby corner. The walls displayed black and white pictures of miners and old maps of the area. Amidst the antique, rustic décor was a six-foot-tall painting of Bigfoot, on the far wall.

An inviting, brick fireplace hosted a corner table, where they sat with a view of the entire restaurant.

While Eddie enjoyed the warmth of the crackling fire, Liliana listened to the thoughts of those around them. Every once in a while, she would share something that she had learned about someone at a table nearby; otherwise, they sat in silence.

"The hostess is wondering if her boyfriend will send her flowers for Valentine's Day," Liliana whispered. "She's wondering if he's been secretly seeing the housekeeper from the motel."

"Oh? Sounds like a soap opera." He looked at the hostess in question. She looked to be about twenty and was blonde and curvaceous. He couldn't imagine why any boyfriend of hers would want to cheat on her. "It must be quite entertaining to hear what other people are thinking."

"I've learned how to block out thoughts; otherwise, it would be too overwhelming to constantly have everyone in my head. And besides, I figure it's kinda like intruding or something. I mean, a person's thoughts are meant to be personal. I wouldn't want someone listening to my thoughts, so I try to be courteous of others."

"I hear what you're saying. Still, at certain times, it's gotta be useful to hear what other people are thinking."

"Oh, it is for sure. I can tell if a teacher is serious when he says we'd better listen because the lecture is going to be on the test, or I can tell if a boy likes me or not."

"Like Tyler." He continued to look straight ahead, surveying the restaurant crowd, but his slight grin revealed his amusement.

"What's that supposed to mean?"

"I think you know." He glanced sideways at her and smiled, again. Then he turned his gaze back to the diners. He continued to look around the restaurant, as he spoke quietly. "I can't hear what you two are thinking, but it's obvious that you're into each other. I heard the giggles last night."

Liliana smiled. "It's that obvious, huh? You're right; I do like him. And I know that he likes me, too, but he doesn't want to lose focus on his brother. I can't blame him." She was silent for a moment and then said, "It wouldn't work, anyway. I mean, I'm only sixteen, and we live a thousand miles away from each other. Long distance relationships never last. It's better if we just focus on finding his brother and just stay friends."

They were interrupted by the approach of their waitress. "I'm so sorry about the wait," she said. "It's crazy here this morning, with this Bigfoot convention, in town."

Their waitress, who appeared to be about twenty, had shoulder length, auburn red hair, sparkling, crystal green eyes, and for a moment Eddie forgot about Jenna and Toby and kidnappers. He was simply captivated by her dazzling smile.

And then, he realized that Liliana was nudging his arm. "I ordered," she said, sweetly but pointedly. "It's your turn…Eddie?"

"Oh, um, yeah." He flipped the menu open, upside down. He had known what he wanted to order for the past ten minutes, but suddenly all thoughts of food were forgotten.

He heard Liliana chuckle under her breath but didn't look at her.

In an attempt to sound confident, he finally said, "I'll have the French toast and bacon."

"Alright, I'll put your order right in. My name's Sarah, by the way. Is there anything else I can get for you, while you wait? Would you like a refill on your drinks?"

Eddie made immediate eye contact with Liliana. For the first time, he wished that he had the ability to read her thoughts and silently communicate. This was Sarah? Their Sarah who they had come in search of? He had pictured meeting her for the first time, had imagined what their conversation would be like, but never had it crossed his mind that she would be so...so beautiful.

"Sure, thanks," Liliana said.

Sarah turned to him. "Would you like another hot chocolate?"

"Huh?...Oh...um...yeah...sure...thanks," he managed to sputter.

"I'll be right back with that." She smiled and then turned toward the kitchen.

As soon as she was out of earshot, Liliana giggled. "Wow, you really like her, huh?"

"Well..."

"She's married."

"She is?" He wondered if his disappointment was obvious.

"Yeah, *and* she's pregnant."

"How can you tell? She doesn't look pregnant."

"I saw her aura. Pregnant women have a different type of aura; it's like a golden glow. You know how they say, 'a woman seems to glow when she's pregnant'? Well, it's because of her aura. There's no doubt about it; Sarah's pregnant. You've fallen for a married, pregnant woman," she teased.

"I haven't *fallen* for her. I just think she's...pretty."

Liliana snickered under her breath. "Oh, is that all? Well, we need to think of what we're going to say before she comes back with our drinks. Do you have any ideas?"

"I don't know. If she's married, there's no way that her husband is going to let her go traipsing off with us, and if she's pregnant she's not going to want to put her unborn baby in danger.

"There is no 'if'. She *is* married, and she *is* pregnant. But, if she doesn't come with us, she'll be in danger, so maybe we can use a scare tactic to try to convince her."

"Scare her into coming with us? I don't know. Maybe it's better if she stays here, or maybe we can convince her to take a short vacation and hide out somewhere."

"Well, we need to at least talk to her, you know? Give her the choice and let her know that she could be in danger."

Eddie sighed. "Yeah, you're right."

"Here she comes, time to turn on the charm."

Just as Sarah approached their table, Eddie mumbled under his breath, "Read my thoughts."

"What?" Liliana whispered.

Through a forced smile, he mumbled, "You heard me."

"Here you go." Sarah placed new glasses on the table. "Is there anything else I can get for you?"

"No thanks, this is fine." Eddie indicated his hot cocoa. As she turned to leave, he called out, "Sarah?"

She turned to him and smiled. "Yes?"

"I know you're busy, but do you think you could sit with us for a few minutes to talk?"

I'm not sure what I'm going to say to her, Eddie thought to Liliana, *but I know you can hear me, and you can hear what Sarah is thinking, too, so if I start to fumble, help me out. Okay?*

Liliana tapped her foot on his, under the table, and he knew that she understood.

"That's really kind of you to offer," Sarah replied, "but I really am pretty busy. I need to get food out to the tables, or the customers are going to get impatient."

"I understand," Eddie said. "We were just hoping that we could chat with you before we have to leave this morning. Do you have a break soon?"

Sarah looked puzzled at his earnest attempt to talk. "Um, no, sorry. Julie is the only other waitress, besides me, for the next hour."

He sensed that she was anxious to escape his pleas for conversation. *Any ideas, Liliana? I can't make her sit and talk with us, and she does have a point. She has a job to do. Maybe we should just wait until she gets off of work.*

Just as Sarah started to walk away, Liliana called out, "Sarah?"

Their waitress turned, this time with a somewhat amused but annoyed expression on her face. "Yes?"

"The truth is," Liliana said, "we came here to surprise you.

See, my friend, Eddie, here, heard that your husband, Danny, was sent overseas with the military. He wanted to check on you, to make sure that you're doing alright. He *influenced* me to come along for the ride." At the word 'influenced', Liliana kicked Eddie hard on the shin, so that there would be no mistaking her meaning. The night before, they had shared stories of their various powers, and Eddie had told her that he could mentally influence the actions and decisions of others. This was Liliana's way of telling him that he should use his "influential charms", now, to convince Sarah to talk with them.

Keep her talking for a minute, Eddie thought to Liliana.

"...so, you know how guys are," Liliana continued, "they watch each other's back, especially during times like this, when they're sent away and have to leave their pregnant wives, home alone. Eddie wanted to make sure that you're doing alright."

Liliana was obviously using Sarah's private thoughts to learn about her husband and personal life. As she continued to spin her story, he concentrated on the beautiful waitress and sent positive thoughts and energy her way.

When he felt that he had complete concentration on Sarah's energy, Eddie interjected into the conversation. "So, it would really mean a lot if you could sit with us, for a few minutes. I know that Danny would be happy to know that I came to see you." He smiled at Sarah. It wasn't difficult to send warm thoughts her way; just looking at her made him smile. He didn't care if she was married or not; he could still appreciate her beauty.

"So, you know Danny?"

"Well..." He didn't want to lie to her. Liliana had stretched the truth a bit and had perhaps implied that they knew her husband, but she hadn't come out and said so. If they were going to get Sarah to believe their story, it would be best if they stuck to the truth as much as possible. So far, everything Liliana had said was completely true; Danny would be happy to know that they had checked on his wife.

"Why don't you get yourself a cup of hot chocolate and join us for a few minutes. We can tell you all about it," he said.

"Well, it's very kind of you to come see me. Maybe later this afternoon, when I get off of work—"

Eddie tried to sound disappointed. "I'm afraid we won't be here this afternoon. We have to head home." He feared that his efforts to influence her had failed, and he conjured up a new wave of positive energy to send her way. His efforts seemed to work, because in a moment, her hesitant expression disappeared. Her face seemed to lighten, and her eyes twinkled in reaction to his smile.

"Alright," she said, "I guess it won't hurt to sit for a few minutes, since you did come all this way to see me. Let me just talk to Chelsea, our hostess, and see if she can cover for me, for a little bit. I'll be right back."

Eddie watched Sarah walk to the podium by the front door. She spoke to the hostess and then both girls disappeared into the recesses of the kitchen.

Once Sarah was completely out of sight and earshot, he turned to Liliana with a smile. "You were brilliant. Thank you."

She grinned in return. "You weren't too bad, yourself." She stared at the fire for a minute and then asked, "Did you do the same thing on me? *Charm* me into coming with you?"

Eddie shook his head. "No, not at all. But, then again, it wasn't necessary. You could hear our thoughts, so you knew we were telling the truth."

"That's true...and I trusted you from the beginning because I read your aura. Good, that makes me feel better; at least I know that I'm here on my own free will."

Eddie laughed. "Yeah, well, I'm not *that* good. I can have a strong influence over someone, but I can't make people do anything they don't want to do. Sarah *wanted* to sit and talk with us; she just had another voice in her head telling her that she should work, instead. I just helped to quiet that other voice, for a while, so that she could concentrate on what she really wanted."

"And what she wants is to sit down and talk with us?"

"Absolutely, otherwise she never would have agreed to it. Believe me, when I was a kid, I tried to convince my parents to let me stay up past my bedtime and not make me eat my vegetables. It never worked because they truly wanted me to eat my veggies, and they couldn't wait for me to go to bed so that they could have some alone time."

Liliana laughed. "That's funny. Still, I'll bet you were able to use your gift to your advantage once in a while."

"Sure, like the time I wanted to go to Disneyland over spring break. My mother kept insisting that she couldn't take the time off of work, but that time I won out and talked her into taking us. Deep down she really wanted to go; it just took a little extra power of persuasion on my part."

"Nice," Liliana said and then glanced up. "Here she comes."

He followed her gaze. Sarah was headed their way with breakfast plates in hand.

She set the plates on the table and took a seat. "So, where are you from?"

"I'm sorry, we didn't introduce ourselves. My name's Eddie, and this is Liliana."

"Hi." Liliana smiled sweetly and then occupied herself with breakfast. Eddie had his sweet talking charm up and running and she was ready to let him do the talking.

"It's nice to meet you," Sarah replied. "Where do you know Danny from? Were you in the military together?"

"Um...not exactly." Eddie glanced at Liliana and took a deep breath as he gathered courage to explain why they had come. He continued to focus positive energy her way.

"The truth is, we don't actually know Danny." When he saw that she was about to ask questions, he quickly interjected, "But, we do know that he is away from home right now and you're alone. We did come here to make sure that you're okay."

Obviously confused, Sarah tilted her head sideways and raised her eyebrows. "We've never met, right?"

"Right."

"And, you don't know my husband?"

"Uh...no."

"So...?"

"Alright, this is going to sound a little odd, but please just hear us out before you say anything. Okay?" When he noticed her confusion start to turn to frustration, he sent her another wave of warm energy. Soon, the frustration seemed to dissipate, and he sensed a juncture of peace settle upon her.

She nodded. "Go ahead."

"I have a friend; his name's Tyler. We only met just a few days ago..."

As he spoke, he glanced at Liliana, who would listen to Sarah's thoughts and be ready to warn him if he needed to boost up the positive energy.

"...and so, that's why we're here," he concluded, after he had explained the entire story. "I know it sounds crazy; it has to, because that's what I thought when Toby first contacted me. But it's all real, every last bit of it. For whatever reason that we can't begin to understand, there really are people after us, and they *are* ready to take us when they find us. Even if you don't care about finding Toby, think about yourself and your baby. If you come with us, we can watch your back and track these people down, before they track us down."

"I don't know what to say," Sarah said.

"Sarah," Liliana began, "I know you must be confused, and you're probably hesitant to run off with a bunch of people you just met, but you can't stay here. I've never done anything crazy like this in my life. My parents would be furious if they knew that I wasn't in school, but I took the risk because this is serious. There *are* people after us, and if I had stayed home, they would have come after me and found me, just like they're going to come after you."

Sarah sat in silence. She picked up a discarded, straw wrapper and began to tie it in knots. Eddie and Liliana turned their attention to their breakfast, as they waited for her to say something.

Finally, she looked up. "I understand that you're in quite the predicament. I get that, but...," she paused as if to search for the right words, "I'm not the girl you're looking for."

They sat in momentary silence, trying to absorb this new bit of information. Was it possible that they had tracked down the wrong person? Toby had specifically told Tyler that Sarah worked at this restaurant, unless...

"Is there another Sarah who works here?" Eddie asked.

She shook her head. "Um, no, sorry."

"You are Sarah *Hughes*, right?"

"I am."

She smiled politely, but Eddie sensed that it no longer mattered how much charm and energy he threw her way; this conversation was just about over, as far as she was concerned.

"My name is Sarah Hughes, but it's a common name." She shook her head, again. "Obviously, you're looking for someone else. I'm sorry that I can't help you."

Eddie glanced at Liliana. *Is she lying?* he asked, silently.

Liliana shrugged.

How can you not know? I thought you could always detect a lie.

Not for the first time, he wished that he could hear Liliana's thoughts. It was like a one-way conversation; he could silently ask her questions, but she couldn't respond.

Help me out, he silently pleaded. *I don't know what else to say. She has to be the right Sarah Hughes. How could there be a mistake?*

"Sarah," Liliana began, "I know that this sounds strange and scary, but if you don't let us help you, the kidnappers *will* eventually show up, looking for you."

"Well, if they do, I'll just explain to them, like I told you, that they have the wrong person. Sarah Hughes is a very common name."

Eddie felt like there was nothing else he could possibly say, but he took one last grasp at hope. "What if the kidnappers find you and they don't take 'no' for an answer? What if they insist that you are the Sarah Hughes they're looking for and they decide to take you anyways? Would you at least think about going away for a little while? Maybe you could take a trip to see family?"

"I have nowhere to go. In fact, I *am* on a trip, visiting family. My home is in Fort Lewis. I came here to live with my aunt, when my husband was deployed, so that I wouldn't be alone. I have no other family, and I'm five months pregnant.

"Don't worry," she continued. "If they show up, I'm sure they'll be able to see that I'm not the person they're looking for, because when it comes down to it, the facts are very simple...I don't have any special gifts. I can't read minds, or tell the future, or make objects float through the air. I'm just plain, old, Sarah Hughes. There's nothing special about me."

That's where you're mistaken, Eddie thought, to himself. He wasn't psychic, he couldn't read auras or hear thoughts, but he was certain that there was something very special about Sarah Hughes, even if she had no powers, as she claimed. He felt drawn to her and wanted to protect her, but he felt that there was nothing else that he could say or do.

"Okay," Eddie finally said, with reluctance.

"*Okay*?" Liliana asked, in quiet bewilderment.

What else can I say to her? he asked, silently.

From the corner of his eye he saw Liliana shrug and shake her head.

"Look," Eddie said, "I apologize for taking up your time with this crazy story, and I hope that we haven't upset you, too much. Hopefully we can find the Sarah Hughes we're looking for. I wish you the best of luck with the baby and hope for the safe return of your husband."

"Thank you," Sarah said, with a sincere smile. She stood, and Eddie and Liliana rose, as well. "It was nice meeting you, even under these strange circumstances. I wish you the best of luck finding your friend's brother. If you like, I can package you up some muffins and juice to take back to the room, for him."

"Thank you," Eddie said. "That would be nice."

"I'll be right back with your check and the muffins."

"Now what?" Liliana asked, after Sarah was gone. "Where do we go from here?"

He shook his head. "I don't know. I hear what she's saying,

but I just don't buy it. You can't tell if she's lying?"

"No, it's weird. Usually, when someone is lying their auras are, well...different. Her aura changed a little, but not like she was lying. She seemed more confused than anything else. I believe her when she says she doesn't have any powers. I certainly didn't hear her think otherwise. But, there was something strange, when I tried to listen to her thoughts, I heard—"

She was interrupted by Sarah's return, to the table. "Here ya go." She handed them the check, a to-go cup with juice, and a white paper bag. "I packed a few extra muffins for the road, since it sounds like you might be gone for a while. My treat."

"Thank you," Liliana said, as she accepted the bag.

"Do you have a piece of paper I could write on?" Eddie asked.

"Um...sure, here." Sarah handed him a pen and the tablet she used for writing orders.

"I'm writing down my cell phone number and address," he told her. "If something comes up after we leave, if anyone comes around and scares you, or you just want to talk to us for any reason, please give me a call. We're flying out to Salt Lake as soon as we leave here, to go meet a girl named Grace; she's the last person on the list. After that we plan to head back to Arizona to figure out the next step. That's where we'll be."

He tore the paper off of the tablet, folded it in half, and handed it to her. "So, please, keep this somewhere safe, and call me if you change your mind."

She accepted the folded paper and placed it in the pocket of her jeans. "Thank you. I appreciate your concern, really I do. Good luck with everything."

*****

"What, no breakfast burrito?" Tyler asked, when Liliana handed him the cup of juice and bag of muffins.

"You were lucky to get that," Eddie said.

"Uh oh, what happened?"

"She's not coming," Liliana said, as she plopped down on the edge of the bed.

"What do you mean, she's not coming?"

Eddie sat in the armchair and sighed. "Sarah claims there's nothing special about her and she's not the person we're looking for."

"Are you *serious*? Did you explain it to her? Did you let her know that her name is on the bad guys' list and they're going to come after her?"

"Yeah, we explained it all, in as many ways as we could think of. She insists that we have the wrong person and there's no way she'll consider coming with us."

Tyler slumped on the hard sofa. "Great! So, now what?"

"Now, I guess we go find Grace."

"I have a question," Liliana interrupted. "Did it ever occur to you guys that if these kidnappers are as powerful as Toby claims, they can track our cell phones and your rental car, or for that matter, any credit card transactions that you make?"

"I hadn't thought about that, but you're right," Eddie said. "I don't know what other choice we have, though. I don't exactly have a lot of money in my savings account, and I can't ask my parents to borrow money any more than you can. Credit cards are all we've got, right now. I guess it's a chance we're going to have to take. But, you're absolutely right about the cell phones; we should turn them off."

After they had located their phones, Tyler said, "Wait a second. It's not enough to just turn them off. The GPS can still be traced. We need to take out the battery, too."

Liliana raised her eyebrows in question. "Really? Are you sure?"

"Well, I don't know from experience, but it's something that I learned from one of my roommates."

Liliana smiled. "At your, uh...special school?"

Tyler grinned in return. "Exactly. I guess you could say it was an enriched, educational experience."

While Eddie checked out, at the front office, Tyler and Liliana loaded their bags into the car. As they pulled out of the parking lot and headed for the airport, Eddie looked back at the restaurant. He couldn't help but think about Sarah and prayed that it wasn't a mistake to leave her behind. "Liliana?"

"Yeah?"

"Back in the restaurant, you said that when you were listening to Sarah's thoughts, you heard something strange. What was it?"

"Yeah, I've never heard it, before, but I'm sure I wasn't mistaken."

"What was it?"

"I heard her baby."

"Her *baby*?"

"Yeah, I heard thoughts coming from her, but they definitely weren't her thoughts. It had to be her baby."

"Really? What was he...or she thinking?"

"I got the feeling that it was a boy. He was trying to tell me that we should take Sarah with us."

From the backseat, Tyler leaned forward. "What are you saying? Are you saying that the baby could hear your thoughts?"

Liliana turned to look at him. "Yeah, I think that's exactly what happened."

9 SARAH

Armed with a fresh pot of coffee, Sarah glanced out the window in time to see her peculiar visitors drive out of the parking lot and head out onto the highway. They must have mistaken her for someone else, but still, something that they had said resonated in her mind, and she hoped that it hadn't been a mistake to send them away.

The hot drips of coffee, down her arm, reversed her awareness back to the task at hand. Too late, she realized that she had overfilled the customer's cup. "Oh no!" she exclaimed. She set the coffee pot on the table and poured the excess liquid into an empty cup. Then she grabbed a napkin and wiped off the outside of the mug.

The customer offered her another napkin which she graciously accepted. "Thank you. I'm so sorry," she said, as she dried her arm; the coffee had dripped down to her elbow.

The man appeared to be in his late fifties. Slightly overweight and balding, he sported a thick mustache and wore a blue flannel shirt. He chuckled and flashed a jovial smile. "Don't worry about it, happens to the best of us. A little distracted this morning, huh? Daydreaming about your man?"

The woman beside him smacked his arm. "Chuck! Don't tease the poor girl." From the familiar way she spoke to him, Sarah assumed the plump woman with the bright, purple, flowered sweater, had to be his wife.

Sarah smiled. "It's okay. I guess I was a little distracted. I was watching some...friends drive away. I'm sorry. Is there anything else that I can get for you, this morning?"

The woman patted her purple, flowered belly. "Oh, no thank you. I'm stuffed."

"Alright then, I'll be right back with your check." The jingle of the bell on the door caught her attention, and she turned to see a sharply dressed couple, who looked to be in their late thirties, walk in. They appeared out of place amongst the other guests, their attire much too expensive for the usual patrons who frequented the diner. She ruled out the possibility that they were locals or even Bigfoot enthusiasts and was curious what had brought them to town.

After she handed the check to the balding man and his wife, Sarah grabbed a couple of menus from the front podium and made her way over to the mystery couple. They had seated themselves by the fireplace, at the same table where Eddie and Liliana had sat, ten minutes earlier.

She noticed the man had manicured fingernails. He had removed his trench coat to reveal a brown, pullover, sweater vest with a lightly checkered, long sleeved, collared shirt, beneath. She couldn't see his shoes, under the table, but from the glance she had seen when he had walked in the door, they had looked to be pricey and completely impractical for the ice and impending snow. No, Sarah thought, this man certainly wasn't a local.

The woman beside him looked equally displaced. She too, had also removed a long trench coat, and Sarah saw that she wore a cream colored, cashmere sweater. Her shoulder length, blonde hair was tucked behind her ears to reveal pearl earrings that matched her pearl necklace. When the woman had entered, Sarah noticed that she wore high heels, shoes that were also equally impractical for the icy conditions.

She realized that she still held the menus and quickly placed them on the table. She pasted on a smile and hoped it wasn't obvious that she had been staring. "Good morning, my name's Sarah. I'll give you a few minutes to look at the menu. Can I start you off with something to drink?"

The couple immediately glanced at each other when she introduced herself. It seemed an odd behavior, but she brushed it off as her imagination. The warning about kidnappers still had her on edge. Surely, this couldn't be them, could it? She pushed the thought aside; it was a ridiculous idea, of course. Whoever Eddie and Liliana had thought they were searching for, it certainly wasn't her. There was nothing special about her, and no one had any reason to look for her.

They're odd, but they're not here to kidnap me, Sarah chided herself.

The man casually flipped through the menu. "Sarah, are you serving lunch yet? We just flew in, from out of town, and our schedule is slightly off." He smiled and seemed nice enough; and yet, a line of goose bumps ran down her arms, in warning.

She made a mental note to take a break as soon as she placed their order. *It must be pregnancy hormones playing havoc with my nerves*, she thought.

"We don't serve lunch for another hour yet, but the place has cleared out enough, the cook might make an exception for you. I can run back and check, if you like."

"Thanks, that would be great."

Anxious to escape their odd stares and her sense of unease, Sarah excused herself to the kitchen, where she was greeted with a friendly smile by her friend, Juan. "Hey, m'hija," he said, "what's up?"

"I hate to ask, but this couple that just came in wants to know if you're willing to make lunch."

The cook glanced at the clock on the wall. "It's no time yet."

"I know. I know. But they seem really...uppity. I was scared to tell them no. I told them I would check with you."

Juan looked at her quizzically and shook his head. He didn't understand her word choice.

"Uppity...you know, um...rich...used to getting what they want."

He smiled in understanding. "Ah, I see...snobbish."

Sarah nodded. "Yes, and I am in no mood today to deal with cranky, demanding customers. So, do you think you could just make them lunch so they'll be happy, and eat, and get outta here?" Sarah pressed the palms of her hands together in a pleading gesture. "Pleeease." She offered a beaming smile.

Juan nodded. "For you, m'hija, anything."

Sarah smiled at the Spanish endearment. "Thank you!"

After she had taken their order, she caught up to her friend, Julie, at the kitchen door. "Hey, would you mind taking my table by the fireplace? I need to take a break for a little bit."

"Sure thing." She looked over Sarah's shoulder, to the table in question. "Who are they? They look a little out of place for these parts. Are they lost?" She laughed at her own joke.

"Yeah, I don't know. I didn't ask, but I know what you mean. They said they just flew in from out of town. Definitely not from around here, that's for sure. Let me know if you find out anything; I'm curious."

"Alright. Have they ordered yet?"

"Not yet, I'll get their order and put it in then I'm going to sit in the office for a bit and take a break."

"Are you feeling okay? Can I get you anything?"

Sarah knew her friend was concerned; it wasn't like her to take a break so early in the day. "I'm fine, just a bit tired. I'll just prop my feet up for fifteen minutes, and I'm sure I'll feel refreshed."

"Take an hour. The morning rush is over, and I doubt we'll get much of a crowd until dinner. Go on, go take a break. I'll call you if I need help."

"Thanks." Sarah offered an appreciative smile, and with relief, headed for the break room.

*****

Sarah plopped into the blue, lounge chair and turned on the television. She had no interest to watch anything in particular and did so more out of a desire for background noise so that she wouldn't feel alone. She closed her eyes, took a deep breath, and let it out slowly.

When her husband, Danny, had been deployed overseas, leaving her alone and pregnant in Fort Lewis, Washington, her aunt had suggested that she stay with her to help run the family inn and restaurant. Grateful for the offer, Sarah had moved to Granite Falls, in December.

She had known from the beginning of her marriage that there was a risk he could be sent into a war zone, but she had illogically told herself that it wouldn't happen to him. She had dreamt that they would get married, she would finish college, and they would buy a little house with an apple tree in the backyard, get a dog, have a couple of babies, and live happily ever after.

Now, seven months later, and only twenty-years-old, she was indeed married and had a baby on the way, but she was alone. Her hopes of a little house and happily ever after, were a wishful dream, for the future. She tried not to worry about the dangers that Danny faced and prayed daily for his safe return. To keep her mind occupied, she had transferred her college credits to a nearby college, so that she could continue her studies to become a teacher. Any free time that she had was spent at the restaurant. Free time meant time to worry, and so she tried to stay constantly busy with work and school.

She ran a hand absent-mindedly through her hair and sighed; then she closed her eyes and rested a hand on her belly. Her momentary respite was interrupted by a voice in her head. *You should go to the airport, now.*

She opened her eyes and shook her head. Was she imagining things? This wasn't the first time, since she had been pregnant, that she had heard a voice in her head, but she had always pushed the idea aside and chalked it up to her imagination. Pregnancy hormones could wreak havoc on emotions, and she had assumed that hearing voices was an adverse product of pregnancy.

It's not your imagination; you need to leave. Follow your instincts. You're in danger, and you know it.

Sarah sat up. Maybe she should go, but how could she justify it? Her visit from Eddie and Liliana, not to mention the strange couple in the restaurant, had her nerves on edge; but really, she had no justifiable reason to think that she was in any sort of danger. Maybe she should just take the remainder of the day off and get some rest.

Her thoughts were interrupted by another voice; but this time, she recognized the source. It was her Aunt Mae. "Hey there! Julie said that I could find you in here. You feelin' okay, Sweetie Pie?"

Her aunt stood in the doorway. Obviously concerned, she pursed her lips and frowned.

"I'm fine, Aunt Mae, just a bit tired, but I'm fine, really."

"Well, that's good. I'll tell you what, it's a bit slow in there, right now, but I expect we'll have a large crowd, tonight. We're running low on some supplies. How would you feel about taking a break from the restaurant, for a bit, and running to the store, for me?"

The prospect of a drive and some shopping sounded like the perfect reprieve to clear her thoughts. "Sure, sounds like fun. Do you have a shopping list?"

"Yep, right here." Her aunt handed her a folded piece of paper. "Try not to take too long though; a storm is supposed to roll in later this afternoon, and I don't want you to get stuck."

Sarah grabbed the keys, for the truck, off the desk. "No worries, Aunt Mae. I'll be there and back before you know it. Call me if you think of anything else you need."

*****

The warehouse store was, thankfully, uncrowded. Sarah loved to shop at the massive store but found that she had little patience to deal with the hordes of people who were often drawn there.

It didn't take long to gather the desired supplies, and though Sarah was tempted to browse the children's clothing section, on the way to the checkout line, she passed up the allurement and made her way to the front of the store. She had just pushed her large cart past a row of books when an overwhelming sense that she was being watched made her pause.

She thought she saw him out of the corner of her eye. A man in a trench coat stood at the opposite side of the store, at the end of a food aisle. Just as she turned to get a look at him, he disappeared up the aisle, out of sight. Was it her imagination? It was winter after all; plenty of people wore trench coats. And yet...he had looked very much like the man from the restaurant.

For a moment she was tempted to investigate. *But, then*

what? she pondered. If she discovered that it wasn't him, she would be relieved, but what would she say if she came face to face with him? On the other hand, if she didn't look to see who it was, she would worry for the rest of the day that she was being followed.

She picked up a children's book and pretended to read the back cover, as she contemplated the best course of action. A glance out of the corner of her eye revealed that the man was nowhere in sight. *It had to be my vivid imagination playing tricks on me again,* she chided herself.

After she had located the shortest line, she drummed her fingers on the cart with impatience. When the line finally moved, she grabbed a giant jar of salad dressing to place onto the conveyor belt but froze with the jar in mid-air, when she glanced toward the food court and caught sight of a blonde haired woman in a trench coat. Her back was to Sarah, so her face was undetectable, but it was too much of a coincidence for Sarah's peace of mind.

She silently willed the cashier to move faster, and as soon as he handed her the receipt, she thanked him and headed for the exit. As she passed the table, on the way to the door, she noticed that the blonde haired woman had been joined by a man in a trench coat. Their backs were to her, and she still couldn't see their faces.

Sarah had stopped to stare and realized that, in doing so, she held up the flow of customers who were in line to exit the store. She pushed her cart off to the side, took out her phone, and pretended to send a text while she considered her options. After a minute of deliberation, she decided that she wasn't mentally prepared for any sort of confrontation and continued on. She resisted the urge to look back and kept her sights on the exit.

The sky began to spit miniscule snowflakes as she walked toward the truck. Her hands shook, not from the cold but from nerves, as she all but threw the boxes from the cart into the back of the truck. Without wasting time to return the cart, to the cart corral, she left it beside the truck, jumped into the front seat, and made a beeline for the exit.

Before she turned onto the street, she checked her rearview mirror to see if she was followed, but there was no one behind her. Maybe her overactive imagination had played tricks on her, after all.

It wasn't until she had exited the freeway and was headed down the quiet highway, to Granite Falls, that she was able to relax. Another check in the mirror revealed an aging, red minivan but no one else. She breathed a sigh of relief and shook her head at her excitable state of mind. Obviously no one followed.

She adjusted the volume on her favorite radio station and turned her thoughts back to her morning visitors. Why would they claim that she was in danger, unless it was true? What could they possibly have to gain from her involvement? They hadn't asked for money, so it wasn't like they would benefit financially. She drummed her fingers on the steering wheel. Was it possible that there was an ounce of truth behind their story?

For a few moments, she noted the evergreen trees, fields of horses, and occasional houses, but then her surroundings became indiscernible as she replayed their conversation in her head, but after reviewing everything they had told her, she was drawn back to her original conclusion. "They must have the wrong person." She spoke out loud but found that her fears weren't suppressed. She couldn't unleash the feeling that she was being followed. She began to doubt herself and wondered, not for the first time, if it had been a mistake to send Eddie and Liliana away.

"But, why would anyone want to find me?" she asked herself, out loud. "What purpose could they possibly have?"

They want to find you, so they can get to me, the voice in her head replied.

The truck swerved dangerously close to the ditch, on the side of the road. With a racing pulse, Sarah realized that she had crossed the white line and quickly straightened her course. For a minute she focused to keep the truck between the lines, but soon her thoughts wandered as she thought about the voice.

She took her left hand off of the steering wheel and placed it on her baby bump. It wasn't possible, was it? Her rational mind told her that she was ridiculous; mothers didn't hear the thoughts of their unborn babies. And yet…what else could explain the distinct voice in her head?

'They want to find you, so they can get to me', the voice had said. Is that the answer? she wondered. *Maybe the kidnappers aren't interested in me at all. Is it possible they're after the baby?*

As she contemplated this new idea, a black, four-door sedan came up from behind and passed her on the two-lane highway. Sarah checked her speed; she was going five miles per hour over the speed limit. *Hmm, they must be in a hurry*, she thought. Just as soon as the car had passed and taken the lead, however, it slowed down. It slowed enough so that Sarah was forced to reduce her speed to twenty miles per hour below the speed limit.

There were double yellow lines, and so she had to follow at the snail speed for two miles. Once it was safe to pass, she took the first opportunity. She looked over to get a glimpse at the driver but couldn't see through the vehicle's dark, tinted windows.

After she had safely passed, she reset her speed, and then glanced in the rearview mirror to see if the car now lagged behind. Her heart skipped a beat when she discovered that the black vehicle now rode her bumper.

With both hands firmly gripped to the steering wheel, she glanced at the road sign. The town was still eight miles in the distance. She debated if she should pull off at the nearest gas station or if she should continue on to the restaurant.

Slowly, she increased her speed, not too much, just enough to get to town faster. She also hoped that the increase in speed would encourage the driver to back off. This was not the case; as her speed increased, the driver matched it and stayed dangerously close to her bumper.

It occurred to her then, that if she slowed, the vehicle might pass her, once more. She didn't tap her breaks to draw attention but took her foot off of the gas pedal and allowed the truck to gradually slow on its own. The car continued to match her speed for a minute, and then, it suddenly swerved around her and narrowly missed an oncoming semi before it shifted back into her lane and continued ahead. For a moment it seemed as though the driver was going to speed off and leave her behind, but then he slowed, and Sarah found herself stuck behind him, once again.

Like a vision of a water mirage in the desert, a gas station miraculously came into view, about half a mile up the road. She continued to follow behind the car at the same speed. Her pulse continued to race as she neared the gas station, and then, just as the car passed the entrance, Sarah slammed on the brakes, careened into the parking lot, and brought the truck to a sudden stop in front of the building.

She looked in the rearview mirror to see if the black vehicle had retreated; thankfully it was nowhere in sight. She wished that she could call her husband. If he were home, he would run to her rescue. But, she couldn't call him, and she was on her own. She wondered if there was enough cause to call the police. What would they say if she told them that she had been harassed on the highway? The car was gone, and she hadn't gotten the license plate. They would probably tell her there was nothing they could do.

Frustrated and feeling helpless, she leaned back, pressed her head against the back of the headrest, and kept watch in the rearview mirror. And then, just as suddenly as they had disappeared, they were back. The black car had returned and was parked at the entrance by the road.

I'm safe; this is a public place, she thought. Her self-affirmation did little to sway her fears as she realized that there were no other vehicles at the gas station. Still, she decided that she wasn't going to sit there and hide. She grabbed her cell phone, stepped out of the truck, and took a firm stance. She couldn't see them but had no doubt that the occupants concealed behind the dark windows were the man and woman from the restaurant. She was also certain that, from behind the veiled windows, they had their eyes trained directly on her.

Her glare didn't falter as she made a production of holding up her cell phone. She pretended to dial a number and then placed the phone up to her ear. *Let them think I'm calling the police*, she thought. For a moment, she wondered why she didn't just call the police but remembered Eddie's answer to that same question. *The people who are after us are more powerful than the police*, he had told her.

They might be more powerful than the police, but it looks like they don't want to face them right now, she thought with glee, as she watched the car pull onto the road and continue the drive, toward town.

She climbed into the truck and immediately pushed the lock button. Now what? she wondered.

Now you go to the airport and find Eddie, the voice in her head clearly responded.

She placed her hands and forehead on the steering wheel. "What am I supposed to tell Aunt Mae?" she asked, out loud.

The voice didn't respond, but she figured that sitting in a parked truck would get her nowhere. Before she had time to reconsider her actions, she pulled a small piece of paper out of her pocket and dialed the number. The phone rang, and rang, and rang. She listened to his message and then the beep. "Hi, Eddie...," she began.

*****

When she pulled into the parking lot, of the inn, she half expected to find the black car waiting, but thankfully, it was nowhere in sight.

The pelting snow had been replaced with large, fluffy flakes. It fell heavily from the low-lying clouds; and already, the ground was white. As she hauled her purchases inside, she noticed the imprints of her footsteps between the truck and restaurant. The snow was piling up fast.

On her second trip through the backdoor, into the kitchen, she ran into Julie. "Hey, how was that table I left you with? You know, the couple who looked like they were from out of town? Did you find out anything about them?"

"Oh yeah, they were quite the pair, weren't they?" Julie replied. "No, I didn't find out much. They said that they were just visiting and checking out the area, but that's about all that I gathered. They weren't quite dressed right to be checking out the local sites if you ask me; but whatever, they left a twenty dollar tip. I'll split it with you, of course."

Sarah was disappointed that Julie hadn't discovered more but hadn't expected that she would. "Don't worry about it. You did the hard work, you deserve the tip. It's yours."

"Really? Thanks! Next time we get rich looking tourists, they're all yours."

"Thanks. Hey, I'm going to head out of town for a couple of days. Do you think that your sister could work and cover for me?" A few drops of water, from her snow covered hair, dripped down her forehead, and she brushed them away with her gloved hand.

"Yeah, I don't see why not. Are you supposed to work tonight?"

"No, I don't work again until Monday."

"Alright, I'll let her know."

"That's great. Tell her I said thank you, alright?"

"I will. Where are you going?"

"I'm just heading back home for a couple of days to say hi to friends and stuff. I should be back within the week."

"Cool, well, have fun. We'll miss you."

"Thanks." Sarah hoped that she was realistic and a week was all that would be needed.

She found her aunt, in the house that they shared, behind the inn. After she had provided a similar explanation for her departure, she packed a bag with a week's worth of clothes and walked back toward the restaurant where she had left her car.

She tossed her duffel bag into the backseat and was ready to hit the road but was soon frustrated to discover that the car wouldn't start. She turned the key twice more, but the results were the same. The car was dead.

That's odd, she thought. *The weather is cold, but it's not that cold. The car should start. It worked just fine this morning.*

She got out of the car, closed the door, and stood in the falling snow. *So much for that plan*, she thought.

A screech of a woman's voice, from across the parking lot, caught her attention. It was followed by a declaration of, "Chuck! Don't let the door close!"

She looked over to see the source of the raucous and spotted the funny, older couple who she had served that morning. They stood outside of the first motel room, next to the office. The woman with the purple sweater was throwing her hands in the air as she shouted at her husband, "My purse was still in there! Now we're going to have to find someone with a key to let us back in!"

"I'm sorry, Bonnie, had I known that your purse was in there, I wouldn't have closed the door. I told you to check to make sure that you had all of your things," replied the man in the blue, flannel shirt.

Sarah chuckled to herself and headed across the parking lot to assist them.

"Hi there," Sarah said. "It looks like you got yourselves locked out of your room. I'd be happy to help."

"Oh, look, Chuck. It's that nice waitress from this morning."

Sarah smiled. "Hi, again! I have a master key. I can let you back in your room. Have you already checked out?"

"Yep," Chuck affirmed. "We *were* just headed out for the airport, until my wife here locked her purse in the room."

"*I* locked my purse in the room? *I* did that? *Really*?" his wife exclaimed.

Sarah fought to contain her laughter as she listened to the couple's tirade. "Here, it's not a problem," she interrupted. "We'll get your purse out in a jiffy." Sarah took out her key ring, found the master key, and let the woman into the room to retrieve her purse.

While she stood beside Chuck, on the sidewalk, a sudden thought occurred to Sarah. If these two were heading for the airport, maybe they could give her a ride. The people in the black SUV would never look for her in a Buick rental, with an overweight balding man and his loud mouthed wife. If she went with them, she wouldn't have to worry about her car until she returned.

"Chuck? Did you say that you're heading to the airport? Are you going there right now?"

"Yeah, as soon as my wife can get a move on," he grumbled.

"I was actually headed to the airport, too, as a matter of fact, but my car won't start. Do you think your wife would mind if I came along for the ride? I'd be happy to chip in gas money."

"You are more than welcome to join us, My Dear. Your company would be like a breath of fresh air."

"Really? You're a lifesaver! Thank you so much. Let me just run, and grab my bag, and I'll be right back."

Sarah popped her head into the kitchen, to find Julie. She informed her friend that she was having car problems and that she was going to borrow a friend's car to drive to Fort Lewis. Then, she grabbed her duffel bag out of the backseat and rejoined Chuck and Bonnie.

"I'm so excited to have another woman to talk to," Bonnie began, as they drove out of the parking lot. "I never get to have a real conversation with Mr. Excitement, over here." She indicated her husband who pretended not to hear and kept his eyes trained on the road.

"Well, I for one am happy to have *pleasant* company for the drive," Chuck said. "Thank you for joining us, Sarah."

Sarah sighed and smiled to herself. It would to be a *long* drive to the airport, but she was thankful that luck had come her way and she had a ride. Now, hopefully with more luck, she would find Eddie and his friends before the kidnappers found her.

10 GRACE

Grace was acutely aware of the rhythmic rain, as it played a somber beat on the black umbrella, overhead. It was held by her boyfriend, Derek, who had remained by her side, as a solid support, since the loss of her grandfather. On her opposite side, stood her mother and younger brother, Ethan, who had remained still as a statue throughout the solemn proceedings.

As the rocketing vibrations of the rifle salute filled the air, Grace observed her grandmother who stood proud and silent as she watched the servicemen. Even through the rain, she could see her grandmother's weakened aura. A plagued sense of heartache warned that her grandmother might not be around much longer. If there had been any doubt, her diminished aura was proof. She had heard tales of broken hearts, stories of spouses who passed away soon after the loss of the other spouse. Grace feared that this might be the case with her grandmother.

She focused her attention on her father and uncle. Dressed in their military blues, they stepped forward, in the wet grass, to pay tribute. Following in their father's footsteps, they had both made a lifetime career in the army.

A tear reached the corner of her eye as she watched the expressionless faces of her father and uncle momentarily falter, but then, they regained their composure and continued on, each exact step carefully measured. Their movements were precise and mechanical as they carefully folded the flag.

Grace knew the task was emotionally daunting for her father, and she was proud of him for his bravery. He had recently returned from an overseas tour of duty, and it occurred to her that standing up in uniform for his father's funeral, to present the folded flag to his mother, was perhaps more difficult than standing up in uniform to face the enemy.

When her mother wandered away from the group to meet her father, Grace realized that the service was over. She watched her father rest his head on her mother's shoulder, saw her mother whisper something in his ear, and then they held each other in a tight embrace.

Her brother, Ethan, who was eleven, huddled close to seek refuge under Derek's umbrella. She tucked him in close, and they stood in silence while they waited for their parents and watched mourners slowly leave the gravesite. A true gentleman at heart, Derek held the umbrella so that she and her brother would stay dry, while he sacrificed himself to the saturating effects of the interminable rain. She felt a weak smile emerge as she watched the water pour off of his hair and then was overcome with guilt. Derek was a wonderful guy; she should be happy that they were together, and yet...she couldn't ignore the fact that she thought of him more as a brother than a boyfriend.

The approach of her parents stalled the progression of her thought process. She would have to dwell on her relationship later.

"Everyone is heading back to Grandma's house," her mother said. "I guess we should probably get over there so we can greet them when they arrive. Are you going to join us, Derek?"

Derek, who stood almost a half foot taller than Grace's height of 5'9", looked down at Grace and smiled as he placed an arm around her shoulder. "I would love to join your family, thank you," he replied, to her mother. "I can't stay too late, though. I still have to pack for the band trip, tomorrow."

"That's right, that is tomorrow, isn't it?" her father replied. "With everything that's happened this past week, I forgot all about it." He turned to his daughter. "Grace, Honey, are you sure you don't want to go? Your ticket is already paid for, and a trip might be just the escape you need."

"No, Dad, I just don't think I could put my heart into playing, right now. It is a competition after all, and I don't think I would be a very good addition to the band. They probably wouldn't appreciate it, if I started crying during the competition."

"Are you sure? It might be a good distraction for you. And if anything, your friends will be there. Derek will be there."

"That's right," Derek said. With his arm still around her, he gave her a squeeze. "The competition will only take up a small part of our time; we also get to spend a day at Disney World, and you can just lay out by the pool at the hotel, if you want to."

"I don't know." Grace hesitated. "I just...I don't think I'm ready for any sort of vacation. It seems like it would be wrong."

"Grandpa would want you to go to the competition," her mother said. "He loved to hear you play the violin."

"I know he did." A lone tear fell from her eye and dripped down the side of her nose.

"Well, look, we're all getting soaked and people are going to start wondering where we are," her father said. "Let's head over to Grandma's house, and we can talk more about it there. If anything, Grace, I say you should sleep on it. You have your ticket, after all, and things might seem brighter tomorrow. If you wake up in the morning and change your mind, I'll drive you to the airport, myself. Will you agree to at least sleep on it?"

"I don't think I'll change my mind, Dad, but yeah, I'll sleep on it. Okay?"

Her father relinquished the shelter of her mother's umbrella and swept Grace into a warm embrace. "I love you, Honey."

"I love you too, Dad."

*****

Grace awoke with a start and glanced at the clock. It was three in the morning. She closed her eyes against her waking reality and tried to regain a hold on the dream that she had been immersed in. She had been driving somewhere with three other people. Although she couldn't recall their names, she could still clearly see their faces, and she could still feel the strong emotion and bond that they had shared. A feeling of anxiety swept over her as she remembered that someone had pursued their every move, and they had needed to get away.

She tossed and turned in an attempt to recapture sleep, but sleep didn't want to be found. Frustrated, she looked at the clock. It was three-thirty. Just as she closed her eyes again and pulled the blankets in close, her internal voice spoke. *You need to go to the airport.*

I'm not going on the band trip, she silently argued.

Get up and get ready, the voice nagged. *Pack your bags, and go to the airport. It will all make sense, in time.*

Grace opened her eyes, stared at the ceiling, and shook her head. None of it made sense, but she had learned long ago to always follow her intuition. It might not make sense, but she also knew that if she didn't listen to her internal voice, she would somehow regret it.

She closed her eyes once again; and immediately, sleep seemed a more attractive option than getting up to go to the airport. Eventually, however, her conscience got the better of her. If her internal voice said that she should go to the airport, she needed to listen.

Regretful to leave the comforts of her pillow and down comforter, she sat up and swung her legs over the side of the bed. She forced her tired eyes open and blinked in confusion as she looked around the room. She was no longer in her bedroom, but rather, a bright sunroom, filled with lush, green, potted plants and several bird cages with brightly colored parrots.

She shook her head and closed her eyes, certain that she must be hallucinating, but when she opened her eyes again, she saw that the sunroom remained and she wasn't alone. Her companions from her dream were there. They sat on white wicker sofas, across from her. A guy with sandy, brown hair, stood behind a girl with long, black hair. His back was to her, as he talked to one of the birds, so she couldn't see his face. The group laughed when the parrot responded to him.

When another girl laughed, Grace realized that, beside her, on the wicker sofa, sat a young woman who appeared to be in her early twenties. She had shoulder length, auburn hair, and striking, crystal, green eyes. Even though Grace didn't recognize her, the knowledge suddenly hit her that they were friends. She closed her eyes in concentration, in an attempt to recall her name. When she opened her eyes a moment later, the girl had disappeared, and the bright red numbers on her clock stared at her. It was four o'clock.

It had all been another dream, another dream that seemed all too real. No time to dwell on it, if she was going to make it to the airport on time, she would have to leave by five-thirty. She had less than two hours to shower and pack. She argued with herself that she wanted to go back to sleep but knew it wasn't going to happen. As much as she didn't want to go on the band trip and celebrate with a group of cheerful teenagers, she knew that she was headed to the airport to meet them, though for the life of her, she had no idea why.

*****

As she made the long hike toward her terminal, Grace's hesitation to go on the band trip continued to nag at her. She felt like she was dragging her feet, awaiting any excuse not to go. With two hours before her flight's scheduled departure, she decided that, rather than going directly to meet Derek and the rest of her classmates, she would stop at a restaurant to get breakfast.

Seated at a tall, round table, she watched travelers hustle by, some struggled with suitcases and strollers; others wandered slowly to pass the time before their flight's departure. Then, her thoughts wandered to her present situation. She couldn't let go of the feeling that her presence at the airport had nothing to do with a band trip. She wished that her internal voice, that had so vehemently urged her out of bed during the wee hours of the morning, would turn itself back on and tell her what to do. It remained silent; however, and so, she sat and waited, waited for...for some sort of an answer that would explain everything.

Overcome with a sudden urge to turn around, goose bumps rose on her arms the moment Grace swiveled in her chair and noticed the woman in line. She couldn't see her face, but she didn't have to. The shoulder length, auburn hair said it all. It was the woman from her dream.

Twisted sideways in her chair, Grace's gaze remained transfixed to the woman as she walked through the line, paid for her food, and then followed an older man and woman to a table.

The woman took a bite of her food and appeared to listen to the older couple in conversation. And then, as though she sensed a watchful eye, she looked up and met Grace's stare. They held eye contact for a moment, and then she turned her attention back to her companions.

Grace pretended to return her attention to her apple-raisin oatmeal, while she carefully watched the woman out of the corner of her eye. Twice, she noticed that the auburn haired woman looked her way, but Grace pretended not to notice.

When the woman stood and walked toward the restroom, across from the restaurant, Grace recognized her opportunity. It was now or never. She didn't want to follow too closely but also wanted to ensure that she got her chance to talk to her. She hadn't planned what to say but knew that she would have to say something; their simultaneous presence at the airport was no mere coincidence.

Feeling much like a stalker, Grace stood in front of a mirror and pretended to fuss with her long, blonde hair, while she waited for the woman to exit the stall. It was with luck that she chose to wash her hands at the sink, next to Grace.

Grace turned to introduce herself and was taken aback when the woman spoke first, "Um, this might sound strange," she said, "but I think you might know some friends of mine. Is your name Grace?"

Stunned, Grace froze, momentarily speechless. She must have appeared disconcerted because the woman immediately followed up with, "I'm so sorry! It was a silly idea." She shook her head. "I don't know what I was thinking. I thought that you might have been Grace, but of course you aren't. I'm so sorry!"

Obviously embarrassed, the auburn-haired woman turned to walk away. Grace regained her composure and called out, "Wait! Don't go. My name *is* Grace."

She swiveled on her heel and stared, unblinking. After an awkward moment of silence, she said, "You're Grace? I mean...really? I thought you might have been, but then, I thought

I was just delusional."

"I know you," Grace told her. "I mean, I don't know you, but I've seen you before. Please don't think I'm crazy. I don't know how else to say this, so I'm just going to say it. I had a dream last night, and you were in it...That sounds crazy, doesn't it?"

The woman shook her head. "Not so crazy...no. No more crazy than a voice in my head telling me that you were Grace. I've heard a lot of crazy things lately, and I think I'm just starting to believe them. I met some interesting people, yesterday. They told me that they were on their way to find a girl named Grace, in Salt Lake. Then, when I saw you back there in the restaurant, a voice in my head told me that you were the girl they were looking for. So no, I don't think you sound crazy at all; if anything, I'm probably the one who sounds crazy."

With raised eyebrows, Grace slowly shook her head. "Wait, there are people looking for me? Who?"

"A few different people...some good, some not so good. Do you have time to talk? My name is Sarah, by the way."

Grace glanced at the time on her cell phone and saw that she still had an hour before her flight would board. It was then that the realization hit her; she hadn't come to the airport for a band trip. She had come to meet Sarah. "Sure," Grace said, "I think we should talk."

Sarah returned to the restaurant so that she could excuse herself from her travel companions, while Grace waited inside of a nearby bookstore and inattentively flipped through a magazine. Sarah found her a few minutes later; and together, they found a quiet bench where they could sit and talk.

Grace explained how she had seen Sarah in her dream and how she had eventually decided to come to the airport, and then she blinked, in speechless, confused awe after Sarah finished her story. When her brain was finally able to formulate words, Grace looked at Sarah and said, "I'm coming with you."

Sarah frowned. "Are you sure?"

"Yep, no one ever has to know. I wonder how difficult it would be to get my ticket switched."

"Hmmm, I don't know. I know that airlines often make special exceptions for people in cases of funerals and things like that....Let's go find out."

*****

"This ticket is nonrefundable." The ticket agent tapped her red, polished fingernails, impatiently, on the computer keyboard. Her tight, severe bun revealed a hint of gray roots, and the dark circles under her eyes said that she was tired of working and had little patience to deal with demanding passengers.

Grace cast a worried look toward Sarah, who patted her arm in reassurance and then faced the ticket agent with an air of authoritative confidence. "I know that, Ma'am, but surely there is something that you can do. My sister isn't asking for a refund, just a destination change. A ticket to Arizona has to cost a lot less than a ticket to Florida. Our grandfather just passed away, and we need to get to Arizona to be with our family."

"Well, we do make exceptions when there is a death in the family, but we would need to get your parents' approval to change the ticket. Give me just a moment; let me go speak with my supervisor."

The ticket agent strode toward the end of the long counter and spoke with another woman who scowled and appeared less than thrilled to deal with another problem.

"I hope this works, Grace. That lady doesn't look too friendly."

Grace eyed the supervisor, who frowned and shook her head while the ticket agent spoke to her. "Don't worry, I can convince her. Along with hearing prophetic voices in my head, I can also influence others."

"What do you mean?"

"Shh," Grace whispered, "they're coming back. Just continue to play along."

When the stocky supervisor stepped up to the counter, it became apparent that the days of tall, skinny flight attendants were long gone. The bulging, shiny gold buttons of her navy blue jacket appeared ready to pop. The ticket agent stepped back to allow her supervisor to take over. Sarah glanced at Grace with a look that said, *Are you sure about this?*

Grace smiled with reassurance. It had been a while since she had used her special talents to influence someone, but she was confident that it wouldn't be too difficult.

"Girls, I understand that your grandfather has passed away. I'm so sorry for your loss," the supervisor began.

As the memory of her own recent loss flooded her emotions, a surge of tears reached her eyes, and she allowed them to flow freely. Her apparent inability to speak would allow her time to focus her energy on the supervisor.

With an unwavering, rigid stare, the supervisor continued, "But, this is a nonrefundable ticket, and with that comes strict guidelines. Now, we do make exceptions for a loss in the family, but we will need your parents' consent to change the ticket."

"I understand that, but our parents aren't here," Sarah told her. "They flew to Arizona, to be with our grandfather, before he passed away."

"Perhaps we could talk to your mother or father on the phone."

While Sarah kept her talking, Grace began to channel positive energy toward the stocky woman behind the counter. The woman's defensive aura slowly faded and then gradually grew warmer. When her aura visibly reached out toward Grace, she knew that she had a solid connection with the woman's energy and was ready to speak.

She eyed the supervisor's nametag. "Donna," Grace began, "please, is there any way that you can help me?" She wiped away a tear. "The next flight to Arizona leaves soon, and we need to get there to be with my family. My sister is over eighteen. Can't she act in place of my mother?"

Grace continued to pour on the positive energy, and the supervisor's mood seemed to visibly transform. Her stern scowl was replaced by an expression of soft concern.

Donna turned to Sarah. "You're over eighteen?"

"I'm twenty. Would you like to see my I.D.?"

With a surprising smile, Donna said, "No, that's not necessary. Let's see what we can do to get everything arranged for you." Her fingernails clicked on the keyboard, for a few moments, and then she said, "It looks like our flight is almost full, but I was able to get you seats next to each other."

A few more clicks of the keyboard and Donna handed Grace the revised ticket off of the printer. "Your flight boards in thirty minutes, Ladies. My condolences to your family."

"Thank you." With a sincere smile, Grace accepted the ticket.

As soon as they were out of earshot from the ticket counter, Sarah turned to Grace. "That was amazing. What did you do back there? It's like that woman's mood shifted from night to day."

"It's something that I learned to do when I was little. When I realized that I could see auras, I learned everything that I could about them. Auras are a reflection of a person's energy. I discovered that energy is something that can be manipulated, and energy has a direct connection to a person's mood and thoughts. So, with a little practice, I learned how to manipulate a person's mood." Grace shrugged. "It's simple, really."

Sarah laughed. "Okay, if you say so."

*****

Seated in the hard, black, vinyl chairs, next to the boarding gate, Sarah recounted everything she knew about Eddie and Liliana. Then, she went on to describe her experience with the black car that had followed her on the road to Granite Falls.

Grace bit her lower lip and looked around nervously as though she would recognize the potential kidnappers if she saw them. "Do you think that the people who followed you will come after you again?"

Before Sarah could respond, they were interrupted by a woman in a bright purple sweater. "There you are, Dear! Who's your friend?" she asked, indicating Grace.

Sarah looked up and smiled at their visitors. "Hi there!

Bonnie, Chuck, this is my...cousin, Grace. She's flying down to Arizona for the family reunion. We weren't supposed to be on the same flight, but since our flight got cancelled last night, and we got laid over, our paths ending up crossing after all, so we get to fly down together."

"Well, isn't that nice," said the heavyset, balding man, who Sarah had introduced as Chuck. "It's a pleasure to meet you, Grace."

Grace shook his outstretched hand. "Nice to meet you."

"We flew in last night from Seattle," Sarah explained to Grace. "We were supposed to catch a connecting flight last night at ten, but it was cancelled, so they switched us to the first flight out this morning."

Bonnie groaned and shook her head. "Looks like we aren't having the best travelling luck. Take a look at the board; looks like our flight has been delayed, again."

Grace glanced up to the departure board and saw that their flight was indeed delayed for an additional two hours. "Well, Sarah, I'm glad that your flight was cancelled last night. I guess everything happens for a reason, huh?" With raised eyebrows and a look that said, *Who are they*? she glanced inconspicuously from Sarah, to her two traveling companions.

Sarah glanced at the couple in question. They were momentarily occupied with a disagreement about the weight of a certain carry-on bag. She rolled her eyes and smiled.

"Bonnie and Chuck happened to be leaving for the airport when I was, and they were kind enough to give me a ride. As luck would have it, they were actually heading for Arizona, too. So I've had the pleasure of their company on this trip."

Grace glanced at the couple. Their auras consisted of an odd tinged hue that she couldn't quite place, but she chalked it up to their argument and flared tempers with each other.

They continued to argue about the necessity of items in the woman's large, flowered, carry-on. Grace turned away and pretended to scrutinize the flight departure board. The momentary distraction allowed her time to mask her impending laughter. With regained composure, she turned back to Sarah and smiled. "It sounds like you found each other at the right time. That certainly was lucky, wasn't it?"

"Wasn't it though?" Sarah returned the knowing smile.

"Is someone going to meet you girls at the airport when you get to Phoenix?" Chuck asked.

"Um, no, I don't think so," Sarah told him. "I think we'll just rent a car and head up to Flagstaff. The rest of our...family is already up there."

Bonnie nudged her husband. "We should give them a ride. It seems silly for them to rent a car, when we could just drive them."

"That's not a bad idea," Chuck said. "What do ya say, Girls? How would you like to put up with us for a little while longer? We'd be happy to take you up north, once we get to town. That'll save you a little bit of money, at least."

Sarah glanced at Grace, who returned the look with an expression that said, *They're your friends, not mine.*

"Um, that's really kind," Sarah began, "but...we wouldn't want to inconvenience you. It's a long trip, and I'm sure the last thing that you're going to want to do is drive three hours out of your way. Didn't you say that you live in the Phoenix area?"

"Yep, but it wouldn't be an inconvenience at all. Our daughter lives up in Flagstaff, and we had planned to go up there for a little visit; it'll be the perfect excuse. We wouldn't hear of you renting a car, when we can take you. So, it's settled then; you just get to put up with us for a little while longer. Isn't that great?"

"That's...great," Sarah said, with a forced smile.

"Great," Grace responded, with an inward sigh.

*****

Grace watched Bonnie and Chuck, who stood up ahead, already in the boarding line. Though undeniably annoying, they seemed sweet enough; and yet, something about them seemed peculiar. Luckily, they were seated at the rear of the plane, and she and Sarah had been assigned to the front, so they would at least have privacy to talk, away from the couple.

Grace squinted in concentration as she continued to observe them. In a controlled battle for energy, their auras shifted back and forth during their continued argument. While both sets of auras were mostly red; which complemented their argument, their auras were also rimmed with a large amount of gray. She found this discovery to be puzzling because gray indicated dark thoughts, or unclear intentions, and it seemed to be contradictory to the bubbly personalities that they had displayed.

"Sarah, do you trust them?"

The ticket agent called for the next group of passengers to board, and Sarah turned to her, as they took their place in line. "Bonnie and Chuck? Yeah, I mean, they seem harmless enough. Why do you ask?"

"I don't know." Grace squinted at them, again. "I agree, they do seem harmless; it's just…something about their auras doesn't seem right."

"Maybe it's just because they're mad at each other…you think?"

"Maybe…I don't know." Grace shook her head. "Just be careful what you say around them. I'm sure they are nice enough, but right now it's probably safe to assume that we shouldn't trust anyone."

"I agree with you there. Until we know what this whole thing is all about and we know who's after us, we probably shouldn't trust anyone."

11 TOBY

From somewhere nearby, a man called out, "Hey, Henry, you there?" The voice sounded vaguely familiar, but Toby couldn't place it.

"Yeah, I'm here. Go 'head," came a garbled reply, over what sounded like a walkie-talkie.

"It looks like the boy's starting to wake up. Just wanted to let you know."

"Thanks, Jesse. I'll send Ashley down with a tray from the kitchen. Come up and see me when you're done and we'll talk."

"Sounds good, will do," the man, who must have been Jesse, responded.

Toby recognized the voice; he had spoken with him on a few occasions and could picture what he looked like. Stylishly dressed, he was a muscular built man, of African American descent. Toby guessed him to be in his early twenties. The last time they had spoken, he had surreptitiously coerced Toby into providing the identities of other uniquely gifted individuals. Toby had worried that once the individuals were identified and located, they would end up no better off than he was now, locked up and held captive. Somehow, Jesse had persuaded him to use his psychic abilities to provide the names; and after that, Toby had shut down and refused to talk.

His eyes remained closed as he lay on the hard, uncomfortable bed and listened to Jesse and the voice on the other end of the walkie-talkie, discuss him. He had tried to pretend that he was still asleep, but obviously the man knew that he was waking up.

Toby slowly turned his head to look at the man who leaned against a desk, near the door.

"How long have I been here? Where am I?"

"Two weeks. And where you are is of no concern, right now. You are...here." He indicated the room with a sweep of his hands.

Toby looked around; except for the desk, single chair, and bed, the room was bare. With the exception of a small, attached room, which he remembered was a bathroom, it was a prison cell.

"*Two weeks*! Are you kidding? How did I lose that much time?"

"You've been...in an altered state of mind."

"An *altered* state of mind? That's putting it mildly. So, now what? Why am I awake, now? Or, maybe I'm not really awake. Are you just a figment of my *altered* state of mind, too?"

Jesse set the walkie-talkie on the desk, folded his arms, and smiled. "No, this is all very real."

"So, why have you decided to talk to me, now?" Toby sat up in bed. He realized too late that this move was a mistake and closed his eyes; his hands immediately cradled his pounding head. Even with his eyes closed, it felt as though the room was spinning, and he decided that it would be best to lie down, once more. He didn't drink, so he had never experienced a hangover, but he imagined that this was what it would undoubtedly feel like.

When the pain had somewhat subsided, he gradually opened one eye and then the other. He slowly turned his head on the flat pillow and looked at Jesse, who eyed him carefully.

"The headache is typical. It should go away soon; it's just a reaction from the sedatives. You've been out for...a while, but you should feel normal in a few hours. I imagine you're probably hungry. Ashley's going to bring you down some lunch."

"Why now?" Toby asked, again. "I've been here for two weeks. Why have you decided to talk to me, now?"

"Well, we tried, once. Do you remember? You provided us with a list of names. You were a great help."

Toby sighed. It was his fault that his brother and several others were now in danger. "Yeah, I remember."

"After that, you didn't show much interest in talking with us, so we thought we'd give you some time to cool off. If you're willing to hear me out and listen to what I have to say, I think you'll find that this place isn't as bad as it first appeared."

"Not as bad as it first appeared? You mean there's another way to view getting kidnapped and held against my will?"

"Actually, there is. I was once in a position similar to you, and once I was able to see the big picture, I realized how fortunate I really was."

"*Fortunate*? That's not exactly the first word that comes to mind."

"Give me a chance to explain, and you might see things a bit differently. At least try to keep an open mind, okay?"

"Yeah, whatever." Toby shook his head, but the movement caused immediate pain, and he placed a hand over his forehead and groaned.

"Hey, Ashley," Jesse spoke into the walkie, "when you bring lunch down for my friend, here, could you bring him a couple of ibuprofen, as well?"

There was a brief pause, and then a girl's voice crackled back in response, "Not a problem, Jess. Anything else you need?"

"I could use a bottle of water. Would you mind?"

"You got it. I was just on my way down. I'll see you in a minute."

"Thanks, Ash," Jesse responded, then he turned to Toby. "Now then, I'm sure you have a thousand questions. Let me explain why you're here, and then you can ask whatever questions you have. You at least willing to listen?"

"Yeah...I suppose."

Jesse nodded. "Good enough. To begin with, I know you're wondering why you're here. I'll try to explain as succinctly as possible. There's a special group who's been commissioned to study people like you...and me. We are, what they call, Indigos."

"Indigos? What does that mean?"

"It would take a long time to explain, and I will explain it all to you in great detail, later. Simply put, for now, 'Indigo Children' is a term that's been coined to describe people who are born with a difference in their DNA. This difference allows them access to parts of the brain which are usually untouched by most people, and thus provides them with special abilities.

"The people who have...relocated you, here, want to study your DNA and learn why you have special abilities. More importantly, they want to discover the extent of your powers and learn what you can do."

"But, why? Why kidnap me? They were already going to take me to some special school. Couldn't they have just studied me there?"

Jesse stared, unblinking, at Toby, and in a moment the answer silently floated into his mind. *Think about it, and you'll see that you already know the answer.*

Toby furled his eyebrows in confusion. "They want to keep it a secret?"

Why do you think that is? Jesse asked, silently.

Toby considered the little he knew of the people who had taken him. They had created a pretense of a school for the gifted so they would have the opportunity to kidnap him. Jesse had said it himself; these people wanted to discover what they could do with his powers.

"Is it like some secret agency with the CIA or something?" Toby asked, perplexed. "Do they want to use our gifts to spy on others?" The smile and lack of response from Jesse told him that his guess must be fairly close to the truth.

He was about to inquire further, when a knock at the door interrupted the conversation. Jesse swiped an ID badge across a screen, and the door slid open. He noticed there was no handle.

A petite girl, about eighteen or nineteen, with bright, red hair, entered the room. She set a large tray on the desk and picked up a small, clear, plastic cup and a water bottle. She offered him the bottle and a sympathetic smile. "Here ya go; this should help."

He sat up, slowly, as she proceeded to dump two white pills from the cup into his outstretched hand. "Thanks."

"I brought the other water bottle there, for you," she said to Jesse, indicating the tray on the table. "Call me if you need anything else, okay?"

"I will. Thanks, Ashley."

With a swipe of her own ID badge, Ashley left, and they were alone, once again. Jesse lifted the silver, dome cover from the plate and peered inside. "Looks like grilled ham and cheese and a cup of soup. Tasty. Why don't you come enjoy it while it's warm? We can talk while you eat, if you like."

"I am hungry," Toby admitted. He stood carefully; his legs shook slightly as he made the four step journey to the desk and sat.

After he had taken a few bites, he glanced at Jesse, who leaned against the wall and appeared to play a game on his phone.

"So, am I right? Is it the CIA or something like that?"

"Something like that." His captor looked up from his phone. "We're called the I.I.A., short for Indigo Intelligence Agency. I guess you could say our agency is like a second cousin to the CIA, but we're the black sheep of the family. There aren't many outsiders who know of our existence."

"Why is that?"

"Well, basically because we do things that aren't considered the 'norm'. The agency is a little...unorthodox. It's an off-shoot of the CIA; we help gather information when requested, but we also have our own agenda."

"So, why kidnap me?"

"They were going to take you to our school, just like they do with most of the other kids they're interested in, but when Cecelia and Frank took you, they discovered rather quickly that your gifts are much more intricate than they had anticipated. They decided that it would be best to bring you straight here, so that we could start working with you. What they didn't foresee, was that you wouldn't want to readily cooperate."

Toby snorted under his breath. "And why should I? Why would I want to cooperate with someone who kidnapped me? Why do you do it?" He looked at Jesse. "I mean, it sounds like you're a lot like me. Why do you work for them? What's in it for you?"

"I understand your skepticism. I was suspicious when I first met them, but I came around quickly, and I'm sure once I explain everything, you will too."

"Explain it then, because right now all I see is a group of

people who want to exploit my powers and hold me hostage."

"Acknowledged." Jesse crossed his arms and ankles and leaned against the wall. "That is one way to look at it, but just keep in mind, there are always two sides to every story.

"They found me when I was seventeen," he continued. "I had been living in an impoverished neighborhood in Chicago, and I'd just graduated high school a year early. I'd been counting my days until I could move away, but the problem was, I didn't know where to go. I didn't have money to go to college, but I sure as hell didn't want to stick around there and find a job, even though I hated the thought of leaving my momma and my brother."

"After I agreed to work for them, they sent me to college, and after that I was trained with the CIA. Once my training was complete, they brought me here, and I've been working for them ever since. Considering where I came from and where I could have ended up, I can't complain. It's a good gig; and though I admit some of their methods might be a little dishonest, at times, their intentions are in the right place. As far as I can see, they want to use our gifts to find the bad guys and stop them. They've always treated me real good, so I can't complain."

"You came here willingly, though. *This* was not my choice. I had to leave my twin brother."

"Yeah, that was unfortunate, but they're trying to rectify the situation. They're trying to find your brother as we speak, and when they find him, they'll bring him here.

"Yeah, speaking of bringing him here, what's that all about? That list of names that you had me create for you...you're trying to bring all of them here? Why kidnap them? Why not recruit them, too?"

"They have their reasons. Ideally, they would recruit them or if they're under age, send them to one of our schools, but it's not always practical. They aren't always willing to wait until the kids are eighteen, and so, on occasion, they deem it necessary to relocate them."

"*Relocate*? You mean kidnap?"

"Well, it's all in the terminology, I guess. They try not to see it that way. Kidnapping holds a negative connotation. We like to think of this more as a...lifetime opportunity."

"Lifetime opportunity...right. And so, the list of names that I provided, everyone on the list has a unique gift? It's worth the risk to *relocate* them?"

Jesse nodded. "Yes, we have trackers who have been watching them. They've listened to their thoughts and have sensed their powers, powers which would be very valuable to the agency."

"Wait a minute. Do you mean that those people on the list were already under your radar? I didn't identify them for you, after all?"

"Oh, you identified them alright, but it was more like an affirmation to see if you could identify the same people who we had already identified. We wanted to see if you had the potential to be a tracker."

An immense sense of relief washed over him. He had thought it was his fault that his brother was in danger. He was curious then about something Jesse had said. "Tracker? Is that what you are? Do you go out and track people down?

"I did for a little while, but now, for the most part, I stay here and work with the people they bring in."

"Like me."

"Yeah, like you."

"So, there are others, here, like me? How many?"

"Right now...there are ten."

"Were they all kidnapped, too?"

"No, not all of them, some were recruited, but yes, a few were...brought here, unwillingly."

"Kidnapped."

"If that's how you want to look at it, yes. But, eventually they all come around when they realize how their gifts can be used to help others. So many of them have never even understood why they have special abilities. They've always felt alone, and that's where I come in. I help them recognize their true potential and help them to see that they aren't alone, that there are others like them. We become like a family. It's our hope that you'll come to feel that way, too. Besides your brother, you have no family. We can offer you a home."

A home. A family. It was a tantalizing idea, but he still couldn't get over the fact that he had been kidnapped and drugged for the past two weeks. That wasn't the way family treated each other. Jesse made the whole thing sound like a fairy tale. According to him, he had been whisked away from a life of poverty and had lived happily ever after. Was it really that simple? Toby had his doubts.

"I sense that you still have your doubts," Jesse read his mind.

Toby was taken aback. Other than his brother, he wasn't used to having anyone else inside of his head.

"Well, you'd better get used to it," Jesse said. "There's no such thing as a personal thought, anymore." *And just remember, they hear every word that you say, too,* Jesse's thoughts invaded his mind while his eyes glanced nonchalantly to the camera, anchored high on the wall, in a far corner.

Toby retorted with a silent reply, *So basically, the moral of the story is, if you can't beat 'em, join 'em. Is that it?*

You're a smart one, no doubt about that, Jesse thought. He stepped toward Toby, patted him on the shoulder, and then said out loud, "I'll give you time to think about what I've said. I'll come back later this evening." He took his bottle of water from the desk, swiped his ID badge, and stepped out. The door automatically slid shut upon his departure, and then he was alone in the windowless room.

*****

Toby paced the room and then did a few push-ups. It felt good to move. His muscles were stiff, no doubt from the effects of the drugs and lying prone, on a thin mattress. Considering the fact that he had essentially slept for the past two weeks, he was surprised to discover that he was exhausted, and it wasn't long before he decided to lie down.

As he lay on his back and stared at the black dots of the

ceiling tiles, he wondered how long he would have to stay in his prison cell.

Unsure of the amount of time that had passed, his eyes were closed when the thoughts of a girl invaded his mind. *Wake up... Come on, wake up.*

Am I sleeping? he wondered.

Wake up, already!

His eyes shot open and he stared at the ceiling, once more. *I'm over here.*

Toby sat up and looked around. There was no one by the door or at the foot of the bed. He shook his head. Was he delusional?

Behind you.

There she was, over his left shoulder, flush against the corner, beneath the camera mounted on the wall. She had light, mocha colored skin, dark brown, curly hair that hung in ringlets past her shoulders, and brilliant, golden brown eyes. He was struck by her beauty and wondered for a moment if she was some sort of angel or guardian spirit, come to rescue him. He rubbed his eyes, blinked once, and looked again. She was still there.

Don't say anything. She placed a finger over her lips and then pointed toward the camera above her head.

Toby nodded, slightly. He understood. His right hand wandered to his disheveled hair, and he wondered at his appearance. Suddenly cognizant of the fact that he hadn't showered or shaved in two weeks, he imagined that he must be quite the sight.

She smiled and her thoughts floated into his mind, once again. *Don't worry about it. It could be worse.*

Who are you? he asked, silently.

My name's Rebecka.

You're one of them?

No, they're keeping me here, just like you.

If you're not one of them, then how did you get in here?

Are you familiar with the term, teleportation? I can transport myself short distances.

You're serious? People can really do that? Do they know you can do that?

Yeah, that's one of the reasons they've kept me here. They think I could be useful.

How long have you been here? Toby wondered.

About six months.

Six months? Why don't you just teleport yourself right out of this place?

Because I can only send myself short distances. They've taken me outside and have made it perfectly clear that I have nowhere to go. We're in the middle of nowhere. Even if I did get out, I'd be wandering around in the wilderness and wouldn't have a clue which way to go.

What's keeping you from just agreeing to work with them and going to their side? Jesse said that a lot of the people here have agreed to work with them.

Oh, they have, Rebecka thought. *That's why I came to see you, because I heard your thoughts. You have no interest in joining them either, do you?*

Hell no! Tyler thought back. *I just want to get out of here.*

You're smart. Don't let them convince you to join their side. They'll try. They'll be all ready to persuade you with money and images of adventure. They'll try to convince you that they are the 'good guys', that they're doing important research to learn more about Indigo Children; but the truth is, they're not. They use us to spy on other government agencies, including the CIA, the group who is supposedly funding their research, and then they use the information that they gain and sell it to the highest bidder, regardless of what company or country they're from.

How did you get here to begin with? How did they find you?

It was silly, Rebecka thought. *I went onto a social networking site, trying to find other people who were like me. I met this guy, who I became friends with.*

I take it this guy wasn't quite as honest as you thought? What happened? Did he turn out to be a balding, forty-year-old, CIA agent?

Rebecka smiled. *Not exactly; but you're right, he wasn't entirely forthcoming about his true identity. I wasn't stupid. I had always heard about the dangers of online chat rooms and all of the warnings; never give too much information to strangers, blah, blah, blah. This guy really seemed sincere, though. He told me all about his high school and debate team. He even sent a picture of his dog!* She laughed and rolled her eyes.

I can't believe how stupid I was. Everyone always says, 'It can't happen to me'. That's what I thought. I knew there was no way that it could happen to me. I had been so careful!

Wait a minute, Toby interrupted her thoughts. *You make an interesting point. This guy who tricked you, how come you didn't hear his thoughts? How come you didn't know that he was lying?*

Because these guys are good. They've practiced their gifts, and they've learned how to block their thoughts if they don't want someone else to hear them.

Did you ever see him again?

No. Rebecka rolled her eyes and shook her head. *I imagine he's already off in pursuit of his next victim.*

So, here I am, she continued. *Until I can figure out a plan, it looks like I'm here to stay. But, that's why I wanted to meet you. You know the saying, two heads are better than one. Maybe between the two of us, we can figure a way out.*

Well...I sort of have a plan, Toby began, *the beginning of one at least. I've been in contact with my brother, and he's in the process of locating some other people who are also of special interest to the agency. As soon as he locates them, they're going to try to find me.*

Really? You've been drugged for the past two weeks, and you were still able to contact your brother?

We've always had a mental connection. I discovered that distance doesn't matter. There were a few times, over the past few weeks, when I was allowed to wake up. Any info that I learned, I passed on to him.

Wow, that's impressive. With her back still pressed against the wall, she slid to a sitting position, tucked her knees up to her chest, and sat in quiet contemplation.

He smiled and tried to focus on blocking his thoughts from her, as it occurred to him how beautiful she was, even in a pair of grungy shorts and a t-shirt. He assumed that he successfully hid his feelings because her expression appeared unaffected.

So, what's your plan? Rebecka queried. *I mean, once your brother finds everyone? How is he supposed to find you, cuz...we don't even know where we are.*

I know. Toby shook his head. *I've been trying to figure it out, but I'm kind of at a loss. Maybe now that we've got each other, we can figure it out, together.*

Yeah, at least we've got each other.

Toby realized that he very much liked the sound of that. They had only just met, but he already liked her a lot.

Rebecka looked at him then and grinned. He realized that he had forgotten to block his thoughts from her.

If she had heard his private thoughts, she didn't mention it, instead she thought, *Wait a minute, if you have someone on the outside, we might have a chance.*

We might have a chance? How so?

I heard rumors that a tracker bailed on the agency about a year before I got here. They say he went into hiding, and they've been unable to locate him. If your brother can find him, he can find out where we are.

That all sounds well and good, Toby thought, *but if the professionals can't find him, how is my untrained brother supposed to?*

There's an author, some lady with a doctorate in something or other, who wrote a book about Indigo Children. In the book, she wrote about the tracker. I think she had interviewed him and spent some time with him and his family. The agency went to see her after his disappearance, to see if she had information on his whereabouts, but of course, if she knew anything, she wasn't going to give it up. They've had someone watching her, but so far there's been no sign of him.

Toby smiled. *It's a long shot,* he thought.

But it's worth a try, she concluded, with a smile.

Do you know the author's name?

I can't remember, but I saw a copy of her book when I was in Henry's office, last month. That's when I heard him and Jesse talking about keeping an eye on her.

Who's Henry?

He's the head honcho around here.

Will you be able to get into his office? You said there are cameras, everywhere.

Yep, everywhere except for Henry's office. I guess he wants a little privacy.

Well, isn't that convenient? Toby grinned. *I think maybe, we might just have a plan, after all. These guys want to know more about Indigo insight and how we can tell the future and stuff. We'll give them incite, just not the kind that they have in mind.*

What do you mean?

Incite. I...N...C...I...T...E, Toby spelled it out, slowly. *We'll start a rebellion and they won't even see it coming.*

Rebecka grinned. *Clever play on words.*

A noise at the door caught Toby's attention, and a moment later, Jesse entered.

"How's it goin'? Jesse asked. "You have some time to think about what we talked about?"

Toby nodded. "A little bit."

"Well, good. The boss has invited you to have dinner with him. He'd like to have a chance to talk and get to know you a little better."

"The boss?"

"Henry. He keeps tabs on everyone around here. I thought maybe you'd like to get cleaned up first before you meet him. Here ya go." He set a stack of clothes on the desk. "You'll find soap and a toothbrush and stuff, in the bathroom. I'll give you time to shower, and I'll come back for you in half an hour. Sound good?"

"I'll be ready," Toby said, with a forced smile.

He glanced over his shoulder but didn't have to look to know that Rebecka had disappeared.

12 REBECKA

Rebecka glanced to the far side of the dining room where Tamara and Paulo appeared to be in deep conversation. She was friendly with them, when the occasional need arose for conversation, but tried her best to keep her distance. From the little that she knew of them, they had willingly agreed to live and be trained at the compound. They believed in Henry and all that he stood for, and therefore, couldn't be trusted.

She expected that her friends, Ashley and Malik, would join her, soon. While she waited, she contemplated her meeting with Toby. They still needed to figure out an escape plan, but they would come to that puzzle when the time came. For now, she was happy to at least have hope. Hope was more than she had possessed two days ago.

It had been during an evening meal, two weeks ago, when whispered discussions of Toby's presence had caught her attention. His identity had piqued her interest, and she had unobtrusively sought him out. On several occasions, since then, she had listened to his thoughts, and to her delight, had discovered that he had no intention of giving in to the desires of the agency. Toby wanted his freedom just as much as she did, and she hoped that he would be the ally she had waited for. The fact that he was good looking was, of course, an added bonus.

"What are you smiling at?" Malik asked, as he and Ashley joined her at the table.

Malik, who was only fourteen, was the youngest member of the compound. Skinny, and tall for his age, with a witty sense of humor, he reminded her of her younger brother, Tommy. Ashley, who was nineteen, easily revealed her Irish background with her bright red hair, fair skin, and generous helping of freckles. They were the only two members of the compound who she remotely considered to be friends. Now, she reminded herself, she could add Toby to that list, as well.

Rebecka mentally checked her facial expression. "Was I smiling?"

Malik chuckled. "Yeah, from the looks of it, you were a million miles away."

"I'll bet she was thinking about a boy," Ashley said, with a mischievous grin.

"A boy, Ashley? Really? It's kind of slim pickings around here, not a lot of boys to be daydreaming about," Rebecka replied.

"Thanks a lot!" Malik said. "What am I?"

"I'm sorry, Malik! You know what I meant! You're my friend. You're like my younger brother. You even look like my younger brother. You—"

Malik laughed. "Hey, don't sweat it. I was just messin' with you."

"Funny, Malik," Ashley said. "For real though, Rebecka, what were you thinking about? I don't think I've seen you smile like that since you came to this place."

"Actually, I was just thinking about this cheeseburger," Rebecka fibbed.

"A cheeseburger, Becka? Really?" Malik chuckled. "You're easy to please. Then again, there's nothing like a good burger. My momma didn't have a lot of money, so my brother and I never got to eat out much when we were kids."

Ashley turned to him. "Oh, yeah? Where did you grow up?"

"Chicago..."

The two seemed to forget about her as they discussed Malik's past, and she was thankful to no longer be the center of attention. She was curious how he had ended up at the compound but forced herself to bite her tongue. Nearby cameras picked up every word that they said. It was frowned upon to discuss unorthodox methods of arriving at the compound; the word 'kidnapped' was not in their approved vocabulary, so she didn't ask the questions that were on her mind. She could only imagine that Malik's mother must miss him just as much as she imagined her own parents missed her.

She swirled her sweet potato fry in ketchup as she casually observed the resident chef, who had just emerged from the kitchen. The rotund, jolly man, who sported a large, white, chef's hat and white mustache, always seemed to be in bright spirits. She had befriended Chef Franco, early on, in her compound residency, and during her free time, he often invited her to help out in the kitchen.

With tray in hand, he was off to personally deliver the evening's meal to Henry. When he spotted her, he circumvented the room so that he could pass her table.

"Ah, La Mia Stella! How are you today? How is your burger? It's to your perfection, no?"

Rebecka smiled. "It's perfect, Franco. Thank you."

"Buono, I am glad that I can bring a bit of happiness to your day. I am off to deliver this to Henry. Would you like to join me when I return? You could help me pass out desserts, this evening."

A dessert delivery, to Henry's office, would be the perfect opportunity to look for the book, and she jumped at the offer. "I'd love to, thanks! But...just so long as I get first dibs on dessert," she replied, with a wink, "something with a bit of chocolate perhaps?"

"For you, Cara Mia, anything. You will be here when I return?"

"Yep, I'm not going anywhere. I'll wait for you."

After Franco was out of earshot, Malik said, "So, you and Chef Boyardee there, you're pretty tight, huh?"

Rebecka smiled. "Yeah, I guess you could say that. He's a good friend."

"So, really, what I'm hearing is, you've got the hook up on dessert. All this time and you've been holding out on me."

She laughed. "I might have a bit of inside persuasion."

"I always knew you were my favorite girl, for a reason."

Ashley cocked her head to the side and eyed him. "Favorite girl?"

Malik laughed. "You know I'm just playin'. I love you too, Ash."

Ashley grinned. "Gee thanks, Malik. You sure know how to make a girl feel special." She glanced at the clock. "I hate to eat and run, you guys, but I promised Henry that I'd check in on that new kid, downstairs."

Rebecka perked up but didn't want to make it seem that she was too interested. "Oh yeah, I forgot about him. He's been here for a couple of weeks, hasn't he?"

"Yeah," Ashley confirmed, "we're hoping to make some progress with him. With luck, he might be able to join us, in a few days."

"Hey, another guy to hang out with," Malik said. "That would be great. I'll bet you'd think so too, huh, Rebecka? You were just saying there aren't enough guys, around here."

Even though it sounded like a joke, he seemed to eye her with suspicion. He couldn't possibly know that she had already met Toby. Could he?

Rebecka ignored his comment and turned to Ashley, who stood to go. "I'll see you later."

Ashley grinned. "See ya. Bye, Malik."

"Bye, Ash." Malik waved and then seemed to be distracted with lunch until their friend had left the room. Once she was out of sight, he turned and eyed her closely. "So?"

She tried to appear confused. "So...what?" He definitely knew that she was up to something.

"So...I might not be able to see auras, or hear thoughts, but I sense emotions more than anyone else in this place. As soon as Miss Strawberry Shortcake mentioned that new kid, I felt your excitement. I don't know how you know him, but you like the guy, don't you?"

Rebecka prayed that no one was paying attention to them on the surveillance camera. She didn't want any sort of suspicion raised before she and Toby could put a plan into place. "Strawberry Shortcake? You mean Ashley?" She tried to stall for time so that she could think of a response.

"Well, you know...the red hair and all. It seems kind of fitting, don't you think?"

She chuckled. "Yeah...sure, it's...cute. I don't know if Ashley would see it that way, but give it a try, maybe the nickname will stick."

"You're totally trying to avoid the question, aren't you?"

"What question?" Rebecka tried to sound dumbfounded.

"What's the story with the new kid? You know more than you're letting on, don't you?"

Rebecka glanced discreetly from Malik to the leering camera and back. She prayed that he would get the hint and drop the subject. "Nope, I don't know any more than you know. Maybe it's like you said, I'm just excited there's going to be a new boy around. Maybe I *am* hoping he'll be cute."

"That's your story and you're sticking to it? Alright, then." He stood and lifted his tray to go. "I'll catch you later, Girl. I've gotta bounce. My TV and video game are callin' my name. I wouldn't want to keep them waiting." He walked around the table, stopped by her side, and leaned against the table so that his back was to the surveillance camera, and faced her. He leaned in close then and whispered, "Just so that you and I are on the same page, *Stella Mia*, I've got your back. Whatever secret you're keeping, I won't let on."

Then he straightened and in a normal voice said, "You wanna come race some cars with me, later? I got an extra control."

She smiled, knowing that she could trust him and grateful for his friendship. "Thanks, Malik, I'll keep the offer in mind. See ya, later."

*****

Henry's office was the fifth and final stop on the main floor, for the dessert delivery route. With luck, the book would still be on his desk, where she had seen it the week before. She pushed the dessert cart to his door, took a deep breath, and knocked. *Here goes nothin'*, she thought.

"Come in," Henry answered.

With a swipe of the access card Chef Franco had loaned her, she opened the door and then turned to arm herself with a dessert plate. The standard thermos of coffee, provided to the guards on night duty, was unnecessary for Henry. He preferred to brew his own, gourmet blend, in his office.

When she entered, Henry removed himself from his work, leaned back in his chair, and laced his fingers behind his head. "Ah, perfect timing, Rebecka. Come in. Come in, please. Helping out Chef Franco, tonight, are you? And what have you brought for me, My Dear?"

Somehow, when Henry called her, 'My Dear', it didn't hold the same endearing connotation as when Franco said it, in his native Italian. Perhaps it was because she considered Franco a friend, and Henry was...well, kind of creepy, in a sly sort of way.

Determined not to let her negative feelings for the man show, she strode toward his desk, with her head held high. "Chef Franco made chocolate tiramisu. Can I interest you in a slice?" She walked around his desk and set it beside his laptop. As she did so, she inconspicuously scanned the area for the book. The last time she had seen it, it had been on the corner of his desk, on the top stack of three or four other books. It wasn't there.

She was instantly grateful that Henry wasn't gifted in the slightest and couldn't read thoughts or emotions. On the outside, she appeared calm and happy to have the opportunity to serve him; on the inside, she was freaking out. Henry was a busy man. She could get by with a minute of small talk, at the most, while she scanned his office for the book, anything longer than that and he would grow anxious to have her leave.

"Mmm, this looks wonderful. He must have a knack of knowing what my favorite desserts are. He never seems to go wrong. Please express my gratitude to Chef Franco." He stared at her with a patient smile, which subtly said, 'Okay you can leave my office now'.

She wasn't ready to leave and pretended to take no notice of the hint. "I will definitely pass on your appreciation. Is there anything else that I can get for you, this evening?" She scanned his desk, once more. Maybe he had moved the book to a different pile.

"Uh, nope. I think that will be all. Thanks so much, Rebecka." There was a definitive request of departure in his tone.

The book was still nowhere in sight, and she wasn't ready to give up. If she didn't find it now, she would have to come back later. She glanced then at the sidebar, which housed a mini fridge, a sink, and a coffee pot. Beside the ledge was a built-in bookcase, and on the ledge itself was a small stack of books. From where she stood, she couldn't tell if the book was housed in the pile, but she had to see. "Oh wait, before I go, let me get you a cup of coffee. Franco insisted that the tiramisu must be enjoyed with coffee."

Henry laughed. "That sounds like Franco, alright. Don't worry about it though, I can help myself."

"No, I insist. I'm already up. Stay seated and I'll pour you a cup." Before he could argue, Rebecka advanced on the coffee pot and grabbed one of four ceramic mugs that hung on a hook, above the counter. With her back to him, she lifted the full pot of coffee and began to pour. She was cognizant of the fact that the hot liquid needed to be poured *into* the cup and not the counter, as she surveyed the nearby stack of books. She had only seen the book once, but the blue spine that stuck out, second from the bottom, resembled the book from her memory.

She turned her attention back to the task at hand and quickly tipped the coffee pot upright, before she overfilled the cup. Would it seem too obvious if she pretended to peruse his literature selection? It wasn't uncommon to show an interest in books, was it? She decided that she would take her chances. Even if he did suspect her behavior as odd, he would never guess her true motivations.

Each movement was calculated, but seemingly casual. In one sweeping motion, she returned the coffee pot to its base, turned and swept the top book off the stack, and pretended to read the summary on the back, as she walked the cup of coffee to Henry's desk.

"Are you interested in land navigation?" Henry inquired.

She glanced at the cover, which revealed a picture of a topography map and a compass. Perhaps she should have looked at the title, before she picked it up. Did he seem suspicious? She hoped it was only her guilty imagination. "Oh, you know, actually,

I've always loved books. Ever since I was a little kid, I would read anything I could get my hands on." This at least was true.

"Well, in that case, my library is open to you, anytime you'd like to borrow a book. I don't have any exciting novels, but if you're into nonfiction, I have quite the selection.

She snatched on to the open invitation and returned to the stack on the counter. Casually, she pretended to glance at each book, until she reached her target, four books down. There it was. The face of the author stared up at her. She prayed it was the face that would provide the needed answers that would lead to their rescue.

"I'm afraid I can't loan you any books from that stack. I'm still going through them, but anything on the bookshelf you are welcome to."

Rebecka glanced up. Henry continued to lean back in his chair. With his cup of coffee in hand, he regarded her with a bemused grin.

She replaced the books on the stack and smiled. "Thanks for the offer. I have to finish making deliveries, but maybe I'll come back, tomorrow, if you don't mind. I'm always looking for a new book to read."

"Of course, My Dear, you are always welcome."

She had no plans to return, anytime soon, but now that she had an open invitation, she would have an excuse to return, if the need arose. For now, she had the name that she had been after.

*****

The tingling sensation, the usual after-effect of teleporting, subsided as she opened her eyes. She pressed her back into the corner of the wall, so that she wouldn't be detected by the surveillance camera.

She smiled to herself as she watched him. He had changed clothes since she had seen him a few hours before and now wore jeans and a t-shirt. It also appeared that he had showered; his hair was combed and from the slight profile that was visible, it appeared that he had shaved. He sat cross legged on the end of his bed and tossed a baseball into the air. She watched him catch the ball a few times before she let her presence be known.

You look bored. What do you say we get out of here for a little while? she thought.

He didn't turn, but she saw an undeniable grin in his profile. *I would love nothing more than to get out of here, but there seems to be a little issue of a locked door and a security camera*, he thought in return. His ball continued to soar into the air; for the sake of the security camera, he didn't skip a beat.

I thought a locked door wasn't a problem for you.

It's not, but I have zero control over the people who are watching the security camera. The second I walk out that door, they'll be all over me.

Well, then I guess today's your lucky day, My Friend. There's actually only one person who is watching the surveillance camera, and...let's just say that he and I have come to an arrangement. In five minutes, he's going to turn off the game room monitor. So, Cinderella, you are free to go to the ball, until the clock strikes nine. Are you game?

Toby hesitated and held on to the ball. She thought he was going to turn toward her, but he restrained himself and soon resumed the toss of the baseball. *You're serious? What kind of an arrangement did you have to make?...Is the security guard your boyfriend?*

The hesitation in his question told her that he hoped the answer was no. *Good*, she thought, to herself. For a moment, she wondered if she should make him believe that she had something going with Bobby, the gangly, pimple faced, security guard. The thought only crossed her mind for a second though; jealously wasn't her style. Besides, she had a strong feeling that Toby liked her just as much as she liked him. There was no need to make him jealous.

Bobby? No...absolutely not. He wishes, but it's not going to happen. I'll admit, I might have led him astray, a little, but I only did it so I could get you out of here.

So, you trust him? You don't think he'll say anything?

Nah, he won't say anything. He knows that if he does, he won't have a chance with me. And, he wouldn't say anything, anyways, because he doesn't want to lose his job.

But, he doesn't have a chance with you anyway...right?

You sound nervous, Rebecka teased, *or is jealous a more appropriate term?*

Hey now, I'm not nervous or jealous...Is Bobby someone I should be jealous of?

Absolutely not! You have nothing to worry about. I'm here because I want to take you out...I mean, get you out of here so we can talk in private...I mean...what is wrong with me? Why can't I just say what I'm trying to say?

What is it that you're trying to say?

Rebecka caught a hint of amusement in his thoughts. *What I want to say is, I like you, and I'd like to get you out of here for a little bit so we can hang out.*

I like the sound of that, Toby thought. *What do I say if I happen to see someone?*

Do your best not to be seen, okay? But if you do see someone, don't act guilty. Just say hi and keep walking with your head held high, like you belong there.

Easy for you to say, but I'll try my best.

Good, I'll see you soon.

Rebecka? Toby turned to look at her. He looked directly into her eyes, and she thought her heart was going to melt. *Thank you.*

Rebecka smiled. *It's my pleasure.*

*****

When he entered the game room, his grin was instantaneous. "Hi," he said, almost shyly.

With cue stick in hand, she sat on the green felt of the pool table, her legs swung over the side. "Hey there. You found me."

"Yeah, it was a little too easy. I kept expecting guards to come pouring out of every door that I passed, but I didn't see anyone. Your security guard friend must really like you."

Rebecka chuckled. "Yeah, unfortunately he does, but I guess

it was to my benefit, this time."

"So, you said the surveillance camera is turned off?" He glanced at the camera mounted near the ceiling.

Rebecka followed his line of sight. "In theory it is, but I would still watch what you say. You never know…"

"I gotcha. Well then, since we don't have a lot of time, what do ya say we make the most of the time we've got?"

"What do you have in mind?" Her pulse sped up as he stepped closer. He stopped when he was about a foot away. For the first time, she was able to look deeply into his eyes. They were speckled green. He was close enough so that the sharp scent of institutional soap, which still lingered on his skin, permeated her senses. She found it to be oddly intoxicating.

"Well…," Toby began, slowly, as he continued to look into her eyes, "are you any good with that cue stick, or is it just for show?"

Rebecka raised her eyebrows, glanced at the stick, and then narrowed her eyes at Toby. "Oh, I'm good. Are you game?"

He stepped back and with his palms face up, summoned her forward with his hands. "Let's go, My Friend. Show me what you've got."

Rebecka jumped off the table. "You're on. You wanna break?"

"You got it."

Toby grabbed the triangle and began to rack the balls. "How long did you say you've been in this place?" He glanced up at her for a second, but continued to set the balls.

"Six months, it's hard to believe that much time has passed. It makes me wonder about my family. They've probably given me up for dead."

"I'm sure your parents are still holding out hope that they'll find you."

A tear welled up in the corner of her eye, and she hurriedly wiped it away. "I don't know. I hope so. I just can't help but think that this has got to be so much harder on them. At least I know that I'm okay, but they don't have a clue. My poor mother's heart must be broken. And my brother…we were so close…I mean…we are close."

"I know what you mean," Toby said. "My brother and I are like that, too. He's my best friend. But at least he knows that I'm okay. I imagine your brother really misses you. How old is he?"

"He's fourteen...three years younger than me, but he's my best friend." Rebecka glanced at the surveillance camera. She was sure that it was turned off, but just in case, decided that it would be better if she didn't express her next thought out loud. *I can't wait to see him, again...if we manage to make it out of here.*

Toby glanced at the camera and then winked at her. *We will make it out of here*, he thought, in return. *Think positive.* He picked up a cue stick. "Now then," he said, "what do ya say we relax and have fun for the next half hour?"

On the first strike, Toby broke the set and sent two balls flying into the far corner pockets. In truth, she had only played pool once before and didn't have a clue how to properly hold a cue stick, but she grabbed it with confidence, anyway, and took a firm stance. She eyed the ball that she wanted to sink into the side pocket, took a deep breath, and prepared herself to hit the white ball.

"You don't want to do that," Toby interrupted.

Rebecka straightened and glared at him. "Oh really? And why is that, exactly? You know what I was planning to do?"

Toby chuckled. "Well, yeah, actually, I do. You were going to try to sink the yellow ball, but actually it was going to ricochet off the side and sink my striped green ball, instead."

Rebecka tried not to show her surprise. She had in fact been planning to sink the yellow ball, but didn't want to give him the satisfaction of knowing that he was right.

"You are so making that up! You didn't foresee that." She tried to sound irritated but couldn't hide her smile.

"You think I'm making it up? You know very well that I'm not because you can hear my thoughts. And I can hear yours, too, don't forget. It's okay if you don't know how to play pool. I'd be happy to teach you."

"I can play pool," she retorted, but even she could tell that her affirmation lacked confidence.

"Of course you can," he said, with a smile. "How about I just help you with your form, a bit?"

"Well…"

"It won't hurt. I promise."

"Okay, but you have to promise not to laugh."

"What would I have to laugh about? Come on. Let me at least show you how to hold the cue stick. You can feel free to aim for whichever ball you like. Okay?"

Rebecka smiled. "Alright. I guess it wouldn't hurt to learn." She held the cue stick out. "What should I do first?"

Toby circled the table and came to stand in front of her. Once again, he stood close enough that she could see the speckled twinkle in his eyes.

"Alright, face the table and pretend that you're getting ready to make a shot."

She grabbed the stick, turned to the table, and attempted two practice strokes.

"Here, let me just make a slight adjustment on your hold. I think you'll find that your aim and accuracy will be a lot better." He reached in from the side and placed his hands on hers to help position the stick in the proper form. The warmth of his hands sent a thrill of excitement up her arms, and she closed her eyes to relish the moment. She hadn't known Toby for very long, but the unique connection that she felt to him was undeniable.

"I've never tried, but I would imagine it's kind of hard to hit the ball with your eyes closed."

She grinned and then opened her eyes. His hands still lay on top of hers, and she twisted her head sideways to look at him. He smiled back and she laughed. "I'm sorry; I guess I was just daydreaming. I really am paying attention. I think I've got it now. Can I give it a try?"

He released her hands and took a step back. "Absolutely. Show me what you've got."

With the cue stick held the way he had shown her, she once again aimed for the yellow ball, took three practice strokes, and then struck the white ball with finesse. The balls seemed to move as though in slow motion, and then, much to her delight, the yellow ball dropped neatly into the side pocket, just as she had planned.

Toby applauded. "Not bad. I'm impressed. I guess, now, it's game on, huh?"

Knowing that they were pressed for time, they played quickly, and it wasn't long before only three colored balls remained on the table. She realized that she only had one ball remaining, while Toby had two.

"I'm chalking that up to beginner's luck," Toby said. He stood at the opposite end of the table and held his cue stick to the floor.

"Luck? I don't think so." Rebecka shook her head. "I've got skills."

"And you had a pretty good teacher, too."

She laughed. "Well, yeah, that too, of course." She glanced at the clock on the wall. "We'd better hurry. You've only got five minutes before Bobby's going to switch the camera back on. If you don't want to risk it, we can just end the game, now."

"What? Walk away and let you win? I don't think so!"

"It's only a game."

"Sure, you say that because you're winning." He circled the table, tilted his head, and squinted at the balls. Then, he squished his way between Rebecka and the table. He took a step back and leaned his back against her. "Excuse me. You're in my way."

Rebecka giggled. "Oh, I am, huh? Well then, let me just move out of the way for you. I wouldn't want to hinder your ability to play." She took an exaggerated step to the left. "Is that better?"

He glanced sideways at her and grinned. "Much better." He leaned over the table and lined up the cue stick. "Now then, let me show you how to win..." He cut his sentence short and straightened.

Rebecka looked at him, puzzled. "What was that? What were you going to show—"

"Shh..." He held a finger up to his lips. "Someone's coming."

They simultaneously stepped toward each other, until they stood side by side. "Did you hear something?" she whispered.

Toby shook his head. "No, I had a brief vision. Hold on for a second."

She looked at him as he closed his eyes, in concentration.

He opened his eyes a few seconds later. "It's that guy who came to my room...Jesse."

"You saw Jesse? Where?"

"He's down the hall, and..." He closed his eyes again. "He's walking this way. He just passed the stairs. Is there anywhere else, besides here, that he could be headed?"

"I doubt it. There's a dance studio, but other than that, every other room is empty."

"So, basically what you're saying is, we're sitting ducks."

"Um, yeah...I think we're screwed."

"*We're* not screwed. *I* am...*you're* not. Get out of here. Now."

Rebecka shook her head. "Toby, I can't just leave you."

"*Yes*, you can. There's no sense in both of us getting caught. They don't know that you use your abilities to move about this place. Don't blow your cover now. Get out of here."

She leaned in close and whispered in his ear, "The author's name is Patricia McCormack."

He pulled her into a bear hug and whispered back, "Thank you. Now go."

She took a deep breath. He was right; she needed to go, but still, she regretted leaving him behind. Still held in his embrace, she whispered back, "I'll see you soon." Then she closed her eyes and focused on her room. Just when the tingling sensation reached her head, she heard the door begin to open, and then she was gone.

13 FLAGSTAFF

A row of aspens that lined the drive, greeted them upon their arrival. The trees, which swayed gently in the breeze, relinquished their hoard of snow, which resulted in a rhythmic splatter on the roof of the Jeep, as they drove up the long, winding lane. With luck, the kidnappers wouldn't expect their return, to Eddie's hometown. The confusion would hopefully buy them time, while they waited for guidance and direction from Toby.

Tyler glanced over his shoulder, to the backseat. Liliana had used his fleece pullover as a pillow. Snuggled against it, she slept in momentary escape from the tumultuous situation that engulfed them. He was hit with a sense of guilt, as he watched the peaceful countenance of her face. He silently questioned the wisdom of bringing her along. Maybe she would have been better off in Seattle.

"They would have found her, you know," Eddie said. He glanced at Tyler. "If we had left her there, she would probably be locked up with Toby, by now."

Tyler turned to him with curiosity. "How did you know that's what I was thinking?"

"It doesn't take mind reading skills. I see the way you look at her. Whether you want to admit it or not, you're starting to care about her. And besides," he continued, "I was thinking the same thing. She's a sweet girl, not the type to run away from home or do anything crazy like that. But it's true...they would have found her. She's better off, for now, if she stays with us."

Tyler sighed. "I hope you're right."

Liliana awoke when Eddie brought the Jeep to a stop, in front of the house. "Are we already at your place? I can't believe I slept the whole way!"

"Don't worry about it," Eddie said. "We're all tired from the trip. No sense in staying awake when you could be resting."

She handed Tyler the pullover. "Thanks for this. I think you're going to need it. It looks a bit chilly, outside."

"No problem." He pulled the fleece over his tousled hair and shivered as he looked out at the fresh, untouched snow. It was hard to gauge from inside the vehicle, but he guessed there was at least two feet on the ground.

A tall, skinny girl, bounded down the cement steps of the house. "Eddie! You're home!" she shouted. She grinned from ear to ear as she ran toward Eddie. Tyler guessed this must be the sister he had mentioned.

Eddie swept her into a giant bear hug and swirled her around. When her feet were planted back on the ground, she turned to the newcomers. "Who are you friends?"

"This is Tyler and Liliana." Eddie indicated them each by turn and then placed an arm around her shoulders. "This is my sister, Abby."

"You were gone *forever*," his sister scolded.

He smiled down at her. "Not forever, only three days."

"Well, three days too many."

"Ha! I missed you too, Little Sis." He turned to Liliana. "Why don't you go on in and get warm. Tyler and I will grab the bags and be right in."

"Alright, thanks." Liliana smiled and turned to follow Abby up the steps.

Once she was in the house, Tyler turned to Eddie. "Do you think we'll be safe, here?"

"As safe as anywhere else, I suppose. If they tracked my credit card, they'll know we flew to Phoenix, but after that, there's virtually no trace of us."

"I hope you're right."

"Hopefully, once Sarah and Grace get here, we'll be able to formulate some sort of plan." They hadn't actually spoken with Sarah, but through a continuous circuit of phone tag, when Eddie had taken the risk to occasionally turn his phone on, he had determined that she had somehow located Grace, and together, the girls were on their way to Flagstaff.

"I'm curious how Grace and Sarah found each other," Tyler said. "That seems like an odd coincidence."

"Yeah, no kidding. My grandmother says there's no such

thing as a coincidence. If they found each other, they were brought together for a reason. Hopefully they don't run into any problems along the way. I imagine they should be here soon. You haven't heard from your brother?"

Tyler shook his head and frowned. "No...I haven't."

"Well, come on. We might as well go inside. You can meet my family, and we'll make lunch. If there's nothing else that we can do besides wait, we might as well relax."

Once inside, the house presented an illusion of safety. Eddie's father sat in a recliner and watched TV in front of a warm and inviting wood stove. Off to the other side of the house was the kitchen, where Eddie's mother stood in front of an open refrigerator and put groceries away. The entire scene was refreshingly normal, and Tyler was thankful for the temporary sanctuary.

"Hey, Son, welcome home!" Eddie's father waved from the chair. "How was Tucson?"

"It was good. I brought some friends home. This is Tyler, and Liliana is around here, somewhere. Abby already stole her away. I told them they could stay with us so they wouldn't have to get a motel room."

"That's fine; your friends are always welcome. Hi, Tyler, it's nice to meet you."

"Nice to meet you too, Sir," Tyler replied.

His dad smiled. "You can call me, Mannie."

"And I'm Claire," his mother said, as she entered the living room. "It's nice to meet you, Tyler." She extended a hand in greeting.

"Thank you for allowing us to stay here."

"It's our pleasure," Claire said. "Have you boys eaten?"

"No, we're starving," Eddie replied.

"Good. Why don't you go ahead and find the girls. I'll make lunch."

*****

"Well," Eddie said, once they had finished lunch, "I guess all we can do is wait. As much as I hate to say it, I should probably get caught up on homework. I don't want to fall behind any more than I already have. I'm going to call my lab partner to find out my missing assignments. Do you two think you can entertain yourselves for a couple of hours? You're welcome to watch TV with my dad, or if that prospect doesn't excite you, I can loan you some snow boots and coats, and you can explore the property."

"I like the idea of staying warm," Tyler said.

"Oh, come on! Where's your sense of adventure?" Liliana elbowed Tyler in the arm. "Let's go outside and play in the snow."

"I've got warm clothes you can borrow," Eddie told him. "In fact, we've got a couple pairs of snowshoes in the garage. Have you ever gone snowshoeing?"

Tyler shook his head. "Nope, can't say that I have. I've lived in the desert my whole life, and my foster family never took me anywhere."

Liliana grinned. "Let's try it! It sounds like fun!" *Don't be a wuss*, she thought to him.

Excuse me? Tyler retorted, silently. *I am not a wuss!*

Good, then come out with me, she thought back.

You're on, Tyler thought, in return.

"We'll go snowshoeing," she told Eddie.

Eddie looked back and forth between them and smiled. "Why do I feel like I just missed something?"

"Nothing important." Tyler glared at Liliana and then turned to Eddie. "Do you have a pair of boots that will fit?"

*****

Almost an hour had passed when it occurred to Tyler that he had forgotten about the cold. He admitted, only to himself, that he was glad they had decided to explore the winter wonderland. He stood back for a moment and watched Liliana follow a hawk that flew from one tree to the next. Her excitement and wonder for life made him smile. If the search for his brother hadn't been at the forefront of his mind, he would have openly admitted his attraction for her.

Caught up in her enthusiasm for bird watching, he found himself looking skyward at the fleeting bird, as he trudged through the snow to catch up to her. He had almost reached her when his left ankle gave way. He stumbled forward over a bulging tree root and landed face first, into the snow.

Startled by his hollers and exclamations, Liliana turned and trudged toward him. She plopped down beside him and helped him into a sitting position. A hint of a smile was quickly replaced with a frown as she wiped snow from his forehead. "That was quite the face plant. Are you okay?"

Tyler sensed that her apparent concern was a mask to hide her amusement.

"I'm great," he mumbled.

From out of the blue, Toby's thoughts invaded his mind. *What are you doing*? his brother inquired.

Oh, thank God! Tyler thought in return. Liliana raised her eyebrows in silent question. "It's my brother," he explained. She wouldn't be able to hear Toby's end of the conversation, but at least she'd be able to hear his own thoughts.

"Good!" she sat up straighter, in alert attentiveness.

We were just out for a little snowshoeing adventure, Tyler thought to his brother.

You and the girl, huh? Toby replied, with a hint of amusement.

He scooped up a glove full of snow and crushed it into a tight ball. *Yeah, we, uh, just sat down to take a breather,* he thought.

Liliana chuckled. "Yeah, sure...that's exactly why we sat down."

A wave of pain emanated from his left ankle; he grimaced slightly at an attempt to bend it but decided not to mention it, lest he worry his brother.

I think I might have a lead for you, Toby thought. *It turns out that the people who are looking for you guys are from an agency called the I.I.A. They're serious, and they mean business.*

The I.I.A.? Does that stand for something?

Yeah, it's short for Indigo Intelligence Agency. It's a long story, but the main thing you need to know is, they're determined to find you. They want to use our gifts for their own intelligence purposes. Basically, they want to use us as spies.

Spies? Really? That's...interesting.

Interesting to say the least, Toby thought in return.

So, did you find out where they're keeping you?

No, not yet. From what I gather, I'm in the middle of nowhere, but that's all I know. I think we might have a good lead for you, though. There's someone on the outside who might know where we are.

'We' might have a lead? Tyler queried. *Who's the 'we'?*

I've met someone else who wants to help. Her name's Rebecka. They kidnapped her, too. She's been here a bit longer and has a little more inside information.

That's cool, Tyler thought. *We can use all the help we can get. Speaking of help, were you able to find everyone on the list?*

Yeah, just about. Sarah and Grace should be here, soon.

Where is here? Toby asked.

We're back in Arizona, at Eddie's house, in Flagstaff.

That's perfect, because the next person who I want you to find is in Sedona, not too far from there. Her name is Patricia McCormack. She's the author of a book about Indigo Children. I don't think she'll know where I am, but she knows someone who does. There's a tracker who used to work for the agency, and he bailed on them. He took off, and they don't have a clue where he is. The author wrote about him in one of her books, and there's a good chance that she might know where he is. If you find the tracker, then he can tell you where they're keeping me.

Nice. We just have to wait for Sarah and Grace to show up and then we can head out to look for her.

Thanks. Please be careful. Word is, these guys are keeping a close eye on her, hoping that the tracker will return. If they see you there, the gig's up.

No worries, Tyler reassured him, *we'll think of something, and we'll keep our eyes open.*

Thanks, Bro. I knew I could count on you.

Of course. Don't worry; I'll be coming to see you soon.

After Toby was gone, Tyler filled in the pieces of conversation that Liliana had missed.

"That's awesome!" she replied, when he had finished explaining the details. "At least now we have a lead."

"Sure, but that's assuming she's been in contact with the tracker. Toby doesn't know for sure."

"Well, it's better than nothing. Do you want to go back to the house and tell Eddie?"

Tyler hesitated, "Um...yeah." Once again, he attempted to flex his ankle, but took in a sharp breath and froze when he was assaulted by the increased pain.

Liliana frowned. "Are you okay?"

He shook his head. "I don't think so. My ankle really hurts. I think it might be sprained."

"Are you kidding? Let's see if you can stand."

With snowshoes still on, so that his ankle wouldn't sink two feet into the snow, Tyler accepted Liliana's arm and carefully got to his feet. When he was steadied, he slowly put his weight on his left leg and was immediately met by pulses of sharp, piercing pain.

"Ow!" He immediately forced the majority of his weight onto the opposite foot. "I don't know if it's sprained or broken, but there's no way that I'm going to be able to walk back to the house."

"Here, sit back down." Concern was evident in her eyes, as she helped him to the ground. "Can you take your boot off?"

"Sure, if you can help me figure out how to get this snowshoe off."

It took a few moments, but eventually the snowshoe was removed. Tyler winced in pain as he maneuvered the bulky boot off of his foot.

"Here, rest your foot on my leg so that it's not sitting in the snow." She scooted in beside him and slid his pant leg up to his calf. "Alright, let me see. I'm going to let you roll your sock down. I don't want to hurt you."

With his sock rolled down, the appearance of his ankle revealed the truth. Already it was swollen and had turned an assortment of colors.

"Ooh, that does look like it hurts," Liliana cooed, sympathetically.

"I think you're going to have to go back to the house to get Eddie. Maybe they have a snowmobile or something that he can bring."

"I could...," Liliana began, "but I have a better idea." She grinned. *Do you trust me?* she asked, silently.

Tyler looked into her eyes. Oh yeah, he trusted her. He was surprised to realize that he trusted her about as much as he trusted his brother, and that was saying a lot.

"Let me see if I can help, okay?"

"Um...okay."

"Just relax and lean back."

With her help, he scooted back to the base of a large pine and leaned against it. His foot remained propped on her thigh, and she gently cupped his exposed ankle, in both hands.

"Will this hurt?"

"You know, I've never tried it on a human, but I've never had an animal complain."

Her tone remained even and calm, and Tyler couldn't tell if she was serious or joking. He laughed in a poor attempt to hide his nerves. "Great, so I'm a guinea pig?"

She chuckled softly and said in the same, calm voice, "If that's the way you want to look at it...yes."

"Hmm, that certainly helps to instill a lot of confidence."

"Just hush and lean back," Liliana chided. "This shouldn't take long."

Gingerly, her cupped hands slid up and down his ankle. Tyler watched with curiosity. When she seemed to find the right spot, she closed her eyes and held her hands firmly in place. Her eyes remained closed, in focused concentration. Tyler smiled. She truly was beautiful.

His skin grew warm beneath her gentle touch, and just when

he thought his ankle would become uncomfortably hot, the heat subsided, and she opened her eyes.

They made eye contact, then. Tyler found himself entranced in her gaze, held by her beauty, and frozen with an unfamiliar sense of passion.

Liliana sat, equally immobile, as she met his gaze with her own.

All sense of practicality and reason was momentarily gone. Tyler gulped and slowly leaned in. He no longer thought about the fact that he shouldn't be attracted to her. He was no longer thinking at all. His motions were directed entirely from his feelings.

For a moment, he wondered if Liliana noticed his aura. He knew that it must reveal his true feelings, and suddenly he didn't care. With his ankle still propped on her thigh, the distance that he could lean was limited, but she quickly caught on and moved to meet in the middle.

He braced himself for the impending kiss, but they were stopped short by the reverberation of a car door. The slam echoed through the trees. Brought back to the present, they both pulled away, but not before Tyler caught the look of disappointment in her eyes. He wondered if she saw the same disappointment written in his.

Liliana turned toward the sound. "Do you think they're already here?"

"I guess we'd better go see."

"Let's get your boot back on and see if you can walk."

She removed her hands from his ankle, and Tyler gasped in awe at the result. It was as though he had never been injured. The swelling and bruising was completely gone.

"That's amazing! I don't know how you did it, but...wow! Thank you!"

Liliana grinned. "You're very welcome. Does it hurt at all?"

He flexed and rotated his ankle and was amazed to find that he no longer had the slightest twinge of pain. "All better!" he proclaimed.

"Alright then, I guess we'd better get back up to the house."

Tyler thought he detected a hint of disappointment in her voice. He was certainly disappointed. What would have happened if they had kissed? Perhaps it was better this way; after all, he reminded himself, they had a mission to complete and they didn't need distractions.

"You're right; we should get back to the house." He laced up his boot and popped his snowshoe back on. He wondered again, as they retraced their steps, if she could read his aura and see how he truly felt about her.

14 SEDONA

At the slam of a car door, Eddie glanced up from his homework and peered out the kitchen window, in time to see two girls wave to a car as it retreated down the driveway. His heart skipped a beat when they turned. Though her face was half-concealed by auburn hair, tossed by the wind, it was undoubtedly Sarah who strode toward the house. He tore his gaze away for a moment, to notice the slightly taller, blonde, by her side. This must be Grace.

He was greeted by a cold rush of wind when he opened the massive, oak, front door. He had wondered if he would ever see Sarah again, and suddenly, there she stood, on his front porch.

His heart raced, his palms grew sweaty, and he fruitlessly tried to push his feelings of attraction for her aside. He reminded himself that not only was she married, she was also pregnant. His efforts to disregard his feelings were momentarily hampered when she dropped her duffel bag on the porch and threw herself at him with a giant bear hug. He circled his arms around her, wrapped her in tight, and held her close for a few moments before he reluctantly released her.

"So," he said, with a smile, "you found me."

She shook her head. "I should have listened to you. You were only gone for a couple of hours and they came for me. I'm positive it was them. I was so scared; I didn't know where else to go."

"Well, you're here now." He held eye contact as he looked into her brilliant, aqua green eyes. They were even more beautiful than he remembered. *She's married*, he reminded himself, again.

He finally forced himself to break his gaze and with a smile, tried to appear equally happy to see the blonde who stood behind her. "You must be Grace." She was beautiful in her own right; a few inches taller than Sarah, she had long, blonde hair and sparkling, crystal blue eyes.

"Hi," she stepped forward and extended a hand, in greeting, "you must be Eddie."

"I am. Please, come inside, out of the cold."

The girls stepped into the entryway, and Eddie closed the door against the frigid elements. "Why don't you follow me into the kitchen? Can I get you both something warm to drink? Hot chocolate? Apple cider?"

"Hot chocolate sounds great, thank you," Sarah replied.

"That does sound good," Grace said. "I'll have one, too, if you don't mind."

"No problem," Eddie replied. They followed him to the kitchen and sat at the table while he turned to the cupboards for mugs and hot cocoa.

The back door opened and closed, and in a moment, Tyler and Liliana rounded the corner.

Tyler beamed at the sight of the newcomers. "Sarah, you made it!"

She smiled in return and rose to give him a hug. "Yeah, I made it, alright. It's nice to finally meet you. I met up with a friend along the way. I didn't think you'd mind if I brought her along, figured it would save you the trouble of finding her yourself."

Tyler turned to Grace. "I'm so glad you're here. How did you two ever find each other? We went to your house, Grace, and your mom said that you'd gone on some band trip to Florida."

After Sarah and Grace had explained their chance encounter, Eddie turned to Sarah. "How did you get here, from the airport? Who dropped you off?"

"It's a long story. It was this couple that I met, back at the diner, in Washington. They happened to be heading to the airport and offered to give me a ride."

Eddie raised his eyebrows. "They just happened to be headed to Flagstaff? Isn't that a strange coincidence?"

"Yeah, that's what I thought, too, but I didn't see any reason to be suspicious. They were just a nice, kind of kooky, older couple."

Tyler took a thoughtful sip of hot cocoa, cupped the mug in his hands, and then pursed his lips in doubt. "And neither of you sensed anything strange about them?"

"No," Grace replied. "I mean their auras seemed a bit shady, but I sensed that it was because they were constantly bickering with each other. I thought it seemed like an odd coincidence that they were coming here, but they didn't give us any reason to doubt them. They dropped us off and went on their merry way."

Eddie hoped that she was right. After their laborious attempts to evade the enemy, the last thing that they needed was to announce their location. It didn't sound like they posed a threat, but it seemed a safe bet not to trust anyone, right now.

"Well," Eddie said, "I guess now we need to figure out where to go from here."

"Oh," Tyler replied, "in all the excitement, I forgot to tell you that Toby contacted me while we were out in the woods." He went on to inform them of his most recent conversation with his brother.

Eddie glanced at the clock. "If we leave now, it will be late and dark, by the time we get to Sedona. I know we're all exhausted. I say we get a good night's rest and head out in the morning. Anyone up for ordering a couple of pizzas?"

"Sounds good to me," Tyler agreed. "That'll give us time to figure out where this author lives and come up with a game plan."

They settled in front of the TV and joined Eddie's father, who was engrossed in a 1980's detective movie. Eddie noticed that Tyler and Liliana sat together on the love seat. "Hey, I forgot to ask. How was your snowshoeing adventure?"

The two outdoor explorers shared a moment of quiet eye contact, and Eddie sensed that a silent conversation passed between them.

Liliana grinned, and then Tyler said, "Snowshoeing...right, it was uh...definitely...interesting."

*****

Eddie stopped at the first gas station he came to, in Sedona, to find out if someone might know where Patricia McCormack lived. Eager to assist, he was promptly offered directions by the gas station clerk and three customers who had overheard his inquiry. No one seemed to know actual street names, but down around a few right hand turns, past a church, two businesses that advertised psychic readings, another which advertised a map to locate local vortexes, up a steep hill, and they quickly arrived at what they hoped was the author's home.

The pueblo style, ranch house had a circular drive and was nestled up to one of the hundreds of majestic, red rock formations that made Sedona a popular tourist location.

"Stay here with the car running...just in case," Eddie said, as he stepped out. "No sense in all of us walking into a trap."

The finely crushed white rock crunched beneath his boots as he strode toward the front door. Overhead, a hawk silently circled. He rang the doorbell and waited while the chimes reverberated throughout the house. He prayed that the author was home. If she wasn't, they would once again be at a stalemate, with nowhere to go.

He removed his sunglasses and tapped them impatiently as he waited for a sign of inhabitation. He turned to the car, where his new friends watched with intent, and shrugged, as if to say he didn't know if she was home or not. Just as he was about to ring the bell for a second time, the lock clicked, and the door swung open to reveal a woman, who appeared to be in her early fifties. Slightly stocky, she had shoulder length, frizzy, reddish blonde hair. Dressed in an ankle length, tie died dress, she was adorned in multiple pieces of necklaces, bracelets, and rings.

Her smile was pleasant, but Eddie sensed an air of suspicion, as she eyed him quizzically. He realized that he should say something, but suddenly found himself at a loss for words.

"Can I help you?" She looked first at him and then over his shoulder, to the car parked in the driveway.

Eddie found his composure and said, "Um...hi...yes. Are you Patricia McCormack?"

"I am. And who might you be?" She continued to eye him with suspicion, and Eddie knew that he needed to quickly assuage any doubts that she might have, about him.

"My name's Eddie. I've driven over here from Flagstaff, with some friends. We were hoping that you might be able to answer a few questions, for us, about Indigo Children. I heard that you're the person to talk to on the subject."

Her composure relaxed slightly, but obvious hesitation was still written on her face. She nodded and said, "You heard correctly. I have done extensive research on Indigo Children. Did someone in particular send you?" Doubt lingered in her voice, and Eddie wondered how many times people had come to her door, in search of advice and answers. More importantly, he wondered how many times someone from the I.I.A. had come to question her, and he wondered if she suspected he might belong to the agency, as well.

He looked around to ensure that no one else had arrived. "Is it safe to talk?"

"Safe? Yes, I believe it is. Though of course we never know for sure now, do we?"

"No, I guess we don't," Eddie said, with a smile. He didn't quite know how to begin, and so he decided the best place to start was with the truth. "I was sent here by a boy named Toby. He said you might be able to help. He was kidnapped by a group called the Indigo Intelligence Agency."

Her eyebrows rose in surprise. Whatever she had thought he might say, mention of the I.I.A. was obviously not what she had expected.

She glanced again over his shoulder and then said, "Invite your friends inside. It sounds like we have a lot to discuss."

*****

The author guided them into a comfortable sun room. The circular room was surrounded by floor to ceiling windows and lined with potted green plants and trees. There was a large, rock, waterfall on one side, and mingled amongst the plants, were a half dozen bird cages, which housed a variety of colorful, tropical birds. As they entered the room, the birds bellowed out a mixed melody of songs and squawks, in greeting.

"Please, have a seat and make yourselves comfortable," the author said. "If you'll excuse me, for just a moment, I'll have my housekeeper prepare a tray of snacks."

Eddie took a seat by himself, on one of the four, pillow lined, wicker, love seats that were positioned around a glass coffee table. Sarah and Grace sat across from him, and Tyler and Liliana claimed the love seat, to his left.

They sat in silence, each left to their own thoughts. He became acutely aware of Sarah's presence, directly across from him. He tried not to stare for any length of time. Instead, he pretended to be entranced in watching a small, green parrot; however, he couldn't help but look at her from time to time. His growing infatuation was absurd; but nevertheless, he felt drawn to her.

Tyler must have decided that the growing silence had gone on long enough, and he took it upon himself to lighten the mood. "Hey, you know, when I was a kid, my grandma had a parrot that could talk. I wonder if any of these birds can say something." He stood and wandered over to the cage which housed a green parrot.

"Wait a minute! I've been here before," Grace exclaimed.

Tyler turned to her with raised eyebrows. "You've been *here*? When?"

"Well...I wasn't exactly *here*, not physically, anyway. It was in a dream, and now that I remember it, all of you were in the dream, too."

"Cool, I guess that's a sign we're supposed to be here," Tyler said. Then he turned back to the parrot and spoke in a high-pitched, parrot imitating voice, "Polly want a cracker?" The bird looked at him, blinked, then let out a high pitched squawk. "Hellloooo," Tyler squawked, in his parrot voice. The bird looked at him and blinked once more.

Grace laughed. "You did that in my dream, too."

He grinned. "Oh yeah? And in your dream, did this bird talk to me?"

Liliana laughed. "I don't think your new friend there wants to talk to you."

Tyler turned to her. "Don't be silly; animals love me. He just needs to warm up a bit, just you wait and see."

He grinned, again, turned back to the bird, and stared in silence, for a few moments. Then, the quietude broke, when the bird squawked, "Hello! Hello!"

The girls giggled at the parrot's response.

"What's your name?" Tyler asked.

"What's your name?" the bird responded.

"I'm Tyler."

"Tyler! Tyler!" the parrot screeched.

"Right, I'm Tyler. What's your name?"

"Freddie."

"Freddie? Nice to meet you, Freddie. What's a handsome bird like you doing, all alone, in this cage? There's a lot of pretty, girl parrots on the other side of the room. It looks to me like they have their eyes on you."

In response, the other parrots let out a raucous of calls and squawks. "See there, Freddie, I think they like you."

"Pretty girls!" the parrot replied.

"That is amazing!" Patricia said, from the doorway. The author reentered the room, strode around the loveseats, and stopped beside Tyler. "How did you do that?" She gazed at him in wonder.

"Do what? Talk to the bird?"

"I have had Freddie for ten years, and I've never been able to get him to talk. You've been here for five minutes, and he's carrying on a conversation." She broke her gaze from Freddie, to stare at Tyler. "Who are you?" She turned to the rest of the group. "Who are all of you, for that matter?"

"It's a really long story," Tyler replied. "Do you have time?"

"Eddie mentioned the I.I.A. and said that a friend of yours was kidnapped. For that, I will make time. Please, have a seat."

Tyler resumed his seat, beside Liliana, and Patricia sat in the empty love seat, to Eddie's right.

"You have a friend who was kidnapped?" Patricia began.

"It's my brother, actually," Tyler replied, "my twin brother."

"I see. And you know for a fact that it was the I.I.A. who took him?"

"I do. Toby has been able to contact me, telepathically. He doesn't know where he is, but he does know for sure that it's the I.I.A. who took him. They want to use him, for his gifts."

Patricia nodded. "Yes, I know. That is what the I.I.A. does. They use teenagers and young adults with special powers, for their own benefit. How much do you know about them?"

"Not much at all. That's why we came to see you. Toby said that you know a tracker who deserted the agency. He said that you might know where he is. We need to find the tracker and talk to him. He's the only one who might be able to give us directions to find my brother."

"You aren't the first people to come around, asking about him. There's been a slew of agents through here. Some have had official looking badges; others have appeared to be college age kids who claim to be his friend. I'm going to tell you, the same thing that I told all of them...I don't know where he is. If he deserted, then it must be because he doesn't want to be found."

"You don't know where he is, or you don't want to tell us where he is?"

Patricia smiled and looked at him in silence. A sound from the doorway broke the tension. "Ah, thank you, Maria," she said, to the housekeeper. "You may set the tray on the table."

As directed, the housekeeper set a crystal tray on the coffee table. It was filled with a pitcher of water and an assortment of sausage, cheese, crackers, and fruit.

"Please, help yourselves," Patricia said.

It had been awhile since breakfast, and they were all happy to sample the refreshments.

"This is delicious," Sarah said. "Thank you."

The rest of the group murmured similar responses of appreciation.

"What can you tell us about the I.I.A.?" Eddie asked the author.

"You don't know much about them?"

Eddie shook his head. "No, we know that they took Toby because he's what they consider an Indigo Child, but we don't really know what that term means, either."

She looked at the members of the group, one by one. "How did all of you get involved?"

"Toby said that they have a list of people who they are interested in recruiting, if you want to call it that, and we are all on the list. I guess they're determined to find us one way or the other."

Patricia nodded in understanding. "Yes, that makes sense. There are always trackers who are in search of people like you. The more powerful your gifts, the more useful you are, and therefore, the more determined they would be to find you. I am curious how you came to find each other, but let me start from the beginning and answer some of your questions. I guess the first place to start, is to explain what an Indigo Child is."

She took a deep breath. "First off, the term Indigo Child was coined in the 1970's. It was given to label children who demonstrated a collection of characteristics. It was noticed that more and more children who were born, held a series of personality traits and special abilities, that hadn't been widely known before.

"On a very basic, scientific sense, it was noticed that these children possessed an indigo hue in their aura. That's where the term 'Indigo Children' comes from. They all demonstrated a heightened sense of the energy in the world around them. Those are common characteristics of all Indigo Children, but just as all people are different, so are Indigo Children. They possess a wide range of personality traits and abilities, some more so than others. If you have drawn the attention of the I.I.A., that tells me that each of you must possess strong abilities, in one way or another."

"What sort of abilities or personality traits are common for Indigo Children?" Sarah asked.

"Well, let me begin with personality traits. Indigos are often curious about the world, they're empathic toward others, highly intuitive, and they often hold a clear sense of purpose for their lives. They can be strong-willed, and they often perceive the world differently. They often don't feel it's necessary to follow the normal way of doing things, and they usually have a higher sense of spirituality. Now, please understand, these are just some traits that Indigos exhibit, the list isn't all inclusive, but they are common personality traits that are seen much of the time."

The group nodded their heads in silent understanding, and the author continued.

"Now then, besides those certain personality traits, Indigos *sometimes* possess one or two special abilities. They can be telepathic or psychic, they can have the ability to affect electronics and harness energy, they can have the ability to influence others, oftentimes, those who can influence others have a dynamic personality that draws others to them. They have also been known to communicate with others of different energy levels, like spiritual beings, and they can see auras.

"Again, that is just a small list. I could go on and on, but I think you get the idea."

"What about healing?" Liliana asked. "Can Indigos heal others by touching them?"

Patricia turned toward Liliana with a look of interest. "Can you do that?"

Liliana nodded.

"Well, that's one that I haven't come across, before, but it would make sense. If Indigos can harness and manipulate energy, it would make sense that they would be able to do it on another person as well. An injury in a body, after all, is just a series of electrons that have essentially gone askew. So, if Indigos can manipulate the electrons to fix themselves, then it would be reasonable to assume that they could heal an injury, as well.

"Wow, that is something to think about." She smiled at Liliana and then was silent for a moment, as though lost in contemplation.

Grace pursed her lips and leaned forward. "Is there an explanation why there are suddenly more people who are born with these characteristics?"

"That's an excellent question," Patricia said, "and the answer is, yes. Actually, there is a very real and plausible theory behind the emergence of Indigo Children. Are you all familiar with DNA?"

The author looked around the room and they all nodded.

"Well, that is the first place to begin. Along with DNA, is something else called RNA. RNA identifies and responds to experiences that we all have, both emotional and physical, and it carries messages to our DNA. In turn, as our DNA receives these new messages, it has the ability to communicate differently. Over the past few years, this variance in DNA communication has begun to occur more frequently.

"After a while, the DNA gets rewired permanently, and we see the changes occur more rapidly. We begin to see a leap in the make-up of people, as consciously aware beings. Have you ever heard of something called a 'critical mass'?"

Most of the group shook their heads, but Eddie said, "I have. I remember hearing something about it, in one of my physics classes."

"You may have," she said, to Eddie. "Critical Mass is a term used in physics when it's referred to obtaining a necessary amount of material to sustain a chain reaction. Critical Mass also has another meaning. It refers to a moment in time that an evolutionary trend becomes the norm. As more and more people begin to change, it is believed that the characteristics held by some, will eventually be the characteristics held by most.

"You've heard that most people only use ten percent of their brain power? Well, as new DNA strands, which have previously been dormant, become activated, people gain the ability to unleash their telepathic and psychic abilities, along with many other abilities. We begin to see this happen more and more often amongst Indigo Children."

"So," Eddie began, "what you're saying is, there's an actual reason why I am, the way I am, and that people like me are becoming more common?"

Patricia smiled. "That's right. As time goes on, researchers believe that the appearance of Indigo Children will become more frequent, as we near a critical mass. Now, again, remember, not all Indigos have such extreme powers, but those who do, have the potential to be true leaders. And it's also why the I.I.A. would like to get their hands on those with special abilities."

"Can you tell us what you know about the I.I.A.?" Eddie asked.

The author nodded. "I can, but just keep in mind that what I tell you is not common knowledge, and if you went to any official agencies with this information, it would be discredited."

"Yeah, that's kind of the impression we've gotten, too," Eddie said. "That's why we're on our own and haven't gone to the police."

"I'm glad you understand," Patricia said. "Everything that I know about the I.I.A. comes from word of mouth from my friend, who you are looking for. His name is Ian. I first met him when he was twelve. I knew his parents; they were professors at the university, where I taught. When they found out that I was doing research on Indigo Children, they brought their son, Ian, to my attention.

"Around the same time, his parents went to a convention on Indigo Children, and that is when the I.I.A., which is short for Indigo Intelligence Agency, also became aware of his abilities, and they took an interest in him. They discovered that his parents, who were professors in psychology, could also be useful, and so the whole family was recruited."

"You mean, Ian's parents joined the I.I.A.?" Liliana asked.

"That's right. They worked to develop tests that could be used to help identify other Indigos, and they became teachers at the school that is run by the I.I.A. As time went on, other groups of children, besides Indigos, were identified. They were given labels like Crystalline Children and Star Children, and they had stronger powers than researchers had ever seen. But basically, regardless of the label that they were given, it was all the same idea. If someone possessed useful powers, the I.I.A. wanted them."

"And they allowed their own son to be used as a guinea pig?" Grace asked.

"They didn't see it that way. Ian was sent to one of their schools, where he was encouraged to develop his abilities. His parents never realized that he was being groomed to be a spy."

"A spy?" Liliana asked. "So that's what this whole thing is about? Who do they spy on?"

"It all depends. Sometimes they use Indigos to infiltrate corporate businesses, to learn their secrets. Sometimes they use them to spy on other countries, and sometimes they're used to spy on our own government. There are active members and there are also 'sleepers'. Sleepers are trained and then are sent out to live in the world, to lead what would appear to be normal lives, until they are called upon to complete a mission."

"What's the point though?" Sarah asked. "Who funds them?"

"The I.I.A. is a small branch that falls under the CIA. There are very few people, even in the CIA, who know of its existence. From time to time, the CIA gets intelligence from them, and that's enough to keep the I.I.A. funded."

"So, what happened with Ian and his parents?" Tyler asked.

"When Ian was seventeen, he graduated and went to live at what he calls, 'the compound'. That was where he was trained to be both a spy and a tracker."

"What exactly does a tracker do?" Eddie asked.

"A tracker is trained to identify other people, who have Indigo traits. Trackers usually possess psychic and telepathic abilities, and they are able to tune in to other Indigos, even from a distance. Ian worked with them for seven years, until he finally discovered the truth. He found out that the intelligence that he reported back was used to sell to the highest bidder, even if it was to another country."

"So, that's when he decided to leave?" Tyler asked.

"That's right. The problem was, Ian knew too much and they weren't willing to let him go. He went to his parents for help, but they were in just as deep. They encouraged him to stay in and insisted that the benefits far outweighed the disadvantages.

"So, the next time he was sent out alone on a mission, he decided to desert. With the help of a friend in the CIA, he obtained a new identity and disappeared."

"Did Ian tell you where the compound was?"

"He mentioned that it was in a mountainous area, near a desert, but he didn't want to tell me specifics. He said that the less I knew, the safer I was, and I was fine with that."

"If you know all of this, then you've talked to him since he left," Tyler said. "Do you know where he is now?"

His question was again answered with a smile. "Ian disappeared because he didn't want to be found. If his whereabouts were known, he would be in danger. He holds too many secrets that could be exposed. The I.I.A. doesn't want him wandering around, with no one to answer to. Even if I did know where he was, I wouldn't be much of a friend if I was willing to reveal his location to the first person who came along looking for him."

"But, we aren't just anyone," Tyler said. "They have my brother. We just want to get him back."

"I would like to believe that," Patricia replied, "but like I said earlier, many people have come to my door in search of Ian. I have no way of knowing that you aren't working for the I.I.A., as well. But, if you are who you say you are, it is possible, even now, that they know you're all here. You took a gamble by coming here."

"I know," Tyler said, "but we didn't have much of a choice. Ian is the only one who can lead us to my brother. Are you sure that you can't tell us where he is?"

Patricia shook her head. "I would like to help you, but my first responsibility is to keep Ian safe. But, I also understand that you are in danger. If the I.I.A. finds you, they *will* take you, especially now that they know you're aware of them. They're going to want you on their side, one way or the other. Let me think on it for a few minutes. I need to go see to a few things. Can you wait here for a few minutes, until I return?"

They nodded, and she promptly departed.

She returned fifteen minutes later, with an envelope in hand and a set of keys.

"It just so happened, that Ian called while I was in the other room," Patricia said, with a wink. "I explained your situation, and he was able to sense your presence. He believes that you are who you say you are. It's not safe to talk over the phone with any details, but he is willing to see you. You're going to have to be careful, though. I don't know how you've managed to travel as far as you have, without getting caught, but if you're using credit cards, they *will* track you. From now on, use nothing but cash. There can't be any trace of where you are, or where you're going. If you're going to go see Ian, you can't let them follow you.

"Take this." She handed the envelope to Eddie. "You'll find enough cash, inside, to get you by, for a while." Then she handed him a set of keys. "You can't take the Jeep that's parked outside. They'll track any vehicle that is linked to you. I have a car parked in the garage. It was left here by a professor, who is doing a sabbatical, overseas, for a year. They would never think to track it. It should keep you off the radar for a little while. Take it, and leave your Jeep parked in the garage. You can come back for it whenever you're ready.

Eddie accepted the envelope and glanced inside. "I don't know what to say. This is a lot of money. Why are you helping us?"

"Because I was never able to help Ian as much as I would have liked, and because he said that he trusts you. You need help, and right now it looks like I'm the only one in any sort of a position to help you.

"Of course, keep in mind, you won't be completely safe. This will help get you ahead of them for a little while, but if there are trackers after you, they *will* eventually find you."

"I don't understand though," Grace said, "if the trackers are capable of finding us, how come they can't find Ian?"

"I don't know. That would be an excellent question to ask him, once you find him. I can't give you an address, because even I don't know where he lives, exactly. I can tell you to go to Roswell. Once you're there, Ian will sense your presence and find you."

"Roswell? As in...New Mexico?" Tyler asked.

"Isn't that the alien place?" Liliana asked.

Patricia smiled. "Yes, it is a popular tourist spot for alien enthusiasts."

"Cool!" Tyler said, with a chuckle.

"Thank you," Eddie said. He gave her a hug in appreciation.

"I wish you all the best of luck." She turned to Tyler and gave him a hug. "I hope that you're able to rescue your brother."

She showed them to the front door so that they could retrieve their bags from the Jeep and transfer them to their new vehicle. When she swung the door open, they were stunned motionless at the appearance of a man and woman on the front walk. They appeared to be in their late fifties. The man was balding and had a rotund belly. The woman was just as rotund and had a curly head of white hair.

"Bonnie? Chuck?" Sarah questioned. "What are *you* doing here?"

Patricia turned to Sarah. "You know them?"

"Um...yeah. They flew here with me from Washington. We kind of met up along the way and became travel buddies."

"Hi, Sarah, so sorry to show up here like this," the man said, sounding truly apologetic.

"Everyone," Patricia began, "I'd like to introduce you to Chuck and Bonnie...Ian's parents."

"Well, let's not stand right here, with the door wide open to the world," Patricia said, noticeably irritated at the arrival of her newest visitors. "You might as well come on in."

"Thank you," Bonnie replied. Without further invite, she stepped into the entryway with her husband close on her heels.

Patricia closed the door and locked it with a resounding click. Sarah noticed that she also bolted the safety chain. It occurred to her that this seemed an odd thing to do, since the enemy was now inside the premises, but she said nothing. Instead, she followed them into the front living room and sat on a plush, sectional couch, between Grace and Liliana. Chuck and Bonnie took a seat on a nearby sofa. Eddie and Tyler took their place behind the girls and stood with glaring suspicion, their arms firmly crossed.

Patricia strode across the room and closed the horizontal blinds, on the three picture windows that lined the room. Then, for good measure, she pulled the heavy drapes across, leaving the room in near darkness, until she turned on a variety of floor and table lamps, which sat upon rustic, wood, end tables. Seemingly satisfied that they couldn't be seen by additional, outside intruders, the author took a seat in a large, oversized, southwestern style chair.

Confused and outraged that she had been misled by the unassuming, older couple, Sarah surprised herself when she found the courage to speak first. "You followed me? Why? I thought you were my friends."

"I know you must be angry," Bonnie began. "Please, give us a chance to explain."

"What is there to explain?" Tyler asked, from behind Sarah. "It seems pretty clear cut to me. You traveled with Sarah so that you could track us all down. What more is there to say? What do you plan to do, now that you've found us? That's the question."

"It's true, we did follow Sarah," Chuck said, "but our motives aren't quite as you would think. Yes, we do work for the I.I.A., but we aren't trackers, not by any sense of the imagination. That isn't our job. Our job is to recruit and test prospective students. That's why we were in Washington. We were there for a recruiting convention. When we got word that two trackers had located a target, we thought there might be a chance it was Ian. We had to see for ourselves.

"It wasn't our son, though," Bonnie said. "It was Sarah. When we got to the diner, in Granite Falls, the trackers were there, too. When they saw us, we had to explain what we were doing there."

"They decided that they were going to use us to follow Sarah," Chuck went on. "One of the trackers felt that Sarah was suspicious of their presence, and they worried that their cover had been blown. So, they decided to turn their hunt over to us and instructed us to follow her."

"We didn't want to! Believe me, Sweetheart," Bonnie said. Her pleading expression and apologetic tone almost made Sarah believe her. "We didn't want you to be in danger, but we also didn't have a choice. When you work for the I.I.A., you have to do as directed."

"They suspected that I was on to them?" Sarah questioned. "It *was* that couple back in the diner, wasn't it? The man and woman who were dressed in fancy trench coats?"

"That was them," Chuck affirmed.

"So, you've been following me ever since and have been reporting back to them? Does that mean that they're going to be here any minute to pick us all up, or is it *your* job to bring us in?"

Chuck shook his head. "No, if anyone brings you in, it's definitely not going to be us. After we dropped you off at Eddie's house, we called to inform the agency of the location, and then we were directed to return to the research facility. Halfway there, we were both overcome with guilt. We saw how the agency took over our son's life, and we knew we couldn't let that happen to you. We turned around and drove all night to come back and warn all of you. We were sitting in the car this morning, trying to figure out the best way to explain it all, when we saw you drive away, so we decided to follow."

Sarah was still skeptical of their sincerity. She wanted to believe them, but knowing who they worked for made it difficult to trust them. She examined their expressions for signs that they were lying. "So, you followed us because...you wanted to warn us?"

Bonnie's expression didn't flicker, and she didn't hesitate when she replied, "Yes, they've assigned a local tracker to find you. They don't know that you're in Sedona, but it won't be long before they do. We came here to try to throw them off, to give you a head start."

"But, won't they be suspicious if they find you here?"

"Not at all," Chuck replied. "They know we come here from time to time, in hopes that Patricia will tell us where our son is." He turned to the author with an intent gaze. She had remained quiet, throughout the conversation.

"I still don't know where Ian is," the author lied.

"Of course you don't," Bonnie said, with a forced smile.

Tyler seemed to sense the tense emotions between Ian's parents and the author. He turned to Bonnie in an attempt to change the subject. "Did you know that they kidnapped by brother?"

She looked to Tyler with apologetic eyes. "I didn't know. I'm sorry to hear that."

"Do you have any idea where they might be keeping him?"

"No, Sweetheart. I'm sorry. Our work has always been restricted to the school and the research facility. More than likely, they would keep him at the training compound. From what I hear, it's a very secure and remote location. When Ian was sent there to train, he was never allowed to tell us where he was."

"Look, kids," Chuck said, "we could talk all day, but the fact is, you need to leave before anyone shows up looking for you. We'll stay and do our best to throw them off your trail. Hopefully that will buy you some time." He turned to Sarah. "I know you must be angry with us. I hope you understand our motive to find our son."

Sarah nodded. "I understand. I do."

Chuck patted her on the shoulder in silent response. Enough

had been said.

"If you happen to see our son along the way, please let him know that we would like to see him, again," Bonnie said.

"I will," Sarah promised.

*****

Sarah and Eddie took turns driving the borrowed, Lincoln Town Car, while Liliana, Grace, and Tyler snoozed in the backseat. As she drove, Sarah glanced at her wedding ring and twisted it so the diamond faced up. A single tear formed in the corner of her eye. Before Eddie had a chance to notice, she hurriedly swiped it away. With her emotions kept in check, she could forcibly hold back the tears but knew she wouldn't be able to, if compelled to talk about her husband. This was not the time or place to be tearful and emotional. She had plenty of other worries to consider, worries like, how she planned to keep her baby safe.

We're going to be fine. The voice in her head interrupted her thoughts. She glanced at Eddie, who gazed out the passenger window. He obviously hadn't heard anything. She thought more about the voice. It hadn't said, '*You're* going to be fine'; she was certain that it had said, '*We*'.

Sarah placed a hand on her belly. Would they have to spend their lives on the run, in order to keep him safe? After a hundred miles or so had passed, she found that she had ended up with a headache but no conclusions.

"Your baby's right," Liliana whispered, from the backseat. "We're going to be fine."

Sarah glanced in the rearview mirror. "You heard him?"

"I did. I sense that there's something special about him."

Sarah glanced in the mirror, again, and smiled at her new friend. "Thank you."

"Hey, Sarah, you about ready for a break?" Eddie asked. "It looks like Albuquerque is just ahead. We can stop and stretch our legs and get a bite to eat, then I can take over driving, for a while, if you want to rest."

"Did I hear something about food?" Tyler yawned as he sat up in the backseat.

"A break sounds good to me," Grace said, as she too awoke. "How close are we to Roswell?"

"We've got about three hours left," Sarah replied, "but it's just about dinner time. If we stop now, and eat and gas up, we should be able to continue on without stopping, until we get there."

They pulled into a truck stop, on the outskirts of town. When Sarah stepped out of the car, she stretched her arms and turned her face skyward. The wind whipped her hair wildly about her head, but she didn't care. It was nice to stand in the fresh air. For the moment, no one knew where they were, and she felt momentarily at peace. She had the feeling that this was like the eye of the storm. It was inevitable that the sense of calm would soon pass, and they would once again be running from danger, but for now, she was happy to enjoy the moment.

"I've got to find a bathroom before we eat!" Grace said.

"I hear ya," Sarah told her, "this baby's pushing on my bladder. I'll come with you." She turned to her travel companions. "Do you guys want to meet us in the restaurant?"

"I'm just going to gas up the car so it'll be ready to go," Eddie said. "I'll meet you girls, inside."

"Well, I'm all about trying the pie," Tyler said. He pointed to the hand painted picture of pie on the restaurant window, beside a sign which declared that they had twenty-four flavors.

"Mmm, my favorite is chocolate cream," Liliana said, as she and Tyler headed for the building.

They walked away, side by side, and Sarah smiled as she noticed how comfortable they seemed with each other. Then, she grabbed her purse out of the car and turned to Grace with a smile. "Right then, let's go find the restroom."

As they walked across the parking lot, Grace sighed and said, "I've seen the way Eddie looks at you, and I've seen his aura when he's around you. You know he likes you, right?"

"*Eddie*? He can't possibly. He knows I'm married; and seriously, I'm pregnant." She placed a hand on her abdomen, for emphasis.

"Of course he knows all of that, but sometimes when you like someone, you just like them, regardless of the fact if it's practical or not."

"Yeah, well, I hope he realizes that he doesn't have a chance with me. I'm madly in love with my husband, and there's not a chance that I would ever leave him."

"I'm sure he knows that," Grace said, "and I'm sure one of these days he'll realize that there are other girls; but for now, he only has eyes for you."

Grace's tone of voice revealed more than her words, and Sarah turned to her in question. "You like him, don't you?" The door chimed as they entered the gift shop area of the truck stop.

Grace located the sign directing them toward the restrooms. She didn't look at Sarah, but walking straight ahead, she said, "Well, it doesn't matter if I like him or not. He's not interested in me.

"And anyway," Grace continued a few minutes later, as she looked in the restroom mirror to fluff her hair, "it doesn't matter if he likes me or not. When all of this is over, I'll be in Utah, and he'll be in Arizona. It's not like it would ever work out between us, anyway. Right?"

"You're probably right," Sarah agreed. "Are there any guys waiting for you back home?"

"Actually, yeah, I do have a boyfriend." They headed for the back of the store, where the restaurant was located. "His name is Derek. He's cute and really sweet, he's just not..."

"Not your soul mate?"

"Exactly! I mean we get along great and everything, but I just don't feel that special spark, you know? Did you know your husband was the one, when you first met him?"

"I did. There was never a question in my mind."

"See, that's what I want."

"Give it time. How old are you?"

"Sixteen...I know, I know, I'm only sixteen and I have plenty of time, but, isn't it only natural to dream about the man you're going to marry one day?"

"Of course it is, and one day, you'll find him. Probably when you least expect it."

"Yeah, you're probably right. It's just that..."

"What?"

"It's just that, when I first saw Eddie, he's just so..."

"Gorgeous," Sarah concluded for her.

Grace laughed. "Exactly! But that's not all of it. I mean, Derek is pretty good looking, too; granted, he's not as beautiful as Eddie. It's just that, I feel this pull or connection to Eddie that I can't explain."

"Well, if he truly is your soul mate, then eventually you two will be together. Destiny has a way of bringing people together, even if they don't try. If it's meant to be, it will happen."

"You're right," Grace said, after a moment. "I guess I just need to find a little patience."

"Sometimes that's easier said than done."

They entered the restaurant and spotted their friends who sat at a booth, by the window. Eddie looked up and smiled. She couldn't help but notice that he kept his gaze on her, as they crossed the room. He didn't glance at Grace. She saw that Grace noticed this too, and she suddenly felt sorry for her friend.

*****

Roswell was quiet and deserted, when they rolled into town, that evening. Sarah smiled as she observed the never ending succession of stores that advertised alien and U.F.O. memorabilia. Even the motels and restaurants seemed to want a piece of the action; she noticed a motel with a picture of a green alien on the sign and a restaurant that was shaped like a U.F.O. She had always assumed that the alien rumors, which revolved around Roswell, were exaggerated stories, long since forgotten, but obviously that wasn't the case. It seemed the alien culture was still a strong component of the town.

After driving up and down the main strip, they did a U-turn and checked into the motel with the massive, green alien sign. Before the girls retired to their own room, they agreed with the boys that they would meet at eight, the following morning.

When Sarah opened the door, the sight of the shabby motel room didn't surprise her. After all, the worn carpet with cigarette burns and peeling wallpaper fit the picture of a cheap motel that accepted cash. The room had two beds though, and after she had closed and locked the door, and double checked that the safety latch was secure, she breathed a sigh of relief. The day's drive was over, and she could finally lie down and rest.

Blinking lights from the fabricated, plastic U.F.O. that sat atop the roof, over the motel office, shone through a crack in the curtains. She rolled over so that the lights wouldn't keep her awake. She had barely fallen asleep, when a voice in her head awoke her, *Rest up, tomorrow will be a day of discovery*. She opened her eyes, unsure if she had actually heard the voice or if she had already been dreaming. The voice said nothing more; however, and she eventually closed her eyes and fell asleep.

*****

The restaurant was something of a 1950's meets U.F.O.'s themed diner. It had black and white tiled floors and red bar stools at the front counter. Standing inside the front entrance, was a five foot tall, wooden carved alien. It held a sign which read, 'Welcome Visitors From Afar'. On each table sat a jukebox in the shape of a U.F.O., and from somewhere overhead, speakers projected a Buddy Holly song.

After they had ordered, Liliana flipped through the jukebox selections. "Anyone have a quarter?"

"No, sorry," Tyler said. "What song did you want?"

"Elvis."

"You're a big Elvis fan, huh?"

"I am. My parents grew up listening to Elvis music when they lived in China, and they continued to listen to it after they moved to America. It's what they thought all Americans listened to, so naturally, I grew up with it, too."

"Do you want any song in particular?"

"Not really, anything will do."

Tyler leaned across Liliana to reach the jukebox. Sarah noticed that his hand gently swept across her arm, as he did so, and she wondered if it had been a purposeful move. He flipped through the selections for a minute and then paused. He rested a hand on the jukebox, closed his eyes, momentarily, and then, seemingly satisfied, sat back in the seat and smiled.

"Did you do it?" Liliana whispered.

Tyler smiled. "Wait and see."

A sorrowful Patsy Cline song ended, and as the new song began, Sarah grinned at Tyler when she recognized the beginning of Elvis', "Blue Suede Shoes".

"That's too cool," Sarah said, to him. "You did that?"

"Did what?" His response sounded innocent, but his wink and smile revealed the truth.

Halfway through their meal, their waitress, who had introduced herself as Melissa, returned to the table. "Are you Eddie?" she asked.

In unison, everyone at the table slowly turned their head toward her. Surprise and curiosity was written on each of their faces.

"Um…yeah…I'm Eddie." He set his glass of juice on the table.

"There's a phone call for you, back by the kitchen."

"For me? Are you sure?"

"Pretty sure. The caller said to look for a dark haired guy who would be with another guy and three girls. You're the only group, here, who fits that description."

"Well, I guess it must be me, then." He stood to follow the waitress.

Sarah found it difficult to eat while she anxiously awaited his return. She somehow managed to get down a few more bites and finished off her glass of milk, before he slid smoothly back into the booth, next to Grace, two minutes later.

Tyler leaned forward. "Well?"

Eddie held up a small piece of folded paper, which he slid neatly into his jeans' pocket. "I have an address and directions," he said simply. "I'll tell you about it in the car."

16 TREVOR

The car restoration shop was located on the outskirts of town. During the short drive, Eddie explained the brief phone conversation which had transpired. After Eddie had confirmed his identity, a man had provided the address and directions and had said that he would be expecting them.

"He didn't tell you his name?" Grace asked.

"Nope."

Liliana leaned forward, from the backseat. "But, it had to be Ian...right?"

"I'm sure it was. I can't imagine who else it would have been. In any case, I think this is the place. I guess we'll find out soon enough."

The gated entrance was surrounded, on either side, by a tall, solid fence. The wood sign, which hung over the gate read, 'Hank's Restoration and Repairs'.

Tyler sounded puzzled when he read the sign, "Hank?"

"Who knows?" Eddie replied, as he drove down the narrow, dirt lane, lined with old cars and trucks. "Maybe Ian works here."

"It's a junk yard," Grace said, when she saw the sea of vehicles, which ranged from shiny classics to barely recognizable heaps of rust.

"No," Tyler corrected, "it's a car lover's paradise."

They parked in front of a mobile home, and when they stepped out of the car, they were immediately greeted by two barking dogs that ran toward them at full speed. Liliana stepped behind Tyler, and Sarah found herself taking a step behind Eddie, as well, unsure if the dogs were excited to see them or warning them to go away.

With an extended hand, Tyler knelt to greet the canines. One was a Rottweiler, the other, a German Shepherd. Neither looked very friendly, and Sarah realized that she held her breath in anticipation of their reaction to Tyler. It appeared that the dogs took an immediate liking to him; however, and in a few moments, they had both stopped barking. After a sniff of Tyler's hand, the Rottweiler rolled onto his back for a belly rub, and the German Shepherd laid at his feet. His tongue hung out with a look that could only be described as a smile.

Sarah's gaze shot up when a baritone voice growled, "What have you done to my guard dogs?"

The man who had just rounded the corner, of the mobile home, strode toward them and stopped in front of Tyler. The German Shepherd obediently stood and meandered to his owner, but the Rottweiler continued to lie at Tyler's feet, even as Tyler stood.

"Are you Eddie?" the man asked Tyler. It was difficult to judge his age, but Sarah guessed him to be in his mid-twenties. His long, red hair was tied back in a pony-tail, and it appeared that he hadn't shaved in a few days. He wore ragged jeans and a plaid, flannel shirt with the sleeves rolled up. Despite his shabby appearance, Sarah could only describe him as ruggedly handsome. She smiled when she noticed Liliana and Grace exchange a grin and decided that they must be thinking the same thing.

Eddie, who had remained by her side, stepped forward to shake the man's hand. "I'm Eddie. Was it you I spoke with on the phone?"

"It was." The man looked closely at each of them, in turn. "Patricia sent you?"

"Yes...she did," Eddie replied. Sarah noticed that the guys, who stood eye level to each other, seemed to be sizing each other up, no doubt trying to decide if the other was trustworthy and who they claimed to be. After an awkward pause, he asked, "Are you Ian?"

The man nodded. "I am, but around here, I'm known as Cameron."

After the remaining group members had introduced themselves, Ian turned to Tyler. "My dogs don't usually take to strangers. Either they've grown soft, or they sense something special about you."

Tyler shrugged. "I have a way with dogs."

"Well, that's good. I'd hate to think that I'd have to replace them. I'm rather fond of my guard dogs." Ian chuckled and then said, "Now then, I imagine you have quite a few questions. Why don't you come inside and we'll talk."

Ian guided them into the mobile home. "Please, have a seat."

The inside was small but clean and comfortable. Sarah noted that it would have been just the right size for a single bachelor, like Ian, but with six people crammed into the mobile home, the lack of space was notable. The kitchen table sat beside the couch, which was about three feet from the bathroom, but somehow, they managed to fit. The girls took a seat on the couch, while the guys sat at the table.

"Patricia told me that the I.I.A. is looking for you," Ian began. "You must all have some pretty incredible powers if they're spending the time and resources to send a tracker after you. I've spent well over a year evading them; so I know, it's not a fun position to be in." He turned to Tyler. "They have your brother, right? Patricia told me they took him."

"Yeah, that's why we came here. We're hoping that you'll be able to tell us where he is."

Ian pressed both index fingers to his forehead. He took a deep breath and shook his head. "If you're determined to find him, and I'm guessing that you are since you came all this way to see me, it's going to be a difficult search. The compound is well hidden, and it's in Mexico."

"Mexico?" they all seemed to ask at once.

He nodded. "Yes, that's the only way they can legitimately hold people against their will. The CIA would never fund them if they knew they could be connected to kidnapping and holding people on United States property. So, the I.I.A. has its own compound, in Mexico. The I.I.A. does favors for the Mexican government from time to time; and in return, they look a blind eye to the comings and goings at the compound. It's a good deal for everyone concerned. If you want to get your brother back, that's where you'll find him."

"How are we supposed to get into Mexico?" Grace asked.

"Oh, it's not difficult. Anyone can get into Mexico; you just have to drive across the border and you're in. It's the getting *back* into the United States part that might prove a little more difficult, unless you have a passport.

"Getting your brother out is the first part you need to worry about, though. If you can somehow manage that, you'll find a way to get back into the U.S."

"Can you tell us how to find him?" Tyler asked.

"I can give you a general idea," Ian replied. "Like I said, the compound is well hidden, and unless you know the exact location, it's virtually impossible to find."

A ruckus of barking dogs caught his attention, and Ian strode purposefully to the window to peer out. "I forgot, school's out early, today. The bus is here. Come on out and you can meet Trevor."

Tyler and Eddie walked beside Ian, as they made their way down the dirt path, toward a school bus that was stopped at the front gate. The girls trailed slowly behind, discussing who Trevor might possibly be.

When they reached the gate, the door of the short bus swung open, and a boy, about eight-years-old, leapt off and ran into Ian's open arms. Ian swept the boy off his feet and swung him around in circles. Then, setting him back to the ground, he placed an arm around the boy's shoulders and turned him to face the group.

"Everyone, I'd like you to meet Trevor."

"Hi, Trevor," Sarah said.

The boy glanced at her for a moment but said nothing. Instead, he knelt to pet the German Shepherd, who had come to greet him.

"Trevor, are you hungry?" Ian asked.

The boy continued to pet the dog, and it appeared that he hadn't heard the question, but after a moment, with his eyes still on the German Shepherd, he said, "Hot Dog. Yes? Hot dog?"

Ian smiled. "Hot dogs, yes. Run to house. Cameron will be there in a minute."

Trevor sprinted down the driveway. The dogs flanked his sides and joined in the fun. Ian turned to the group for explanation. "He's autistic."

"Is he yours?" Sarah asked.

Ian shook his head. "No, his mother is a friend of mine. You met her this morning, Melissa, the waitress from the restaurant."

"Oh, right," Sarah said. "So, you watch him while she's working?"

"I do. She's a single mother, well, sort of; her husband ran off, and she hasn't heard from him. So, I help her out so she doesn't have to pay for child care. Trevor and I have a good relationship; we understand each other."

They reached the mobile home, where Trevor sat on the bottom step of the porch. A dog leaned against each of his legs and panted happily.

"Inside, Trevor? Hot dog? Let's go."

Trevor bounded up the steps, and everyone else followed. While they took their previous seats, Ian located a hot dog in the fridge and placed it in the microwave. "It's his favorite food," he explained, as he handed the boy the heated hot dog. Trevor eagerly accepted the plain wiener and began to chow down.

"Some children who are identified as autistic, are actually Indigo Children," Ian said, nodding toward Trevor.

"He's an Indigo?" Grace asked.

"He is. Well, sort of, more specifically, he's what they call a Star Child."

"A Star Child? Patricia mentioned that term," Sarah said. "What is that exactly?"

"There are several theories, but one that is now commonly accepted, is that there are some people who have ancient, extraterrestrial DNA. For thousands of years, the DNA remained dormant, but now it's believed that this DNA has begun to awaken in some children who carry the strand. In these cases, the children, who are referred to as Star Children, are able to tap into the powers of their extraterrestrial ancestors."

"You're serious?" Tyler said. "You're saying that Trevor

is...what? Part alien or something?"

"Yes. It's not that uncommon of a notion. I'm not saying that his parents are aliens or anything. I'm just saying that one or the other, carried the dormant alien gene that had been passed down generation after generation, and for whatever reason, the gene decided to become active in him.

"It sounds crazy, I know," he went on. "Some nights, he'll walk outside, stare up at the stars, and talk to them. I can hear his thought process, and it's like he's carrying on a full conversation with someone. There have also been nights when I've seen him talking to the stars, and I swear I've seen lights in the sky flying back and forth overhead."

"For real?" said Tyler. "That's awesome! Does he have any special abilities?"

"He does. Like some children who are autistic, he is extremely gifted in specific areas. In his case, he loves cars and can tell you anything you'd ever want to know about them. He also has psychic tendencies, and he can communicate with animals. He can also communicate with beings from other planets."

When Ian's phone rang, he glanced at the caller ID. "It's a client, calling back about an old car I've been trying to locate for him. Give me just a few minutes. I need to step into my office and get on the computer." He retreated into a back room, and they found themselves left alone with Trevor.

"Do you think that's all for real?" Grace asked. "I mean, do you really think there are people who have alien genes?"

"It's not the first time I've heard theories on the idea," Eddie said. "And I think Ian, probably more than most, knows what he's talking about. After all, he did get paid by a government agency to find people with special powers and stuff. I'm guessing the government wouldn't waste that kind of time and money if it wasn't for real."

While they spoke, Sarah noticed that Trevor had gradually scooted closer to her. He now sat on the floor, with his back against her legs.

"I think he likes you," Tyler said.

Trevor looked over his shoulder and smiled at Sarah. Then he stood, grabbed her hand, and said, "Outside."

"You want to go outside?" Sarah asked.

"Outside," he stated, again.

She glanced toward the office, where Ian had retreated. She then glanced at Eddie, who shrugged his shoulders and grinned. "Okay...sure," she said, after a moment. She smiled at Trevor. "Lead the way."

Her friends stood to follow, but Trevor held out his hand and said, "No."

"You don't want us to go outside with you?" Grace asked.

"No."

"Okay." To make a point that she wouldn't follow, Grace sat on the couch.

Tyler winked at her. "We'll wait right here."

"Thanks," Sarah said. She smiled and then turned to follow Trevor out the door and down the front steps of the porch. As soon as her feet touched the dirt, the dogs ran out from under the porch, in anxious greeting, and sniffed her legs. Trevor grabbed her hand, and without saying a word, led her behind the mobile home and out toward the endless rows of old cars.

Uncertain if she was supposed to say something or simply enjoy the walk, she strolled leisurely beside the boy, hand in hand, in the warm sun. A slight breeze stirred the dirt around them as they walked, and birds in a nearby tree sang happily.

"This is...a...1965...Ford Mustang," Trevor reported, in a mechanical voice. "It was...first introduced on April 17...1964. Here is a...1959...Thunderbird," he said, moving on to the next car. "The Thunderbird...was first introduced in...1955. There have been over...4.4 million Thunderbirds...produced.

"It's a nice car," Sarah said. Ian had been correct; Trevor did seem to know a lot about cars.

For the next few minutes, as they strolled along, Trevor continued to point out various facts about vehicles. When they reached a lone shade tree, he came to a halt and turned so they faced each other. He let go of her hand and placed both of his hands on her small, protruding abdomen. Then, he closed his eyes and turned his face skyward. She looked down at him in wonder. He was smaller than the average eight-year-old, yet he was a beautiful child. He had blonde hair, dimples, and sparkling blue eyes, eyes that seemed full of wisdom behind his quiet exterior.

He stood in immobile concentration for almost a minute and then his serious expression turned into a thoughtful smile. He opened his eyes, and his gaze returned to her belly.

"I like...you," Trevor said. "You...will...be...my friend."

She was unsure if he spoke to her or the baby and was unsure if she was supposed to respond, so she said, "Um, I like you, too."

He didn't make eye contact but kept his hands and gaze on her belly. "They want you...Stay...Stay here." He was answered by a small but undeniable kick, from within. He took hold of both of her hands and pulled her down to sit in the dirt, beside him.

She took her place and sat cross legged, beneath the large oak. She wasn't thrilled to sit in the dirt but welcomed the cool reprieve offered by the large tree. Beside her, Trevor picked up a small stick and began to draw pictures in the dirt.

She watched in fascinated silence, as the boy drew in animated concentration. The subject of his drawing was unclear, but she assumed that the picture would eventually reveal itself. The branches overhead swayed and whispered gently in the breeze, and his words floated back to her mind. 'They want you', he had told her, or had he been talking to the baby? Ian had said that the boy was psychic. Did he know that she and her friends were in danger?

She glanced toward the mobile home to see if Ian had come in search of his young friend, but he was nowhere in sight. She looked, then, at the drawings in the dirt. There was an unmistakable planet with five surrounding moons. Below the celestial images were, what appeared to be, hieroglyphics of some sort.

Sarah pointed to the characteristic symbols, with interest. "What does that mean?"

Trevor glanced at her briefly and then looked toward the sky.

He placed one hand on her belly, again, and sat in silence, for a moment. Then he smiled.

He wants us to stay here, the now familiar voice, in her head, said. *He thinks this is a safe place, for us.*

Sarah looked at Trevor in wonder. "Can you communicate with my baby?"

Trevor looked at her and smiled sweetly. Then he stood and dragged a foot back and forth across his drawings, erasing all evidence of their existence. She accepted his outstretched hand, and he helped to pull her to her feet. Once she was upright, he didn't let go. Hand-in-hand, they continued down the dirt lane, as though they had never stopped.

"This," Trevor said, when they stopped in front of an old rusty truck, "is a...1946...GMC truck."

It looked like it had once been red, in its earlier years, though it was difficult to say for sure, considering that the majority of the truck had rusted over.

"It's uh...nice," Sarah commented, uncertain what she was supposed to say about the aged vehicle.

Considering Trevor's mechanical voice, Sarah was pleasantly surprised at his sincere laugh. As he continued to laugh, she smiled and laughed with him.

"It's not nice?" she asked.

He vigorously shook his head and said, "No!" then laughed some more.

"What's so funny?" a voice, from behind, asked.

Sarah turned to find Ian behind them. "Oh, hi, you found us. I'm not sure. I told him the truck was nice, and he started laughing."

He turned to Trevor. "That is funny. She's funny, huh?"

"Funny," Trevor replied.

"What's wrong with the truck?" Sarah asked. "Other than the obvious fact that it's all rusty?"

"Nothing," Ian said. "I have plans to fix it up, one day. This car lot belonged to Trevor's grandfather, Hank, and this truck was his favorite. He always said that he was going to fix it up and make it look like new, but he passed away before he had the chance."

"How sad. So, that's how you met Trevor? Because he was Hank's grandson?"

"That's right. When I first moved to Roswell, in search of...a new life, I didn't have much of a resume, so to speak. I had always worked for the I.I.A. and had never done anything else, but I did know a lot about cars. When I was growing up, I read every book I could get my hands on, about fixing cars. I have sort of a photographic memory, and I convinced Hank that I could help him out. So, he gave me a chance, and it turns out, I had a knack for car restoration. Hank accepted me. He never asked questions about my past, and I felt like I was a part of the family.

"So, after Hank passed away, you just stayed on here?"

"Yep, he left the place to me. Trevor's father was furious; he felt that he should have inherited the place, but he had never shown an interest in it. He knows nothing about cars. He's spent the majority of his life bouncing in and out of jail, for dumb things like DUI's and petty robbery. Finally, Melissa told him that she wanted a divorce. He told her that he wouldn't give her the satisfaction and took off. She has no clue where he is, and they're still legally married. As far as Trevor is concerned, I'm the only father figure he has in his life."

"It sounds like you've really made a place for yourself, here. You think you'll stay for a while, then?" She thought about his parents and their search for him. She wondered if he knew or even cared.

Ian smiled and nodded. "Yeah, that's the plan. All my life I felt like I was different and never really fit in. I've never felt more normal than I do right here. I like this town, and I love Trevor. We understand each other."

He didn't say so, but reading between the lines, Sarah suspected that Trevor's mother might also have a slight influence on his desire to stick around. Other than his obvious affection for the boy, she wondered about his feelings for Melissa; not that it mattered of course, it wasn't any of her business.

"Did you know that your parents are looking for you?"

Ian looked her in the eyes, for a moment, but said nothing. Finally he said, "I suspected they were. After I took off, I knew the I.I.A. had a search team out, looking for me. They're scared about everything I know and who I might tell."

"You knew all of this when you deserted but were still willing to take the risk?"

"I had to. I looked at what my life had become, and I wasn't happy. They owned me, and they ruled every second of my day. At first the job seemed exciting, you know? It was like in the movies, the idea of being a spy and having adventures seemed like fun, but soon the exhilaration wore off, and I began to see the truth."

"And what was the truth?" They had wandered back to the shade tree. Trevor located his stick and resumed his place in the dirt.

"The truth was, I was just a pawn, a pawn for a group of people who wanted to use my knowledge and gifts, to gain power and money. When I saw that they were willing to sacrifice the freedom of others, like me, and the security of their own country, for their own greed, I knew that it was time to get out.

"I went to my parents for help, but they were just as stuck and weren't willing to take the risk. Even though they knew the truth, just as well as I did, they enjoyed the comforts of life that the I.I.A. provided, and they didn't want to give up their research. I knew that I was on my own and would probably never see them again, but it was a chance I had to take.

"How did you know that my parents are looking for me? You've seen them?"

There was an accusatory tone to his voice. Sarah hoped that he didn't suspect she worked for the I.I.A., as well. "Yeah, I saw them, but I didn't know who they were, when I first met them. They found out that the I.I.A. had tracked me down, in Washington. When your parents first heard the news, they thought it was *you* the I.I.A. had found. They came to see for themselves. When they got there, the trackers instructed them to follow me. I thought that they were just a quirky, older couple. I had no idea who they were. I swear!"

Ian smiled. "A quirky, older couple, that's a good way to describe them. I admit my parents are a bit odd."

Sarah laughed. "Yeah, just a little, but I like them. I know they deceived me, but it was only because they were trying to find you. They really miss you, you know."

Ian sighed. "Yeah, I know, but I can't see them." He shook his head. "I've made a new life for myself, here. I'm finally safe. If I were to see them, or even call them, the I.I.A. would find me, in no time. As long as I stay here, I stay safe, and I can keep Trevor safe." He looked down at the boy in the dirt. He hadn't drawn strange symbols, as before; instead, he had drawn what looked to be, Ian's two dogs. She wondered if she should mention the hieroglyphics but decided that it could wait.

"Keep Trevor safe? What do you mean?"

"If the I.I.A. knew of Trevor's existence, they would snatch him up in a heartbeat."

"But, he can't talk...I mean, he can, but...you know what I mean. What good could he possibly be, to them?"

"They would love to get their hands on him, for research. They've barely begun DNA research on Indigos. If they were able to do DNA research on a *Star Child*, and one with his powers...they would have a hay day."

"So, you see yourself as his protector....his guardian?"

"That's a good way of putting it. Who better to protect him than a former tracker? If I keep Trevor close, I'll always know if he's in danger. As long as we stay in Roswell, we're fairly safe, at least for now."

"How so?"

"It's kind of a long story; I'll give you the abbreviated version. When I was first trying to figure out my plan of escape and where to go, my first thought was to get as far away from the compound as I could. But then, I thought, it wouldn't really matter how far I went, because a good tracker would eventually find me.

"So then one day, I started thinking about Star Children. Everyone in the agency knows of their existence; they have Star

Children working for them, in fact. But, they only seem to send trackers to certain parts of the world in search of them, areas where a large majority exist. So, I began to graph the pockets of areas where the majority of Star Children have been found."

"And Roswell was a major area for Star Children?"

"No, just the opposite," Ian said, with a grin. So then, I began to look at areas where Star Children are rarely found, and I began to see a pattern. There were quite a few spots, but the ones that stood out the most were Roswell and Kazakhstan. Do you know what both places have in common?"

Sarah shook her head. "Um...no."

"Roswell, as you know, is the supposed place where U.F.O.'s crashed in 1947."

"Right...and Kazakhstan?"

"Kazakhstan is a location where there have been over a dozen reported U.F.O. crashes, since 1941, alone."

"Are you kidding?"

"No, not at all."

"How come I've never heard of that?"

"Well, there are a lot of world events that never make it in the news, here in the U.S., but in Kazakhstan, U.F.O. crashes are a pretty big deal."

"Why are crashes so frequent there?"

"No one knows for sure, but some scientists have theorized that there might be some sort of a vortex, that has a direct line to other galaxies."

"So, each place has a U.F.O. connection; I get that, but what's the connection with the lack of Star Children?"

Ian smiled. "That's just it! There isn't a lack of Star Children; they're just as plentiful in Roswell as anywhere else. I've never been to Kazakhstan, but I suspect that if I were to go there, I'd find them there, as well.

"So, how come the I.I.A. has never found Star Children, here?"

"That's exactly what I asked myself. I believe that it has something to do with the vortex. Perhaps it puts off some sort of protective sonar that prevents trackers from sensing the presence of Star Children."

"But, *you* can sense that Trevor is a Star Child."

"Right, but only when there is close, physical proximity. About six months ago, I sensed that there were trackers near the New Mexico border, and that was too close for my peace of mind, so I took a weekend trip to Mexico to try to deter them away. Once I was there, I realized that I could no longer sense Trevor's location. I got scared that they might have taken him, and so I called Melissa. She assured me that he was home, safe and sound. I realized then that there was something behind my theory. As long as I'm in Roswell, and close to Trevor, I can sense his powers, as well as other Star Children in the area, but outside of Roswell, I can't feel their presence."

"How come no one else in the I.I.A. has ever figured this out?"

Ian shrugged. "Probably because the idea has never occurred to them. They're so busy focusing on where Star Children are, they've never bothered to look at where they *aren't*."

"Huh…" Sarah grinned. "That's smart; you know that, don't you?"

Ian grinned. "Yeah, I was pretty pleased when I figured it out. Still, I never let my guard down. I know that one day a tracker is bound to stumble upon the area. For now, though, it's about the safest place I can think to be."

"Unless you want to move to Kazakhstan," Sarah joked.

"I have my passport, just in case."

She wasn't sure if he was joking or not, but suspected that he was serious.

"So, when Trevor told me that I should stay here, do you think that's what he meant? He knows that I'll be safe, if I stay?"

Ian glanced down at the boy, with interest. "He told you to stay?"

"He did; or rather, I think he told my baby." She placed a hand on her stomach. "Trevor seemed to be talking to him."

Ian smiled. "I wouldn't doubt it. He has a way of

communicating with...others."

It suddenly occurred to Sarah that Ian might be able to shed some light on her gifts, or lack thereof, and the real reason why the I.I.A. was interested in her. She explained how she had first met Eddie and Liliana, in the diner, and how she had eventually ended up travelling with them. She went on to explain that she and Liliana could both hear her baby's thoughts, and he listened intently throughout her story.

"So, what do you think?" Sarah asked, after she had finished her story. "Liliana thinks there is something special about my baby. Do you think, maybe, it's him they're after? I mean, you're a tracker, or rather, you were. If you were still a tracker, would you be interested in my baby?"

"That's an interesting question. I can't say that I've ever tracked an unborn baby, but now that you mention it...," he paused for a moment as if he were listening to someone. "Please, don't think this is weird; you can totally say no if you're uncomfortable, but would you mind if I placed a hand on your stomach?"

Sarah shook her head. "Um...no, Trevor already did. I don't mind. Go for it."

"He did, huh?" He looked down at the boy who appeared to be unaware of their presence. "He must sense something special about your baby, too."

Ian stepped in close, so that he stood about six inches in front of her, and placed both hands on either side of her stomach. He said nothing but closed his eyes, and Sarah was suddenly aware of each breath he took. She was acutely aware of his presence, aware of the smell of his cologne, the array of freckles on his muscular arms, and the warmth of his large hands on her abdomen.

She realized then, that her alluring observations were leading her thoughts astray, and she inwardly tried to shake them off. Even though she was madly in love with her husband, she reminded herself that it was only normal to be attracted to a handsome man, especially one who currently had his hands on her stomach.

With a noticeable chuckle in his voice, Tyler asked, "Are we disturbing you?"

Ian removed his hands from her abdomen and turned around. Her four friends, who had apparently become tired of waiting in the trailer, had come in search of them. Eddie looked back and forth between them and eyed Ian with a look of disdain.

"I'm sorry, we got to talking...," Ian began.

Tyler grinned. "It looks like it."

To offer an explanation, Sarah said, "I asked him to see if he could sense anything special about my baby that might explain why the I.I.A. is after me."

"Oh!" Grace said. She grinned at Liliana. "Right, so what's the verdict, Ian? Did you discover anything?"

Ian addressed them all, but it was Sarah who he looked at, when he spoke. "Sarah's baby is definitely special. I sense that he has powers stronger than we have ever seen in a Star Child."

"A Star Child?" Sarah asked. "Are you sure? How can you tell?"

"Well, for one, Star Children often exhibit a greater variety of powers than the typical Indigo. I sense that his list of powers is a long one. In addition, he and Trevor, here, already seem to have some sort of a mental bond. Even as we speak, they're communicating, telepathically, with each other. That is very common among Star Children.

"When you said that you could hear your baby's thoughts, did it occur to you that babies don't typically learn a language for at least a year? If your baby is already communicating with words, that tells me that he is highly gifted and more than likely, an old soul."

"Wow, so I *was* right," Sarah said. "They don't want me; they want him." She placed a hand instinctively on her belly.

"It's true. I suspect it is your baby they're after, but don't sell yourself short. I sense that you have several abilities within yourself that you've been denying. I think you have a psychic voice within yourself that you stopped listening to, a long time ago. Am I right?"

Sarah looked at him in awe. "How did you know?"

Ian smiled. "Because that's what I do. I used to get paid to know these things, remember?"

She didn't reply, but the look of shock on her face, was answer enough.

"I think it's time you start looking within yourself again, to discover who you are. Your baby is going to need you, and the more you know about your own abilities, the more you'll be able to help him."

As he spoke, she was captivated by Ian's green eyes, and she wondered if he felt the same chemistry. She was thankful when Tyler broke the growing discomfort.

"Ian, do you think you could give us some ideas of how we can find my brother?"

Ian turned to Tyler. "I was thinking about that; and you know, I think I might have an idea. It's a crazy one...very crazy, but I think if we plan it right, it just might work."

17 THE PLAN

Tyler grinned and proclaimed, "You're awesome!"

Simultaneously, Grace cried, "You're crazy!" She turned with a glare, which made him laugh. She couldn't believe their absurd plan was under serious consideration.

"Sure, you think it's funny," Grace said, as she combed her fingers through her hair. "You're not the one who's going to have to walk into the lion's den!"

Tyler grinned. "I'll be waiting right outside of the lion's den, ready to catch you."

"And I'll be by your side the entire time," Eddie told her.

She turned to Eddie. "So, you think this is a good idea, too?"

"I think it's about the best damned plan we're ever going to come up."

Ian interrupted, "If you want to go through with it, we'll need to spend the rest of the day working out the details, and we'll need to find something for the two of you to wear. I don't think it should be too difficult. Eddie, you look to be about my size; I think my old uniform should fit you. And Grace, Melissa is about your size; I'm sure she has an old uniform that you could wear."

"Melissa was in the Air Force?"

"After she got married, she moved back here, to her home town. We can go see her this evening and see what she has for you."

Grace sighed and with obvious reluctance said, "Fine." If this ridiculous plan was going to be a success, she would have to give it all she had.

*****

Melissa's small, two bedroom house, had a wrap-around porch and a small garden in the front. The house was small and quaint but comfortable inside. Trevor's mother invited them to sit and then excused herself to change out of her uniform.

Trevor pulled Sarah over to a bookshelf, near the television, and showed her his collection of cast iron, antique, model cars which he'd inherited from his Grandpa Hank. He was busy explaining details of each car, when Melissa returned to the living room and took a seat on the couch, beside Ian.

"So, what's up?" she asked. "On the phone you said you had a big favor to ask."

"First of all, I need you to promise not to ask questions and especially promise that you won't tell anyone about our visit," Ian told her.

"Of course, if there's anything that I can do to help, you know I will."

"Thank you. I knew we could count on you."

He went on to explain Grace's need to borrow an Air Force uniform, and then she followed Melissa into her bedroom, to try it on. Grace turned in a circle and then cranked her neck to get a view of her backside. The free standing, oval, full length mirror showed off the perfect fit of the navy blue skirt and light blue, button dress shirt.

"I promised Cameron that I wouldn't ask questions, and I won't," Melissa said. "I just hope you know what you're doing."

She met Melissa's gaze in the mirror and shook her head. "Not really. I'm going to need all the luck I can get."

"Well then, I wish you luck," Melissa said, with a friendly smile. "Here, let me show you how to do your hair."

*****

Back in the living room, Ian and Melissa went over identification of rank and how and when to salute, until Eddie and Grace had all of the information memorized.

Sarah sat on the floor, with her back against the couch, and watched the interaction. Trevor scooted in close beside her, and she wrapped an arm around his shoulders.

"Don't go," Trevor whispered to Sarah. Grace watched with curiosity as Ian took a seat beside Sarah, on the floor.

"You don't have to go you know," he said, to her. "You're

welcome to stay. I know your husband is gone, right now. Maybe...maybe you would be better off if you stayed here, for a while, at least until we know that things are safe." He glanced discreetly from Sarah to Melissa and back again, and Grace saw that he didn't want to say too much in front of Trevor's mother. "If you want to stay, I can find a place for you."

"I don't know," Sarah began. "My aunt is waiting for me back home—"

"And if you go home, what do you think will happen? They *will* come for you, again. Even if your friends succeed at this plan, the people who are interested in your baby won't give up."

Sarah stared at him and for a few moments and said nothing. "I'm scared," she said, finally. "You're right; I can't go home."

"I don't know what this is all about," Melissa interrupted, "and I promised that I wouldn't ask questions, but I know Cameron. If he thinks it's best that you stay, maybe you should consider it. Obviously my son likes you, and he's a hard one to win over. I don't have a lot of room, here, but you're more than welcome to stay with me. We have an opening at the restaurant, for a waitress. Do you have any experience?"

"Actually, I do. I work at my aunt's restaurant, back home. But, I don't want to impose on you. It's a generous offer, but—"

"No 'but's!" Melissa reproved. "I would actually welcome the company. With my husband gone, it gets lonely around here. It would be nice for some adult conversation."

"I don't have any of my stuff here, though. And I don't have a clue how I would explain this to my aunt, much less my husband!"

"I'm sure we can think of something," Ian said. "If you want to stay, we'll figure out a way."

Grace glanced at Eddie, who looked back and forth between Ian and Sarah, as the conversation unfolded. Judging from his expression, it appeared that he didn't like the idea of Sarah staying behind. She silently agreed that Sarah and her baby probably would be safer in Roswell, and though she hated to admit her selfish reasons, it occurred to her that if Sarah did stay, Eddie might pay more attention to her.

"I know it's hard, Sarah, but Ia…Cameron's right." Grace realized that she had almost called him by his real name and hoped that Melissa hadn't noticed the fumble. "You have to do what you think is best for your baby."

Eddie's sharp glare, directed at her, went unnoticed by everyone else. He was obviously not happy that she had voiced her opinion. *Oh well*, she thought, *he'll get over it.*

When all was said and done, Sarah decided to stay in Roswell. As they drove back to Ian's place, Grace and Liliana sat with her in the backseat and discussed her possibilities for the future. Grace admitted, to herself, that she would miss her new friend, but knew Sarah's decision was a wise one. Roswell and Ian would provide safety for her and the baby.

*****

"If we get caught, I don't know how I will ever explain this to my parents." Grace eyed the entrance to Edward's Air Force Base, as the car crept, slowly forward. Each vehicle in line was admitted, only after careful examination and questioning, by the security guards.

"We're not going to get caught," Eddie reassured her. "It's time to think positive and put on your game face. Are you ready?"

"Ready as I'll ever be." She sat on her hands in an attempt to hide the visible tremors. Dressed in jeans and a t-shirt, she looked like any other visitor who had come to see the air show.

The car moved forward another few feet, and Grace bit her lower lip, in anticipation. Ian's explanation of their plan continued to replay in her mind.

"How are we supposed to get in to a secure Air Force base?" Eddie had asked. "Even if we do have uniforms, we don't have identification."

"There aren't many ways," Ian had agreed.

"There's an air show this weekend," Melissa interjected. "I thought about taking Trevor, but didn't feel up to the long drive, just for the weekend."

"There is?" He turned to Eddie and grinned. "It's perfect. You guys are all set."

Eddie shook his head in confusion. "How so?"

"Whenever there's an air show, they open up the base for visitors. They get thousands of spectators. All you have to do is drive in, no one will look twice at you."

When they reached the gate, Eddie explained to the guard that they had come for the air show. The guard nodded, told them to have a nice day, and they were admitted without hesitation. Grace breathed a sigh of relief. Ian had been right.

Eddie glanced sideways at her, with a grin. "See, piece of cake. Nothing to worry about."

"Sure, that was the easy part. Now the real fun begins."

As promised, there were large crowds gathered for the day's events. They eventually found a parking lot with no one in sight then took turns changing in the backseat, while the other stood on the lookout for anyone who might wander by.

Grace stepped into the parking lot and made her first appearance to the world as Airman First Class Smith. She looked at herself in the car window to examine the tight bun in her hair. It looked perfect, just as Melissa had taught her.

"You look great," Eddie said, from behind.

She took one last glance at herself in the window and then turned to him. "I do?" The compliment caused her pulse to beat faster.

"Absolutely, I'd believe you're in the Air Force."

She looked him up and down, in careful examination. He was stunning in Ian's uniform. To complete the ensemble, Ian had given Eddie's hair a short, buzz cut, and Grace admitted, to herself, that he pulled the look off well.

She couldn't tell him that he looked 'hot', and so instead she said, "You're nametag's a little crooked. Here, let me adjust it." She reached out and adjusted the nameplate, and then gave him a firm pat on the arm. In her manliest voice, she said, "There you go, Sergeant Martinez. You look good. Don't forget your hat."

"Thanks. I guess we might as well do this thing, huh?"

She let out a deep breath. "I guess so. It's now or never."

They got back in the car and followed Ian's instructions until they located the building that housed the office of Colonel Davis. After they had exited the car and ensured that their hats appeared straight and proper, they strode toward the entrance.

Curious why Ian had possessed an Air Force uniform, he had explained that it had been a necessary disguise, for certain missions. "Martinez was the best name that they could come up with for you?" Grace had asked. She observed his red hair and freckles. "You don't look much like a Martinez."

"Well, people often believe what they read," Ian had said. "If anyone ever noticed anything odd, they probably didn't want to insult me."

Luckily, Eddie did look like he could be named Martinez; at least that was one less concern. They had decided that Melissa's last name, Smith, was generic enough so they wouldn't have to worry about tracing the uniform back to her, if Grace should happen to be caught.

They located a directory board and saw that Colonel Davis' office was located on the second floor. They rode the elevator up together, and when they stepped off, Eddie said, "I'll be just a few steps behind you."

"Alright," Grace said, with a forced smile. She was acutely aware of each step, as her dress shoes clicked on the shiny floor. She glanced over her shoulder, once, to make sure that Eddie still followed. He offered a smile of encouragement. At least he had her back.

It was Sunday, and very few people were working. She realized that, any time she passed someone, she held her breath in anxious anticipation. She didn't want to obviously stare, as she tried to observe the rank on each uniform, but worried that she would neglect to salute an officer and would get stopped for reprimand. Along the way, she received a few smiles and friendly nods, but no one stopped to question her presence. As she continued in the direction of Colonel Davis' office, the conversation she'd had with Ian continued to play in her head.

"Colonel Davis is the main liaison between the I.I.A. and the

Air Force," Ian had explained.

"The Air Force is also a part of the I.I.A.?" Eddie had asked.

"They play a small role. The Air Force makes it their business to be involved with anything that has to do with aliens. If the I.I.A. discovers a genetic link between Star Children and extraterrestrials, the Air Force wants to be the first to know. So, they've made a point to make themselves a part of the I.I.A. In turn, the I.I.A. gets unlimited access to the secret, underground, tunnel system.

"Secret, underground, tunnel system?" Grace questioned.

"Yep, it branches off in several directions. One of the main branches spans from Edward's Air Force Base to Area 51."

"You're serious?" Eddie asked. "Area 51? That's not where we're going is it?"

"No, but the tunnel has several branches that lead to a variety of locations. You'll start off in the main tunnel that leads North, toward Area 51, but then you'll branch off and head east. That's where the main I.I.A. office is located, about forty miles northeast of the base."

"There's a tunnel that runs for forty miles?" Eddie asked.

"That's nothing. The tunnel from Edwards Air Force Base to Area 51 is about three hundred miles or so."

"How have they managed to keep it a secret?"

"Just like any other military secrets, there have been some leaks and rumors, but they've always been negated. The military claims that the tunnels are just stories. It's been said that the tunnels couldn't possibly exist because a tunnel of that extreme length wouldn't have enough air ventilation."

"That's right though, isn't it? How *do* they have enough air?"

"There are several substations and outlets along the way, through various other military and government installations, and some through secret tunnels and caves in the desert. The I.I.A. offices are an example of one the stops."

"Why can't we just go straight to the I.I.A. office?" Grace asked. "Wouldn't it save a step?"

"You wouldn't be allowed in, especially without identification.

Security is tight and military personnel never come through the front gate. The military doesn't want anyone to know that they have ties or connections with the I.I.A. If you arrive, in uniform, through the tunnel, no one should question your presence. Of course, there's always the possibility that a tracker could be there and might recognize you, so try your best to stay unseen."

So, the plan was simple, in theory. Inside Colonel Davis' office, inside of a locked cabinet, was a special I.I.A. pass, which would allow them access into the guarded tunnel entrance. Ian had explained that Colonel Davis never worked on Sundays, and his secretary usually didn't, either. As a cover, Grace carried a plastic garment bag with uniforms. If questioned to explain her presence, she would say that she had been asked to deliver his dry cleaning. Eddie followed at a distance, just in case someone happened to be there. Grace would be able to explain her presence, but it didn't take two people to deliver dry cleaning. If the Colonel's secretary was there, Grace would draw her away, so that Eddie could gain access.

When they rounded the corner, they were pleased to discover that the Colonel's office waited in darkness. They glanced up and down the hall, but it remained vacant. Grace tried the door and discovered that it was locked, as expected. She stepped aside, and Eddie placed his hand on the doorknob. A few moments later, the doorknob easily turned, and they were allowed access, inside.

After Eddie quietly closed the door, behind them, Grace smiled in admiration and whispered, "That was amazing!"

They made their way through the first room, past the secretary's desk, and entered a second room. On the door was a gold engraved nameplate, which proclaimed it to be Colonel Davis' office. They left the lights out; the sunlight that shone through the window provided enough light. A large desk, in the middle of the room, showcased several framed pictures of a woman and teenage children, whom she assumed to be the Colonel's family. They skirted the desk and continued toward a tall, metal, wall cabinet, with two doors.

When Eddie jiggled the handle, he found it to be locked, as well. Grace watched with fascination as he effortlessly opened it. There were four I.I.A. badges, which hung on lanyards, from a hook, on the inside of the door. Eddie removed two and handed one to Grace. She placed it around her neck and then tucked it under her shirt so that it would remain undetected. They wouldn't have an opportunity to return to the Colonel's office, and Grace hoped that he wouldn't notice the absence of the badges, anytime soon.

After Eddie closed the cabinet door, he held his hand over the handle once more, and then checked to make sure that it was locked. He made sure to relock the office door, as well, and then they retraced their footsteps down the hall.

Grace stopped into the first restroom they came to and left the garment bag hanging on a hook, in a bathroom stall. She looked in the bathroom mirror, to see if anything about her appearance looked out of the ordinary, but she had to admit that she did look the part. She patted her bun to make sure that she didn't have any hairs dangling out of place and then stepped out to the hall to meet Eddie and begin the next round of their adventure.

*****

After a few wrong turns and a couple of stops to look at the map, they arrived to the north side of a dry lake bed, located in the southwest corner, within the base boundaries. From a distance they could see small airplanes land and take off. The lake bed appeared to house a small airport. Ian had explained that certain government officials and various other dignitaries, who wanted to keep their arrival anonymous, were given special permission to fly in. The lake bed provided more anonymity than the more public and visual area of the runways, on the main part of the base.

They located the small, lone garage; and just as Ian had described, a few military vehicles were randomly parked around its perimeter. A man in camouflage sat in a metal, folding chair, next to the front door. With a coffee cup in hand, he casually flipped through a magazine and appeared to be on break, but Grace knew better. Ian had explained that this building was guarded twenty-four hours a day. Inside, she knew they would find at least one more guard, who would hopefully grant access to the elevator, which would lead to the masked tunnel below.

Grace was thankful that, in their pretense of uniforms, Eddie outranked her. As Technical Sergeant, he would naturally explain the purpose of their visit, and she, as an Airman First Class, would hopefully nod and smile and follow quietly behind.

The guard closed his magazine and eyed them closely, as they neared the building. Grace held her head high and strode forward with what she hoped was a confident look that said she had every reason to be there.

"Good morning," Eddie said. He pulled out his I.I.A. badge and held it up for the guard to examine. Grace noticed the guard's rank and quickly joggled her memory of Ian's rank identification lesson. The guard was a Staff Sergeant, which was one rank below Eddie. This could be a good sign; it would hopefully mean that he wouldn't question Eddie's presence.

"Morning," the guard replied. He set his magazine on the folding chair and examined the badge closely. "You're new?"

Eddie glanced casually at Grace and nodded with a smile. "That's right, just transferred from Nellis, about a month ago. I'm working under Colonel Davis."

At hearing the Colonel's name, the guard seemed to relax slightly and turned to Grace. "You new around here, too?"

Thankful that they had role played various scenarios on the drive from Roswell, she was prepared for the questioning. "Oh no, I've been here since basic."

She noticed the guard eye the rank on her uniform. "You plan on going in, too?" he asked, warily. "We don't usually get many visitors through here."

Grace showed the guard her badge and was thankful when Eddie spoke for her.

"She's been assigned to me. Colonel Davis has some business he needs me to attend to, and I've brought her along to type up some documents, once we get to our destination."

The guard's aura had begun to show signs of suspicion. It was time to turn on the charm. She focused on his energy, while Eddie continued to talk. When his aura brightened, she smiled sweetly and said, "You must get awfully bored sitting out here by yourself, all day, Sergeant."

The guard looked at her and she was relieved when he smiled. "You're right; it does get pretty boring. It's always nice to have someone to talk to when we get visitors through here."

"Well, good, then you'll have something to look forward to when we return."

"I will definitely look forward to that. When you go inside, you'll want to head to the back of the building. Sergeant McDaniel will ask you to sign in. Make sure you have your badges ready to show."

The guard picked up his walkie-talkie and said, "McDaniel, I've got a couple of visitors for you." He was answered by a buzz and a click at the door. "Go ahead. He'll be waiting."

She followed Eddie into a large garage. It took a few moments for her eyes to adjust from the sunlight to the dim lighting. Once she could see again, she noticed that the room was fairly bare. There was a tall, red toolbox, some stacked tires, and three Humvees, parked within. Ian had said that the garage had to be presentable as a working repair shop, in case of any surprise inspections, by uninvited guests. She suspected that the Humvees were present, just for show.

The clicking of her dress shoes, on the cement floor, seemed to echo throughout the metal building and up to the tall, tin roof, above. It was a good thing that they weren't sneaking in, because Sergeant McDaniel could surely hear their approach.

He stood beside a small table and folding chair and examined an expansive, terrain map of the base, which covered approximately ten feet of wall space and reached about seven feet tall. Grace guessed that his examination of the local topography was merely feigned interest, so that he could gauge their approach, without appearing anxious.

When the sounds of their footsteps neared, he turned to greet them with a frown and a stern voice. "How can I help you?" He appeared to be in his early fifties. A few inches shorter than Grace, he had a stout but muscular build and a short mustache. His beady eyes seemed to judge their every move. His suspicion of their presence was obvious, and she worried that it might prove more difficult to charm their way past him.

"We have a pass from Colonel Davis," Eddie explained. He held out the badge, and Grace did the same. Sergeant McDaniel took his time and examined each badge with care. Then, he picked up a small gadget that looked like a retail scanner, and scanned the back of each one.

Grace held her breath in anticipation, but they seemed to have passed the guard's test. "Go ahead and sign in," he said. "Make sure you notate the correct date and exact time."

She signed her name, or rather Airman First Class Smith's name, below Eddie's signature, noting the time from a small digital clock that hung on the wall, above the table.

"Where are you headed today?" McDaniel asked.

Ian had made sure to run them through this part of the charade several times until they knew it by heart. Any alteration in the order of their words and not only would they not be admitted, but several armed men would burst through the doors to question them and take them into custody.

"We're on our way to Disneyland, for the day," Eddie told him.

"Very good, Sergeant, have a good trip." McDaniel pressed a small, obscure button, located beside the map. The wall and map slid sideways and exposed a large door. The sergeant then pushed another button, and the door silently slid open to reveal an elevator big enough for a vehicle, an elevator which offered admittance to the unknown, world below.

Eddie and Grace stepped in, simultaneously. There was only one button. The door slid silently closed after Eddie pushed it, and she felt the elevator slowly descend. She glanced discreetly at one of two cameras mounted on the ceiling and waited impatiently to reach the bottom. Claustrophobia started to set in, and she grew anxious for the door to reopen. It occurred to her that the telepathic abilities shared by Tyler and Liliana would be a useful gift, at the moment. She wanted to talk to Eddie but knew that their every word would be monitored, so they stood side by side, in silence. If the I.I.A. ever reviewed the video footage from the elevator, they would be instantly recognized, but hopefully, their mission would be accomplished before then, and the discovery of their intrusion into the tunnel would be of no consequence.

"We're going to Disneyland?" she had asked Ian, with a chuckle, when he had explained the password.

"Sure," he'd replied, "every destination within the tunnel requires a different password. If you're going to Area 51, you say that you're going to visit some friends from Mexico."

"Mexico?"

"Sure, the big talk these days is about illegal aliens venturing into the U.S. from Mexico. If you're going to Area 51, you're going to see aliens. It's their idea at a sense of humor."

"Nice." Grace had chuckled and shook her head. "So, what's the meaning behind Disneyland?"

"I.I.A. is for Indigo Children. Children go to Disneyland."

"Hmmm, creative."

"Yeah, well, at least it makes it easy to remember. Every destination has a password that sort of makes sense. If you travel to multiple destinations, frequently, you don't want to get the passwords confused."

"Well, now at least I'll be prepared if I want to visit Area 51, anytime soon," Grace had joked.

When the elevator touched bottom, a door opposite the side they had entered, slid open. They stepped out onto well packed dirt and looked around. They found themselves standing in a tunnel that was about twelve feet wide and ten feet tall. The fluorescent lights that lined the ceiling, about every ten feet, buzzed slightly. Thankfully, there was no one in sight.

Just as Ian had described, they found three, electric golf carts, parked and waiting. They picked the first one and climbed in. Safe out of the eyes and ears of the elevator, Eddie turned to her and said, "That was nice back there. What you did with the guard, outside, I mean. I could sense that he suspected something unusual about us, and you...you did something, didn't you? I recognized it, because I've done that trick myself. You tapped into his energy, to convince him to let us through?"

Grace grinned. "I'm not the only one around here with a few talents."

"I can see that." Eddie smiled in return, and inwardly Grace jumped for joy. She had been sitting idly by, the last few days, as she had hopelessly watched Eddie pine after Sarah. Now that they were alone, she hoped that he might finally notice her.

He turned the key and pulled the map and directions out of his pocket. The tunnel ran in two directions. After double checking the map, he handed it to Grace and headed the golf cart in the direction that, they hoped, would lead them to the I.I.A. facility.

Underground, it was virtually impossible to detect which direction they traveled, and so they had to rely strictly upon the map and directions Ian had provided. Twice, they came upon a fork in the tunnel, and each time, they stopped to recheck the map. The last thing they needed was to come up top only to discover that they had entered Area 51 or some other top secret location. They were prepared to answer questions once they arrived to I.I.A. headquarters, any other destination, and they would literally be at a loss for words to explain their presence.

When they came to the second fork in the tunnel, Eddie turned the map upside down, turned it around again, and then drummed his fingers, impatiently, on the steering wheel.

"What's wrong?"

"Well, look." He tapped the map. "In the drawing, Ian shows that we should turn *right* here, but in the written directions, it clearly says that we should turn *left*. I don't know if we should believe the drawing or what he has in writing. I'm kind of leaning toward what he has written, but I'm not sure. If we take a wrong turn now, we could be screwed."

"I think the picture is probably more accurate," Grace said. "I mean, if he's driven through here several times, I'm sure he knows what it looks like. I think we should go with the map, instead."

He shook his head. "I don't know. I'm leaning more towards what he has written, and we can't waste time sitting here all day trying to figure it out. I'm going left, and hopefully when we get to the next intersection, it will be clear if we went the right way."

"Yeah, but the next intersection is twenty miles ahead," Grace pointed out. "If we turn the wrong way, we'll have to backtrack twenty miles."

"Well, unless you have a better idea of how to figure it out, I'm going left." He proceeded along the tunnel before Grace could argue further.

They had driven all of thirty seconds, when a voice in Grace's head told her that they should turn around and take the tunnel that had led to the right. She had learned long ago, that the voice was always correct, and any time she had ever ignored the voice, she had always come to regret it.

"Eddie, I think we're going the wrong way. I think we should turn around and take the other tunnel."

"Look, we don't know for sure, and we've already started this way. I say we just keep going."

They continued on for another minute, and then a clear vision took over her mind. She vividly saw them drive down the other tunnel, and the voice in her head became louder as it shouted, *Turn around now!*

With as much authority as she could muster, she shouted, "Eddie, stop!"

He glanced at her, slowed the vehicle slightly, but continued on.

Grace placed a hand on his arm, willing him to feel the vision that she saw.

The golf cart came to a slow halt, and he turned to look at her. Her hand remained on his arm.

"The tunnel on the right *was* the correct way." She spoke slow, clear, and with confidence. "I saw it Eddie. I saw us drive down the other tunnel. Trust me." She looked into his crystal brown eyes and willed him to believe her. She willed him to feel the same knowledge that she held in her mind. She willed him to turn around.

He was silent for a moment as he held her gaze. After a few moments he said, "I believe you. I believe you, Grace." The tunnel was wide enough that he was easily able to maneuver a U-turn, and in less than two minutes they were headed up the opposite tunnel.

They continued the drive for a minute without speaking, and then Eddie broke the silence. "I'm sorry, Grace. I should have listened. We're in this together. I'm just anxious to get there and get out of there, but if I take us the wrong way, we aren't going to get there any faster. If I do anything dumb like that again, just smack me or something, okay?"

She laughed. "Um...okay." His concession of stubbornness touched her, and if anything, it made her attraction for him stronger.

The remainder of the trip passed quickly and without incident, and soon they arrived to, what would hopefully prove to be, I.I.A. headquarters. They parked beside the only other vehicle, an electric golf cart, identical to the one they drove. Unlike Edward's Base, there wasn't an elevator. Instead, they found a long series of winding, rock steps. The air, below ground, was cool and had a musty, damp odor. As they climbed their way to the surface, they were guided by dimly lit wall lamps that lined the stairway. The air around them became noticeably warmer and smelled fresher. By the time they neared the top, it seemed they must have climbed the equivalent of three flights of stairs. A line of bright light greeted them, from beneath the space under the door.

"Alright, you ready to do this again, Airman Smith?"

"Ready as I'll ever be, Sergeant Martinez. Game face on." She took a deep breath and touched her hat to ensure that it was still in place.

Their infiltration into Edwards Air Force Base had been nerve wracking to the extreme. Fear that men with machine guns would discover their masquerade, had caused her heart to pound and hands to tremble; however, that venture suddenly seemed like a walk in the park, in comparison to marching straight into the headquarters of the enemy.

Eddie twisted the door handle and peered out. They were immediately assaulted by a blast of warm air. They stepped outside, onto fine, brown gravel, and looked around with caution, to assess their position. There was no one around, but they knew that the video camera, mounted atop the building adjacent to them, announced their arrival. Ian had explained that the grounds were monitored by security cameras which were attended twenty-four hours a day, by security guards, in a building near the front gate.

Grace glanced back at the door, from which they had arrived. The tunnel entrance looked like a small shack, built into the side of a hill. The rear of the property was backed by a small mountain. The other three sides of the perimeter were guarded by a tall, barbed wire fence. Ian had described the premises with precise detail and had also drawn a map. The entire property sat on twenty acres and housed a total of nine, plain, brown, modular buildings.

The lack of guards present didn't negate the fact that their every move was closely monitored. Any sign of hesitation or fear and security would be upon them. As long as they walked tall and with confidence, no one should suspect anything unusual about their presence. They had reviewed the map one final time, before they had climbed the stairs; the layout of I.I.A. headquarters was memorized. Their targeted destination was two buildings down and three buildings to the right.

Grace was thankful that the buildings had only a few small windows near the ceiling; their parade across the graveled lot would hopefully go unnoticed, by the occupants within. They had successfully reached the second building without spying anyone, but when they rounded the corner, they were greeted by a middle aged man with salt and pepper gray hair, a mustache, and a beer belly. He sat on the second step of the small, wooden porch, with a cigarette in one hand and a cup of coffee in the other.

"Good afternoon," he said, with a smile. "What brings the military up to our neck of the woods, today?"

It was Eddie who spoke. "Colonel Davis sent us to check out a few things and grab some files from his office. He's detained for the day, entertaining some important bigwigs at the air show."

"So, he sent you to do his dirty work, huh?" The man chuckled. Grace wondered if he was joking or if 'dirty work' actually referred to the illegitimate business of the I.I.A. and its associates.

Graced laughed in return. "Yeah, lucky us. Everyone else gets a day of fun and we're stuck working."

"Well, good luck to you. I was in the military, myself, in my younger days. I was an Army Ranger; I know all about taking orders from higher command. They'll walk all over you when they want to."

"That's for sure," Eddie agreed.

"Well then, do you know where you're headed?"

"Yep, I think we're that third building, right on the end, down there."

"That's right. No one's been there in a couple of weeks. Should be locked up, do you have a key?"

"Oh yeah, we're all set," Eddie reassured him. He of course didn't require a key to open a lock, and the last thing they wanted was for the man to locate a guard to let them in and have their every move watched.

"Okay then, I wish you a speedy journey."

"Thank you," Grace replied, with a sweet smile.

"Well, at least we know that our appearance here doesn't seem unusual," Eddie whispered, after they were out of earshot. "This might be easier than I expected."

They found the inside of the rectangular building to be plain and simple. It housed four desks, a large table, a few file cabinets, a copy machine, a water cooler, and a small restroom. Just as Ian had described, the maps to the Mexican compound were located on the large table, near the back wall. They were massive, about two feet by three feet, and Grace immediately applied herself to the copy machine to shrink them down to size, so that the copies would fit inside of a file folder.

While she copied, Eddie began to search for the access card that would be needed to log into the computer system. Ian had explained that the card would either be found within the Colonel's desk or in his file cabinet.

Over the whine of the copy machine, Grace listened to the heavy thuds of Eddie's footsteps and squeaks of the floorboards, of the thin, modular floor. She turned, with a start, when he slammed his palm on the side of a file cabinet. The resounding vibration caused a picture frame to topple, which in turn landed on a mug full of pens.

"What's wrong?"

"It's not here! It's...we came all this way, and it's not here."

"What do you mean? It has to be here." Grace left the copy machine and crossed the room, to Eddie.

"Ian said that the access card is always kept in the Colonel's desk, and he said that a second, spare card is kept in the last file, at the back of the second drawer, of the file cabinet. They're both gone."

"Do you think the Colonel could be in Mexico?"

"He could be; but if so, it doesn't explain where the second card is. And, it doesn't help us a whole lot, right now, when we need it. It's not like we can just come back again. We need the key now."

"Let me think for a minute." Grace sat in the Colonel's black, swivel, leather chair. She turned so that she faced his desk and placed both hands on the glass top. With eyes closed, she focused on the feeling of the room. She sensed the commanding officer who had last sat in the chair; she felt his lingering presence and tried to imagine where he had placed the card. Then she saw it.

"It's in the third drawer down."

"The third drawer?"

"Yeah, let me see." She pulled the drawer open and reached into the empty space behind the last file. Between the metal slats she touched what felt like a credit card. She gripped it between her fingertips and pulled out what looked like a hotel room key.

"It got pushed back in the second drawer and fell down," she explained.

"You're amazing." His relief was obvious, and she was rewarded with a smile and hug.

All too eagerly, Grace accepted the hug. She tried to ignore the fact that his aura revealed only colors of friendship. He obviously didn't feel the same adoration for her that she felt for him, but she was confident that she would eventually be able to win him over.

He released her from the embrace and glanced to the copy machine. "Are the maps done?"

"They should be. I just shrank down the last one. It should be sitting on the copier. Let me put the originals back, and we should be good to go."

"Not yet, we have to find the password, too. The card won't do us much good if we can't log into the system. It should be..."

Eddie trailed off as Grace flipped the access card around so he could see the backside. "You mean this password?" She grinned and tapped the small piece of paper that had been taped to the back.

"That's the password?"

"I assume so. It has nine figures with a combination of letters and numbers, just like Ian said it would."

"Well, that's certainly convenient. I guess they aren't too concerned about a security breach, are they?"

"Nope." Grace grinned, again. "Lucky for us. Now, can we get out of here, please? I don't think my nerves can take much more of this spy business, today."

"I hear ya. Let's get out of here while luck is on our side."

Stretched out on the bed, Liliana leaned against a stack of pillows, propped against the headboard, while they waited for Eddie and Grace to return. She had flipped through the channels until she stopped at a classic movie but couldn't stay focused on it; her gaze continued to discreetly wander to Tyler. His legs dangled over the arm of an oversized chair, as he leaned back and took a nap.

Daydreams of a future with Tyler mingled their way between her growing concern for Eddie and Grace. She fantasized that he was running after her on a sandy beach. When he finally caught up to her, they tumbled about in the sand as the waves teased their bare toes. Twinges of guilt pulled at her conscience. Such a fantasy should have no place in her mind, when worry for her two friends should be at the forefront of her thoughts. Eddie and Grace had willingly put themselves in danger, and all she could think about was her feelings for a boy.

"So, after I catch you and we tumble about in the sand, what happens next?"

Caught off guard and immediately embarrassed, Liliana looked up. His eyes were still closed, but his quirky smile revealed that he was awake.

Liliana found herself at a loss for words. "I...uh...um...that's not fair; those were private thoughts."

He opened his eyes and grinned. "There's no such thing as a private thought," he teased. Her flushed cheeks must have been obvious, from across the room, because he added, "Oh, come on. It's no big deal."

With swift agility, he flipped himself up and over the arm of the chair and came to sit on the edge of the bed, beside her.

Still leaning against the pillows, her pulse began to race, as she looked into Tyler's eyes. Whether it was his close proximity and her full awareness of his presence, or the fact that she still blushed, the room suddenly grew warmer. His body heat seemed to radiate straight toward her. The damp tips of his hair glistened from his recent shower, and she found the fresh scent of hotel soap to be surprisingly intoxicating.

"So tell me, where is this beach of yours?" His eyes seemed to twinkle with amusement.

"Are you laughing at me?"

He shook his head. "You can hear my thoughts, Liliana. Does it sound like I'm laughing?"

She paused for a moment to assess his thoughts and observe his aura. He wasn't laughing; in fact, he seemed to be fascinated with her daydream.

"The beach...it's um...in Seattle. There's a place I like to go, near the Sound. It's never crowded. I was just imagining that I could take you there someday, just you and I, when all of this crazy stuff is over."

"I'd like that. You didn't answer my question, though. After I catch you and we tumble about in the sand...what happens next?"

"I didn't get that far," she said, with a grin.

"Well, when you do, let me know, okay? I'd...like to know."

"Do you think you'll ever get to come to Seattle? I mean, after all of this is over, where will you go? Will you have to go back to your foster family?"

His mood and aura visibly darkened. "I don't know. With luck, my brother and I will be together, again. I hope to God we don't have to go back, but if we don't, I don't know where the state will send us. Will they find us a new foster family? Maybe. But, my brother and I will both be considered runaways, so who knows...maybe they'll just send us to juvie and keep us there, until we turn eighteen. I don't know what will happen. Right now I just need to focus on getting him back, and then I guess we'll worry about the future after that."

He met her gaze with his own and leaned in closer. "I would love to come see you in Seattle, Liliana. Other than my brother, I've never felt closer to anyone in my life. I feel a connection to you."

Her response came out almost in a whisper, "I feel it too."

He leaned in close. His warm breath was almost upon her lips, and then, he sat back, and said, "You have perfect timing."

She frowned. "Um...excuse me?"

"It's Toby," he explained.

"Oh." *Perfect timing, indeed*, she thought.

As she listened to their one-sided conversation, trying to make sense of it all, she tried to fill in the blanks.

"We were just talking about what we're going to do, after we rescue you," Tyler explained to his brother, with what seemed like a defensive tone. He was silent for a moment, and then said, "You'll like her. I can't wait for you to meet her." Another moment of silence passed, and then he said, "Eddie and Grace should be back soon and then we'll take a look at the maps and see what we're up against. If all goes as planned we should be there tomorrow." He grew silent again, as he listened to Toby, then he laughed. "It's a crazy idea, but I think you're right. In the long run, it will probably be the best plan. Everyone else is going to hate it, but I guess I've gotta do what I've gotta do. Don't worry, Bro, no matter what, I am coming for you." He was silent for a moment, and then he glanced at Liliana and smiled. "Hey, you know me," he said, to his brother. "I won't do anything you wouldn't do. I'll see you soon." She wondered if he was talking about her or his plan. She tried to gauge his thoughts, but he was obviously blocking them from her.

"What is your crazy plan, and how come I'm not going to like it?" She flopped down on the bed and repositioned herself against the pillows.

I had hoped you wouldn't hear that, he thought.

So...what? You thought that you would just rescue your brother and I would never find out the plan? We're all in this together, Liliana shot back, silently.

He took a deep breath and slowly released it. "You're right." He sat on the edge of the bed, beside her. "It's just that...I've been trying to consider the best plan of action, and I seem to keep coming back to the same idea."

"And that is?"

"I think the only way to get Toby out, is to let them kidnap me, too."

Liliana was silent for a moment, in an attempt to comprehend what he had just said. "Kidnap you?...We're going to Mexico to try to rescue your *kidnapped* brother, and you want to get yourself kidnapped, as well?...You...you understand that sounds a little crazy, right?"

"I do, but there is actually a rhyme and a reason to my scheme. I think it just might work."

"Okay, well, before you go and do anything completely crazy, let's make sure that we have a plan that will *definitely* work. I don't want a plan that 'just might work'." She looked into his eyes. "I want to make sure that I get you back, safely."

"Say that again."

"Say what again?"

"You said that you want me."

"I did not!" She giggled and slapped his arm. "I said I want to make sure that I get you back, safely!"

He shrugged and leaned in toward her. "Same thing."

Just as Liliana thought that this was finally going to be their first kiss, they both looked up when they heard voices at the door. A few seconds later, Eddie and Grace entered the room. They were dressed in their Air Force Blues and sported beaming smiles.

Eddie grinned. "I hope we're not interrupting anything."

Tyler sighed. "Not at all."

*****

From the edge of the gas station parking lot, where pavement met sand, the desert presented itself to Liliana as a future of vast and uncertain possibilities. She watched a large collection of tumbleweed roll past and was surprised at the amount of greenery that dotted the terrain. A large jackrabbit darted back and forth between prickly trees and cacti, while a hawk circled overhead. According to the map, the low lying mountains, in the distance, were their final destination. Somewhere amongst the canyons and caves, was the compound.

Liliana sighed as she thought about Tyler. He was ready to put himself in danger and literally hand himself over to the enemy.

Grace had reassured her that everything would be okay, and Liliana knew that she spoke the truth, but she was also aware that Grace's visions of the future could change as other events occurred. A vision of the future wasn't set in stone.

She hadn't heard his approach and was startled when he spoke, from close behind. "I'll be fine." She turned to find him directly behind her. She was surprised that she hadn't sensed his presence.

"You must have been having a good daydream. I'm surprised that you didn't hear me thinking about you."

"You were thinking about me?"

"I was." He smiled and placed a hand on her shoulder. "Turn around and tell me what you see, out there."

Liliana looked out, toward the mountains. It wasn't Seattle; the mountains weren't as lush and green, and there was no ocean, but it was beautiful in its own right. "I see a desert and some cactus."

Tyler stepped in, close behind, and wrapped his arms around her. This was the first time that he had physically reached out to her, and she felt a slight thrill at his touch. Wrapped tight in his embrace, she felt safe. She knew the sense of security was a façade to her peace of mind, but she savored the moment, knowing that this might be the last time they would be together.

"I see a desert, too. You know what else I see? I see the future. Out there, we have the opportunity to take back our lives. We have the opportunity to stand up to the I.I.A. and let them know that they aren't going to control us. I'm done running, and if putting myself in danger is what it's going to take, to keep us all safe, then that's a risk I'm willing to take. I'm going to be fine. And one day, hopefully soon, you can show me that beach of yours." With his arms still around her, he gave her a gentle squeeze.

She turned, in his embrace, so that she faced him. "I hope you're right; I really do." Movement out of the corner of her eye caught her attention. She glanced over and sighed. Eddie and Grace were headed their way. Her brief moment of peaceful reverie with Tyler was over.

"Well, the car's all gassed up and ready to go," Eddie announced. Tyler released her from his embrace but continued to stand close. If Eddie noticed the obvious fact that she and Tyler had become more than just friends, he didn't say anything. "I guess we need to sit down and finalize our plan."

Before he could say more, an old, green, Chevy truck pulled in, beside them. When the swirling dirt cleared, Liliana noted two men in the front seat and two more in the bed of the truck. Their dirt smeared faces gave the appearance that they had just come from working in the nearby fields.

The driver called out something, in Spanish, and Eddie took a step forward. He called something back, in Spanish, and all of the men in the truck laughed. Their exchange of dialogue went back and forth a few more times, and then the driver gave a final laugh and drove away.

"What was that all about?" Grace asked.

"They wanted to know how much they could pay to buy you girls."

Grace looked astonished. "*Buy* us? You're serious?"

"Yeah, two pretty girls like you...you'd go for a pretty penny, down here."

"And they were ready to pay you?"

"Sure. Unfortunately, a slave market does exist, down here. Girls get kidnapped and sold. They probably would have paid for you and then turned around and sold you to someone else."

Liliana watched the truck drive out of sight. "What did you say?"

Eddie smiled. "I told them that you belonged to me, of course."

Grace raised her eyebrows. "Belong to you?"

"It was either that or I ask them how much they were willing to pay."

Grace laughed. "Well, in that case, I'm happy to belong to you. I didn't realize that you spoke fluent Spanish."

"Yep, it's funny, when I'm around Native Americans, they assume I'm one of them, and when I'm around Mexicans, they assume I'm Mexican, so sometimes it works in my favor to have both sides going for me. My dad's side of the family is Mexican, so I grew up learning to speak English and Spanish."

"I know the feeling," Liliana said. "My grandparents only speak Chinese. I like it though. I'm glad that I can speak two languages."

"Yeah, me too," Eddie agreed.

"Sorry to interrupt," Tyler said, "but I think I just figured out how to put our plan into action."

"What are you thinking?" Eddie asked.

"Okay, so we know that the first problem is to figure out how to get into the compound. We know the entrance is camouflaged; it might take us all day to find it. And besides that, we know there are cameras on the premises. As soon as they see us wandering around, they'll be all over us, and it won't do any good if we all get captured."

"So, you have a plan that keeps us all from getting captured?"

"I do. I'll wander in and let them take me. I'll be able to see how to get in and then I can mentally communicate with Liliana and give her the directions. Once inside, Toby and I will work to get proof of their existence and find out what they've been up to."

Tyler had told her about his crazy plan, but now that the plan was ready to be put into action, she didn't like the sound of it. She turned to him with a frown. "Why do you need to get proof? Don't you think that might be dangerous? Can't you just try to find your brother and get out of there?"

"No, we need to do more than that. If we just get out of there and run, they'll eventually track us, again. We need to make sure that they're going to leave us alone, for good."

"How do you plan to do that?" Grace asked.

"I'm under no illusion that a couple of teenagers are going to stop them. I mean, they're a government agency with a lot of power behind them. So, why not pit one agency against another? That's where you come in, Eddie. When you said that you could speak Spanish, you gave me an idea."

"Did I? Why do I get the feeling that this plan of yours is going to be completely crazy?"

Liliana groaned. "That's what I'm afraid of."

Tyler laughed. "It wouldn't be a great plan if it wasn't a little crazy." He turned to Eddie. "I'm thinking that you can easily pass as a Native Mexican. If you can lead the Federales to the compound, we can let them take over."

"But, I thought that the I.I.A. had an agreement with the Mexican government to be left alone," Liliana said.

"Sure, but what if they thought the I.I.A. was trying to get drug money past them, without forking over their fair share?"

"The Federales are the police though, right?" Grace asked. "Why would they want a share of drug money?"

"The Federales try to make a show at stopping drug runs across the border, but they're also aware that they can't stop everyone, and so they agree to look a blind eye, now and then, for a certain fee. If they thought that the I.I.A. was trying to get money past them, without paying up, they would take it upon themselves to try to stop them."

Liliana raised her eyebrows, in question. "How do you know all of this?"

"One of my old roommates from my, uh...special school, used to be in a gang. He told me a lot of stories."

"Hmm...I see, but what happens when they raid the place and find out that there's no drug money?"

"It doesn't matter. Once they're in, they'll find me and Toby, and whoever else they're holding captive, and the compound will be shut down. Before that happens; however, we'll make sure the I.I.A. knows we have enough proof of their existence, so they won't come after us, again. I know it won't shut them down, it'll just put a slight damper on their operations for a while, but hopefully it will keep them away from us, for good. What do you think?"

"I like it," Eddie said, with a grin.

Liliana shook her head. "I don't like it...but it is a smart plan; I'll give you that."

Eddie turned to Grace. "What do you think?" Her eyes were focused on the gas station and she didn't comment. "Grace?"

Her eyes remained fixed on the building. "Someone's here."

Eddie followed her gaze. "Who? Who's here?"

"I'm not sure, but I can feel him...I think it's a tracker."

Liliana turned toward the gas pumps and closed her eyes to listen to the thoughts of the nearby patrons. She noticed that Tyler did the same. Unfortunately, every thought was in Spanish, and she couldn't understand.

"I can't understand a word that anyone is thinking," Tyler grumbled.

"Me neither." Liliana chuckled. "Anyway, I don't see anything odd, but if Grace feels that a tracker is nearby, we should probably get out of here."

"Agreed," Eddie said. "I guess it's time to hit the road and put this plan into action."

*****

Eddie pulled off the road and into a grove of trees, which provided cover from any passersby, then he turned to Tyler. "So...now what?"

"Now, we figure out which direction the compound is and I wander around until they find me."

They stepped out of the car, into the Mexican wilderness. Liliana took a deep breath of fresh, mountain air. The temperature was noticeably cooler than it had been at the gas station. She stood close to Tyler, who had spread the map out on the hood of the car. He looked back and forth from his surroundings to the map a few times, before he spoke. "Alright, I think I'll wander through the woods, parallel to the road, for about a half mile or so, and then I'll make my way out to the road. It looks like the entrance to the compound should be near there. I'm sure I'll be noticed on the security cameras, fairly quickly. I'll let you know when we're ready for you to lead the Federales in. Until then, I guess just hang tight and watch my back."

"You've got it," Eddie said. "You take care of yourself." They shook hands and then drew each other in, to what Liliana thought of as a man hug, a quick half hug with a fist pound on the back.

Grace stepped in to give him a hug and said, "We'll be waiting for you. Be careful, okay?"

"I will," Tyler assured her.

Then Eddie and Grace wandered away to look at a lizard on a nearby rock. Liliana assumed that their feigned interest in the reptile was supposed to give her a moment of privacy with Tyler.

"So…," she said, "this is it, huh?" She stood in front of him and looked up into his beautiful eyes.

"Yeah, there's no turning back now."

She sighed. "No, I suppose not."

Then, without another word or warning, he swooped her into his arms and kissed her. The kiss was everything she could have hoped for and more. In that moment, their thoughts and emotions seemed to be as one.

With obvious reluctance, Tyler set her back on the ground but continued to hold both of her hands in his. "I expect another one of those when I come back," he told her.

She smiled. "Oh, I'll give you more than one, you can count on it."

They were silent for a moment as they stood beneath the trees and looked into each other's eyes.

Finally, he broke the silence. "I'd better get going."

"You be careful. You hear me?"

"I promise." He squeezed her hands and then let go. "Alright, guys, I guess this is it. With luck, I'll see you soon."

After one final round of goodbyes, Tyler wandered into the trees, with nothing but the access card hidden under the lining of his shoe. Liliana stood silently beside Grace and watched his departure until he had disappeared, entirely.

19 PROOF

From the protection of the treetops, a concealed chipmunk scolded Tyler. A slight breeze rustled the leaves; but otherwise, the forest lay silent. Through the trees, he spied a section of dirt road, about thirty feet below. Somewhere, on the other side of the road, he would find the entrance to the tunnel. With luck, the guards would find him first.

Can you hear me, Liliana? he asked, silently.

I'm right with you, Liliana thought back. *Are you doing okay?*

Yeah, I'm good. I think I should be pretty close to the entrance.

Okay, be careful. Keep me posted.

The rocky terrain down the hill was slippery and slow going, but he eventually made it to the road without breaking a leg. Ian had warned that security cameras were located indiscreetly throughout the surrounding premises and along the road which led to the entrance. If he was in the right location, security should already be alerted to his presence.

He didn't have to wait long. He had wandered along the road for about two minutes, when an ATV zoomed up at breakneck speed and came to a sudden stop, two feet away. Ten seconds later, he was surrounded by three men with hand guns, who had appeared from behind nearby trees. If he *had* wanted to run, he wouldn't have had a chance.

"Hey, it's that kid," one of the guards announced to the rest of the security team. "He's not an intruder; he's one of them." He then turned to Tyler. "What are you doing out here, Kid? Henry's not going to be happy when he discovers you're out."

They obviously mistook him for Toby, a misconception which could play to his benefit. "I, uh, just wanted to get some fresh air. Sorry. I wasn't planning on staying out long. Actually, I think I'm a little lost."

"Well, come on. I'm going to have to take you back. Hop up and you can ride with me." He patted the seat behind him.

Tyler did as requested and climbed onto the rear of the ATV.

The guard called into his walkie-talkie, to announce they were headed back to the tunnel, and then cranked his neck around to make sure his passenger was seated. "You holding on, Kid?"

He grabbed ahold of the rear bars. "Yep, I'm good."

They flew down the road for about a quarter of a mile. The guard parked the ATV about ten yards from the base of a rock outcropping. From there, they made their way across uneven ground, strewn with lava rocks, until they came to what looked like a dead end. They were surrounded on three sides by tall boulders. Just when Tyler thought there was nowhere to go, he followed the guard around the tallest boulder, on the left, and saw that they were standing atop a rock stairway.

"Prepare yourself, Kid. Henry's going to want an explanation. Next time you decide to take a walk, you need to let someone know. Take someone with you who knows his way around, so you don't get lost."

"Yeah, I know, that probably wasn't the smartest move, on my part."

"Well, hopefully the boss is in a good mood. Follow me."

Tyler nodded and followed the guard down the stone steps.

When they reached the bottom, they came to a metal door. The guard entered a code into a security panel and was answered by a soft buzz. He pressed the handle on the door and Tyler found himself in the middle of a long, carpeted corridor. If he hadn't known that he was under a mountain, he would have thought that he was in a hotel. He couldn't help but wonder if Toby was behind one of the many doors that they passed, along the way.

They stopped at the last door, on the right. Opposite the door was another flight of stairs, which led down. The guard knocked and waited. In a moment, the door slid open, sideways, and they were greeted by a tall, distinguished looking man. He was clean shaven, had salt and peppered silver hair, and wore an expensive suit.

"What is this I hear about you wandering about in the woods, Toby?"

Tyler couldn't sense if the man was angry or simply curious.

He tried to read his thoughts, but they seemed oddly blank, as though he intentionally blocked them from Tyler.

"I'm sorry; I just wanted some fresh air."

"Well, next time you want fresh air, you need to go through the proper channels. You can't just wander about, unescorted. I would ask how you got out in the first place, but I don't think that's necessary. I've been hearing about some of your many talents, including your little outing to the game room, the other night."

Tyler wondered what else they knew about Toby's 'talents' and what his brother had been up to.

"I need to get back out to my post, Henry," said the guard. "Is it okay if I leave him here, with you?"

"That's fine, Jake. A job well done, thank you."

"No problem, Sir. Take care, Kid," he said to Tyler and then retreated in the direction from which they had come.

"Well now, Toby, I would hate to think that you were trying to escape, just when we were starting to come to some sort of an understanding. Would you like to explain what you were *really* doing out there?"

Tyler decided that it was as good a time as any to let him know his true identity. He would find out soon enough, anyway.

"Actually, Sir, the truth is—"

He was interrupted by the appearance of a man who had just arrived at the top of the stairs.

The newcomer glanced back and forth between them. "Hey, Henry, what's going on here?"

"Hi, Jesse. Our friend, Toby, was just about to explain what he was doing, outside of the compound."

Jesse glared at Tyler and shook his head. "That's *not* Toby. You're Tyler, aren't you?"

"Tyler?" Henry's gaze swiveled from Jesse to Tyler, and he stared at him with intent. "You're Tyler?"

Momentarily speechless, Tyler looked back and forth between the two men and then presented Henry with an awkward grin. "Um...hi."

Henry didn't respond but turned back to Jesse. "How did you know?"

"Because, I just came from talking to Toby, just a minute ago. And because I can hear the thoughts of this one." Jesse nodded his head in Tyler's direction.

Tyler made a mental note to immediately block all thoughts.

"What are you doing here?" Jesse demanded.

Tyler had practiced his cover story, repeatedly, during the long drive, and was prepared for their inquisition.

"Obviously, I'm here to find my brother."

"But, how did you find us?" Henry asked.

"We're twins. We have a connection, you know? Wherever he goes, I go."

"I should have known that Toby would find a way to contact you. I don't know why we didn't expect it. We've been out looking for you, and here you come, waltzing in our back door. Did you think you were going to break him out?"

"Break him out?" Tyler scoffed. "Are you kidding? With all of those armed guards, outside? I'm not crazy. No...I want to join you, if you'll let me."

"Forgive me for being a bit...skeptical, but your brother hasn't exactly been cooperative. Why should we believe that *you* want to work with us, when he has refused?"

"Well, for one, I'm not my brother. We might look identical, but we don't act the same, and we don't think the same. We never have. He's always been the more...cautious one; I guess you'd say."

"So, you just decided to run away from home and join him in Mexico?"

"I'm sure you're aware that we've lived with a foster family most of our lives. They haven't exactly been nurturing, to say the least. With my brother gone, there was no way I was going to stay there, by myself. My home is wherever Toby is, and if this is where he's going to be, then this is where I want to be, too."

"Hmm, I see. Jesse, can I speak with you for a minute, in my office?" He turned to Tyler. "Stay right here. There are cameras everywhere, so don't think about going far."

Tyler smiled. "I'll wait right here."

The door slid shut after Jesse followed Henry into his office. Tyler closed his eyes in concentration, and although he couldn't audibly hear their words, he could hear their thoughts which were formed before their words were spoken.

Do you believe him? Henry asked. *Could you hear what the boy was thinking?*

The boy's smart, just like his brother; I can sense that, Jesse responded. *I could tell that he was blocking his thoughts from me, so it's hard to say. I think he might be for real, though. I know he and his brother are close. Maybe if he's willing to work with us, he can convince Toby to cooperate, too. I'd say it's at least worth a shot.*

Is there any word on the others?

No, there's been no sign of them.

Why don't we bring him in and ask?

The door opened, and Tyler, who leaned casually against the wall, acted as though he wasn't aware of the conversation that had just transpired behind the closed door.

"Tyler, why don't you come on in to my office, for a few minutes? I'd like to get to know you a little better."

Tyler accepted the invitation and sat in a plush, upholstered chair, in front of a massive, mahogany desk. Jesse sat in a matching chair beside him, and Henry took a seat in a black, leather chair, behind the desk. The man leaned back and cracked his knuckles, one at a time.

"So, I understand that you would like to join us. I think that we might be able to come to some sort of an arrangement."

"I'd like that," Tyler replied.

"I can't help but wonder, though, what ever happened to your other friends?"

"My friends?"

"Yes, you see, we're interested in recruiting as many talented, young individuals, such as yourself, as possible. I'm afraid there may have been some sort of a misunderstanding. I'd like to have the opportunity to sit down with them and explain the great work that we do here and invite them to join our team. I wonder if you might know how I could contact them."

Tyler knew that he had to lie and lie well. Jesse would try to search his mind to discover their whereabouts and observe his face for implications that he may be lying. He also knew that, in order for any great lie to be plausible, there was a need for a substance of truth.

"My friends...I assume you're referring to Eddie, Liliana, and Grace."

"That's right. I understand that you were all together. When was the last time you saw them?"

Here goes, Tyler thought, *time to put on the poker face.* "I was with them in Arizona, two days ago." This, at least, was true. "That's when I decided to break off from them and come down here. They tried to stop me, but I told them that I wanted to be with my brother."

"And you haven't heard from them since?"

Tyler shook his head. "No."

"Well, that is unfortunate. They would be a valuable asset to our team; that's for sure. Would you happen to know how to contact them? A phone number, perhaps?"

He was sure that if the man wanted their phone number, he was powerful enough, and had enough connections, that he could access it. Tyler shook his head and tried to look disappointed. "No, I'm sorry."

"Well then, I guess we'll have to just keep trying on our own. I'm sure we'll find them, eventually." His words were casual, but his menacing tone was undeniable.

Tyler didn't respond, and Jesse finally broke the uncomfortable silence. "Well, I'm sure that you would like to see your brother." He turned to Henry. "Would you like me to put him in the empty room, next to Toby?"

"That would be fine. Perhaps, later this evening, Tyler, after you've had dinner and have had a chance to see your brother, we may talk again."

Tyler smiled. "Sure, I'd like that."

Jesse stood to leave, and Tyler was happy to follow. Not only was he anxious to see Toby, but he was ready to leave the vicinity of Henry's uncomfortable, speculative stare. Tyler knew that the man didn't believe his story, but he was also confident that Henry wouldn't turn him out into the Mexican wilderness, either.

Just as Tyler reached the door, Henry called out, "I'm sorry, Tyler, one more question, if you don't mind."

Tyler turned. "Yes?"

"You mentioned Eddie, Liliana, and Grace. What about your friend, Sarah? Where was the last place you saw her?"

He didn't care if Henry believed him or not, he wasn't about to give any indication of Sarah's whereabouts. She and her baby had to be protected at all costs. "She wasn't interested in coming with us. She stayed in Washington."

There was nothing more to say on the matter, and before he had a chance to hear Henry's reaction, he turned and followed Jesse out the door and down the second set of steps. They walked down another hallway, identical to the one they had just come from, and made casual small talk along the way. Jesse wasn't nearly as intimidating as Henry, but Tyler wasn't fooled either; the man couldn't be trusted.

They stopped at the end of the hallway, and Tyler watched carefully as Jesse slid his access card through the security box, beside the door. The door slid open, and Tyler followed Jesse into the room.

Tyler grinned at the sight of his brother, who leaned back in bed, his eyes on an open book. Upon hearing Jesse's entrance, Toby glanced up from the pages and did a double take.

"You're here." He set the book on the bed and swung his legs over the side.

Tyler grinned. "I told you I'd find you."

"I'll tell you what," Jesse said, "I'll leave you boys alone so you can get caught up, and I'll come back in an hour with dinner."

"Thanks, Jesse," Toby said.

Jesse smiled, nodded, and then was gone. The door slid shut, with a resounding click.

Tyler followed Toby's gaze to the video camera, mounted on the ceiling. *Watch what you say*, Toby thought.

Gotcha, Tyler replied, silently. Their every word would be monitored, closely. The boys would have to engage in idle small talk for a few minutes.

"So, I can't believe you made it here," Toby said.

"Yeah, it was a long trip. You're kinda out here in the middle of nowhere."

"I wouldn't know. I haven't been outside since I got here."

"Well, maybe we can work on that. You know, I think if these guys realize that they can trust you, they might give you a little more freedom and wouldn't keep you locked up." Silently he said, *Just go with it. Let them hear what they want to hear.*

Toby smiled indiscreetly; his brother understood.

"Yeah, I don't know," Toby said. "You really want to work with these people?"

"I do. What do we have going for us, back home? Nothing, that's what! If we stay here and work for them, we could actually have a place to call home. We could have a purpose. We could finally put our powers to use and maybe help someone else out, along the way. Each day will be an adventure."

Wow, I'm convinced, Toby thought, *sounds good to me. Too bad they aren't as honest as they pretend to be.* Out loud, he said, "I don't know, maybe you're right."

"Of course I'm right. This is a great opportunity. We have a chance for a new start at life. I say we embrace it and take all these guys have to offer. After all, what do we have to lose?"

Tyler glanced indiscreetly from the camera and back to Toby. *Do you think they're getting all of this?* he asked, silently.

I'm sure they're soaking up every word, Toby thought.

They were interrupted when the thoughts of someone, other than his brother, invaded his mind. *Oh my gosh, Tyler! I knew I heard another voice, in here. You made it!*

He smiled when he spotted her. She stood below the video camera, pressed against the corner of the wall. *You must be*

Rebecka, he thought. *My brother's told me a lot about you.*

She was beautiful and could easily have been a model. Toby had given him a hard time about falling for Liliana; he wondered just how close his brother and this girl had become.

Hey, Brother, Toby thought, *pretend to take a nap, so we can all chat silently and they don't get suspicious.*

"Would you mind if I lay down for a bit, just until dinner?" Tyler asked. "I'm exhausted from the trip."

"Not a problem. Go ahead and take the bed. I'll just sit at the desk and read for a bit."

They each took their unsuspecting positions, so that the watchful eyes in the security room would hopefully ignore them, and then Tyler filled them in on their plan.

Well, I think it sounds like a good idea, Toby thought. *We just need to think of a way to get evidence.*

Any information that you might want is kept in Henry's office, Rebecka thought. *Anything of real importance would be on his computer. I've watched him. To get on the computer you have to have an access card and password.*

Oh? Could that be like the access card that I have hidden in my shoe?

Are you kidding? That's awesome! Rebecka thought. *If you weren't pretending to be asleep right now, and I was actually supposed to be here, I'd hug you.*

I can't take all of the credit; Eddie and Grace actually got the card, so you'll have to thank them when you see them. So, what do you think? We wait until night and then break into his office?

It's not as easy as all that, Rebecka thought. *The surveillance cameras are monitored, twenty-four hours a day. The second they see us, they'll have armed guards at the door.*

So, then we have to make sure they don't see us, Tyler thought.

Toby drummed his fingers on the desk. *How do you propose we do that?*

Can we disable the cameras? Tyler wondered.

We could, Rebecka thought, *but as soon as the guard realizes* that the cameras aren't working, he'll have a dozen guards patrolling the halls to make sure everyone is where they're supposed to be.

Hmmm, Tyler thought, *then I guess we need to think of something else.*

They each fell into silence while they tried to think of another idea.

Wait a minute! Toby thought. *If we can't disable the security cameras, why can't we disable the security guard?*

Disable the security guard? How do you plan to make that happen? Tyler questioned, silently.

The same way they disabled me when I first got here. They keep sedatives in the nurse's office. Rebecka sometimes delivers desserts and coffee to the staff members. If she can make the guard sleep for a while, then we can go wherever we want.

That's a good idea, Rebecka thought, *but then we're faced with the problem of getting the sedatives out of the nurse's office. Any ideas there?*

Tyler grinned. *I'll bet we can come up with a plan.*

*****

"How was dinner?" Jesse asked.

"It was great, thanks," Tyler replied. "I haven't had a meal that good, in a long time."

"That's good to hear. You ready to go up and see Henry? He's waiting for you."

"Sure. Lead the way."

Toby interrupted their departure. "Hey, Jesse, I've got a bit of a headache. Do you think I could get some medicine from the nurse?"

"Sure thing. Come on with us, I'll drop you off on the way. You can stay there until I come back down."

The nurse's office was located in the center of the hallway. Tyler had been briefed on the layout of the tunnels. The rooms in this hallway were the sleeping quarters for all of the residents. The hallway above, where Tyler had first entered, held Henry's office, the offices of other agents and officials, and the kitchen.

There was a third tunnel; which Tyler hadn't yet seen, which held labs and testing facilities. Rebecka had explained that the third tunnel also held a second exit to the outside world.

Jesse made sure that the nurse was in her office and left Toby in her care. Then, Tyler followed him toward the end of the hallway, to the staircase. Tyler's target was the security room. Rebecka had said that it was the last room in the hall, across from the stairs.

Tyler knew that a guard sat behind the closed door, with a careful eye trained on the surveillance monitors. The goal was to distract the guard, long enough for Rebecka to swipe enough sedatives from the nurse's office. Each step of their plan had to be timed with exact precision or they would all be caught.

Jesse led the way up the stairs and Tyler followed close behind. When he made it to the fourth step, he knew it was now or never. The cameras would catch his every move, so he had to make the fall look believable, but he also didn't want to fall so hard that he might actually break something. With a holler, he slipped forward. He fell on his hands and face and then half rolled, half slid and came to a stop at the bottom. His leg stuck out in an awkward angle. Unsure if the guard had seen the fall, he decided to holler, for good measure, "Ow! Ow! My ankle, I think it's broken!"

Jesse hurried down the stairs and knelt by his side. At the same time, the door to the security room opened and the young guard, who appeared to be eighteen or nineteen, came out to kneel by his other side.

Okay, Toby, the guard's out. Tell Rebecka to do her thing, Tyler silently called, to his brother. According to the plan, Toby would lie on a cot and keep the nurse distracted. The medicine cabinets were located in a back room. Rebecka would teleport in, locate the needed sedatives, and would hopefully be in and out before she was noticed.

"Man, are you okay?" Jesse asked.

"I don't know. My ankle really hurts."

"Dude, that was an awesome fall," the guard said. "I saw it all on camera. I mean, don't get me wrong it looked like it really hurt, but it was pretty funny."

Jesse glared at the guard who said, "Yeah, I'll just shut up now, sorry."

"It's okay," Tyler said. "I admit it wasn't one of my finer moves." He made a show of rotating his ankle and winced sharply, as though in pain.

Jesse sighed. "I should get the nurse."

"No, if anything, I should at least be able to walk down there on my own. Do you think you can help me stand?"

"Yeah, yeah here, we can each take an arm." Jesse indicated to the guard that he should help. They each took an elbow and assisted Tyler to a standing position. He slowly attempted to put weight on his "hurt" ankle and immediately lifted it.

"Ow! This sucks."

"Maybe you just need to walk it out," Jesse said. "I'll help you walk down to the nurse."

"Yeah, sure, maybe if we just take it real slow."

"Do you need me?" the guard asked. "Cuz, I should be in the control room, right now."

"You're in there by yourself?" Jesse asked. "No one's watching the cameras?"

"Nope, most of the time there's only one guard on duty, in there."

He narrowed his eyes in suspicion. "Your brother's in the nurse's office, right now."

"Yeah, he had a headache."

"Hmm...convenient."

Toby, Jesse knows that something's up. Tell Rebecka to get out of there, now, Tyler thought.

Stall him for a minute, Toby thought back. *She's still trying to find the right medicine.*

I don't know if I can. Tell her to hurry.

Jesse turned to the guard. "Get back in the control room, and see if there's anything suspicious going on in the nurse's office."

"The nurse's office?" the guard questioned. "What am I

looking for?"

"I don't know. I just have a strange feeling that these two might be up to something." Jesse stared intently at Tyler, in an obvious attempt to read his thoughts.

"I just *fell* down the stairs," Tyler said. "Believe me; I wouldn't hurt my ankle on purpose. We aren't *up* to anything."

"Well, we'll see about that." Jesse turned to the guard and snapped, "Go on. What are you waiting for?"

"Are you okay if I let go of your arm?" the guard asked.

"Yeah, I'm fine," Tyler assured him. The guard slowly released his arm, and when he was confident that the patient wouldn't fall over, he hurried back to the control room.

Toby, tell her to get out now! Tyler thought.

She's got it, Toby thought back.

The guard poked his head out of the security room. "I don't see anything unusual, Jesse. His twin was lying on a cot; the nurse was with him. It all looked fine."

"Okay, well, that's good. Still, keep a close eye on those monitors from now on. I want to make sure that nothing gets past us."

"You got it, Jesse. I'm all over it." He returned to his post and the door slid shut.

Jesse released his arm and looked squarely at Tyler. "If you and your brother are up to something, you won't get away with it, so don't bother trying anything."

Tyler shook his head. "We aren't up to anything."

"For your sake, I hope not. I like you two. I'd hate to see anything bad happen to you."

"Understood," Tyler said and smiled. "Do you think you could help me down to the nurse, now?"

*****

Two hours later, right on cue, Rebecka informed Toby that the guard was out for the count.

You're sure? Tyler heard his brother ask, silently, from his room.

Positive, Rebecka thought. *I'm standing in the control room, right behind him. He's out good.*

You didn't give him too much of the stuff, did you? Toby asked.

Hmmm…I hope not. I wonder how much I was supposed to give him?

Are you serious?

Tyler heard a chuckle in her thoughts. *No, I read the directions on the bottle. I gave him just the right amount. Don't worry. Now hurry up and get down here. I'll meet you at the bottom of the stairs.*

Even though Tyler could have easily unlocked the door with a simple touch, it was faster to use the access card which had remained hidden in his shoe, throughout the day. The plastic card served a dual purpose; it would open any door within the compound and when inserted into Henry's computer, would grant them access to his records and files.

Within moments, Tyler was out. He released Toby from his room, as well, and a minute later they met Rebecka outside of the security room. From there, they followed her up the stairs, to Henry's office.

When they reached the door, Toby whispered, "You don't think Henry will still be in his office, do you?"

"No, he always goes home after lights out," Rebecka whispered back. "There are others who might be in their offices though, so we need to hurry and get inside, before anyone sees us."

Tyler pulled out the access card and ushered everyone in. Then, he slid the door shut and looked around. "I'll work on getting logged into the computer. Why don't you guys check out the file cabinets and see if there's anything worthwhile. Rebecka, we're going to need a flash drive. Do you have any idea where I might find one?"

"Yeah, there should be something in his desk. Let me see what I can find."

Tyler inserted the access card, entered the password, and

suddenly a world of information awaited him. Now, he just needed to figure out where to go.

"I found a flash drive," Rebecka announced. "Here ya go."

"Thanks." He accepted the small device and inserted it. "Now then, what sort of information should I be looking for?"

Toby and Rebecka peered over Tyler's shoulders.

"I would start with the access list," Rebecka said. "Anytime someone uses their access card, their entry gets documented. The list will show who entered the compound and when they entered. There are some people who might not want the public to know that they were here."

"Perfect," Toby said.

"Okay, what next?" Tyler asked, after the access list had been downloaded.

"Well," Rebecka said, "besides the C.I.A., I know there are other groups and individuals who provide funding, for their own gains and purposes. They wouldn't want a list like that to become public knowledge."

It took a few minutes, but Tyler eventually found what they were looking for. Not only did the list include dignitaries from other countries, it also included certain politicians and a few celebrities.

He saved the list of names to the flash drive and then noticed a folder labeled, 'tunnels'. After he clicked on it, his eyes widened when he realized that the new page contained a list of hidden tunnel locations and their corresponding passwords. Not surprisingly, Edwards Air Force Base was among the list. Another click and Tyler opened maps of the underground locations. With a few more clicks, the tunnels folder was also saved. "You never know when access might come in handy, again," he explained. "And I'm sure they wouldn't be happy if proof of the tunnel locations became public knowledge."

"Good thinking," Toby said. "See if you can find the list with our names on it. If other people on the list start to go missing, it could spread suspicion toward the agency."

Tyler located and downloaded the list. He found their names, along with Eddie, Liliana, Grace, and Sarah, and at least fifty others. He also downloaded a few interesting emails, emails he was certain the agency wouldn't want falling into the wrong hands.

He removed the flash drive and held it up. "I think we have more than enough information, here, to secure our safety."

"So, what happens next?" Rebecka asked.

"Eddie should arrive with the Federales in the morning. Before they get here, we need to make Henry aware that we have this information. And then, in theory, we just need to sit back and wait until Henry and his friends are detained."

Tyler removed the access card from the computer and placed it in his pocket with the flash drive.

"Can you think of anything else we should do, before we go?" Toby asked.

"Nope," Tyler replied. "I think we've done enough damage for one evening."

His brother spun toward the door and stared with intent. "Shh, someone's coming."

Rebecka looked up and turned an ear to listen. "Are you sure? I don't hear anyone."

"I don't hear him, either, but I can see him, in my mind. There's a man who just walked into an office, down the hall. Would anyone else have reason to come in here, besides Henry?"

"No, I don't think so."

"He went into a room a few doors down. Come on. Let's get out of here before he comes out, again."

Toby peered into the hall to ensure that it was clear and then ushered Tyler and Rebecka out of Henry's office. He closed the door, but before they could turn for the stairs, they were stopped by a muffled noise that came from a room, down the hall.

Tyler looked down the hall; every instinct told him that he should run. They still might have time to sprint down the stairs and remain undetected, but for some unknown reason, he stood frozen, not from fear, but from curiosity. He saw that Toby was equally as curious.

"What are you two waiting for?" Rebecka whispered. "Come on."

"Whoever's down there...I feel like we know him," Toby said.

"Yeah, well, whoever it is, you don't want him to catch you here, do you?"

Before they had time to contemplate further, they heard a door open. They stood motionless, afraid to breathe, as they watched a man step into the hall. His back was to them, but he seemed oddly familiar.

"It can't be," Toby said.

"Is it?" Tyler asked.

"Who? Who is he?" Rebecka whispered.

The man turned toward them, then, and he appeared just as shocked at their appearance, as Tyler felt.

"It's Dad," the twins said, in unison.

With strong-willed insistence, the girls conquered the battle of dinner selection. They would not be eating in their motel room.

"We've spent a week hiding from the I.I.A., and now you want to throw that all away by parading yourselves in public?" Eddie had argued when the girls proposed that they go to the restaurant, located on the bottom floor of their motel.

"Do you really think a tracker is going to be looking for us, *here*?" Grace had retorted. "This is probably the last place they would expect us to be; and besides, if they are looking for us, they're going to find us whether we're in a motel room or in a restaurant. We'd actually have a better chance to escape out in the open. If they come to our motel room, there's no other exit except for the door."

"She does have a point," Liliana had agreed.

Eddie had made an attempt to look serious but failed horribly when he tried to hide a smile. "Why do I feel like I don't have a choice?"

Grace had grinned. "Because, you don't. Come on, it'll be fun. This might be the last night that the three of us get to spend together. Don't you want to have a little fun?"

As the only male in the group, and the eldest of the three, Eddie felt a weight of responsibility to keep the girls safe. At the same time, he had to admit that a couple of hours spent downstairs, did sound more appealing than sitting in their cockroach infested, rundown, motel room.

"Fine," he had agreed. "But Grace, if you get any visions or feelings that something might be wrong, you have to promise that we'll leave, right away.

"Does that mean we can go?" Her eyes twinkled with merriment, and he couldn't help but smile in return.

"Do you *promise*?"

"Of course. I'm not stupid. I promise, if anyone even looks at us cross-eyed, we'll get out of there. Is that good enough for you?"

"Until we're all safe, it will never be good enough, but I guess it will have to do."

"Thank you! Let me get changed and then we can go." She turned to Liliana. "I have a couple of dresses in my bag. They might be a little long, but otherwise they should fit. Would you like to borrow one?"

"Sure, thanks." She examined the dresses that Grace had laid out on the bed. "I don't know how you have such a wide assortment of clothes. I just packed enough to fit in my small bag. I feel like I've been wearing the same clothes for days."

"That's only because I packed for a vacation to Florida. I planned to lay out by the pool every afternoon and hang out with my boyfriend every evening."

Their conversation piqued his attention, and he turned to Grace with interest. "You have a boyfriend?" He shouldn't be surprised. After all, Grace was stunning. She probably had a handful of guys lined up and waiting, back home.

Grace had looked slightly embarrassed, and it was obvious that she didn't want to answer. "Um...yeah. I mean, we're dating, and I call him my boyfriend, but he really isn't more than just a friend. You know? I just don't feel that...spark."

"Well, give it time. Sometimes the best relationships start out as just a friendship."

"Yeah...maybe." She had promptly changed the subject and then excused herself to the bathroom to change.

So, now he sat on the edge of the bed and waited for the girls to 'pretty up', as Grace had explained. He contemplated the fact that she had a boyfriend. He found that he was both jealous and relieved and couldn't decide which emotion was stronger. He couldn't deny that she was gorgeous and fun to be around, but a relationship with Grace could never work. For one, there was no way her parents would approve of a long distance relationship, with a college student from another state. There was also the fact that he couldn't shake off the attraction that he felt to Sarah. He knew that she was married, and he had no desire to break up her marriage; but nevertheless, the draw to her was there and it wouldn't go away. It wouldn't be fair to Grace if he was with her, but his thoughts were of Sarah.

Then, he reminded himself that Jenna waited back home. He needed to decide if he would ask her out when he returned.

Life had been easier when his sole focus had been on school. Just a week ago, he had been concerned with his research project and had told himself that he wouldn't get involved with a girl until he was finished. Now, only a week later, three girls occupied his mind. How had that happened?

*****

The moment they entered the restaurant, all eyes turned to the beautiful blonde and the exotic Chinese girl, who were both donned in flattering, form fitting dresses. Eddie's protective instincts kicked into overdrive; he stepped between the two, placed a possessive hand around each girl's waist, and steered them to a table in the corner. His body language and facial expression stated that the girls were his, and no one ought to get any ideas.

The town wasn't exactly a hot tourist location, and it appeared that they were the only Americans in the restaurant. The tables were filled with some families but mostly men who looked like they had just gotten off of a long day of work on the farm, men who would like nothing better than to befriend the beautiful girls. He began to question the legitimacy of his agreement to eat out; perhaps room service would have been a better idea, after all.

Grace placed a hand on his forearm. "Relax. Look, there's no sign of any trackers. We're fine, and the place looks fun. See, they're getting ready to start a band, and there's a dance floor. Let's just enjoy dinner, okay?"

"Yeah...it's not trackers that I'm worried about," he mumbled. But then he saw the happiness written on her face and didn't want to spoil the mood. "You're right. We're here; we might as well have fun."

After the waitress took their order, the girls watched the

band set up on stage. Eddie brooded over the conversation that would take place in the morning, with the Federales. He had gone over the dialogue in his head, visualized how it would play out, and had considered various questions they might ask. He hoped that he was prepared.

Liliana tapped his shoulder. "What did he say?"

Snapped out of his musing, he turned to her. "Who?"

"The guy at the microphone."

"Oh, um, it sounds like their fiddle player is out tonight, so he apologized that they might sound a little off."

Liliana turned to Grace. "You play the violin, don't you? Isn't that kinda like a fiddle?"

"Um, sort of, I guess so. I'm not going to get up there and play, though. I don't know any Mexican music."

"Oh, that's too bad. It would have been fun to hear you play."

Their food arrived a few minutes later, and while they ate, they listened to the band and watched patrons take to the dance floor.

Grace tapped her foot to the music and grinned at Eddie. "This is fun. Aren't you glad that we came? Much better than sitting in a motel room."

"It is fun," Eddie agreed. "Though I think the band would sound a little better if they had a fiddle player." He winked at Liliana.

"Oh, absolutely," Liliana caught on. "A little bit of fiddle music is exactly what they need."

Grace laughed. "I told you, I don't know any Mexican songs."

"Haven't you noticed that they've played some American music, too? Maybe you know some of the same songs."

Grace didn't respond and looked toward the stage.

Eddie took advantage of her hesitation, grabbed her hand, and pulled her to her feet. "Come on."

"Where are we going?"

"I'll introduce you to the band." He hauled her to the front of the room before she could argue.

He waited until their song ended and then beckoned the

guitar player to the edge of the stage. He explained, in Spanish, that Grace was his friend from the U.S., and that she would love to join in and play the fiddle.

The band leader looked Grace up and down; and for a moment, he wondered at the wisdom of putting her on stage. He immediately explained that Grace was his girlfriend and let him know, in no uncertain terms, that she was his and his alone.

"I understand," the man told him, in Spanish. "I will guard her as if she were my own daughter."

"Thank you."

"Can she sing?"

Eddie looked at Grace, who waited patiently, with a smile on her face. He knew she didn't understand a word that they said. "I have no idea, but it wouldn't surprise me."

"Ah, well then, maybe we can get her to sing for us, too."

She nudged his arm with her elbow. "What did you say to him?"

"I said that you're very happy to help them out."

"Oh, well, okay then. He doesn't mind?"

"No. He's happy that you're willing to play."

The man presented Grace with a wide grin which revealed several missing teeth. He offered her a hand and in Spanish said, "We will be honored for you to join us."

She looked blankly at Eddie for translation.

He nudged her in return. "Go ahead."

She accepted the band leader's hand and he pulled her up, onto the stage. He then handed her the fiddle, and she tried it out to get a feel for it. Apparently pleased, he grinned and spoke to her in broken English. "Do you...know...Elvis, "Jailhouse Rock"?"

"You speak English?"

"Only little."

"Yeah, I know "Jailhouse Rock"."

He smiled. "Good."

Eddie called up to her, "I'll be right back there at the table, with Liliana. Have fun!"

She looked uncertain but managed a weak smile.

"Um...okay."

He resumed his seat and turned his chair so that he faced the stage. When the band leader announced that Grace would join the band, for the rest of the evening, the men at the table nearest to them, whooped and hollered.

One of the men turned to him. "That's your girl?"

"She is." His clear, firm response, left little question in the matter.

"She's very pretty."

"Yes. Yes she is," Eddie agreed.

Their discussion stopped, then, when the band started up. The song was sung in heavily accented Spanish, but it was still enjoyable. Eddie wasn't surprised that Grace had an impressive talent for the fiddle. She looked natural onstage, even out of place as she was, with a bunch of Mexican guys in cowboy boots.

"I hope you don't mind my saying so, but I can see that you like her," Liliana said. "Your aura seems different, tonight."

"I'm just trying to make sure that she's safe. I'm looking out for you, too. I feel responsible for you both."

"Oh, I get that, and I appreciate it. I do. There's something else, though. When you're around her, I sense that you like her, but you don't want to admit it. Am I right?"

Eddie was silent, for a moment, as he thought about the truth behind her words. She saw right through him and had hit the nail on the head. The band started another song, and he turned to watch, with rapt interest, so that he wouldn't have to immediately answer her question.

"I don't want to hurt her," he said finally. He turned to Liliana. "If Grace thought there might be a chance for her and me, she would get her hopes up. I don't want to disappoint her. The odds that it would ever work out between us are slim to none. Like I said before, I'm trying to keep her safe, not just physically, but emotionally, too."

"Relationships are never a sure thing, but I've always believed that it's best to follow your heart. If the two of you are meant to be together, it will find a way to work itself out."

"You're right, but what if we aren't meant to be together? Just because two people like each other, doesn't necessarily mean that they should be together."

"But, you admit that you *do* like her?"

He shrugged. "Yeah, I do. I'll admit it. But, life is going to go on. I have a life to get back to and so does she. Long distance relationships never work out." Eddie sucked in his breath when he saw Liliana's reaction to his words. "I'm sorry. I didn't mean that. I'm sure that you and Tyler will stay together. You two are obviously meant for each other."

"You think so?"

"Of course. I can't see auras, but I imagine yours lights up when you're around him. I can definitely see it in your face, the way you smile at him, and the way he smiles at you, too. The two of you seem natural together; it's like you've been friends for years and not just a couple of days."

"That's exactly how I feel. I feel like I've known him forever. I hope that we can find a way to still see each other once this is all over. Who knows where he'll end up. If the state thinks he's a runaway, do you think they'll lock him up?"

"I doubt it. Besides, if the Federales find him tomorrow, they'll inform the state that he was kidnapped. When that happens, they'll just return him to his foster family."

"That's a good point. I hadn't thought about that. From what he says though, his foster family isn't very nice. There's probably no way that they'd let him fly to Seattle, to see me."

"You just have to think positive."

Liliana smiled. "You're right." She was silent while she listened to Grace and the band, and then said, "I'm worried about him, Eddie."

"I know, but everything's going to be okay. We have to believe that. Tomorrow, I'll lead the Federales to the compound, and everything will be set right."

The song ended, then, and Eddie and Grace applauded.

Eddie watched while the singer spoke with Grace. He pointed to the microphone, something else was said, and then she set the fiddle down and followed him to the front of the stage.

"We are in luck this evening," the singer announced, in Spanish, to the restaurant patrons. "Our special friend, from America, has agreed to sing for us."

Throughout the evening, between traditional Mexican songs, the band had added several songs by Willie Nelson and Garth Brooks to the mix. It was obvious that the members of the band were big fans of American country music. Eddie was surprised that Grace knew the music; many of the songs had originally been performed well before her time.

When she stepped up to the microphone, the crowd cheered. She glanced across the room, to their table, and Eddie and Liliana both gave her two thumbs up. She turned and said something to the band, and then they started up a familiar tune. He was held captive by her beautiful voice and found it impossible to break his gaze from her sparkling eyes.

Three songs later, Grace bowed to the audience when they roared in appreciative applause. Then the band leader stepped up to the microphone and called out, in Spanish, "I think this pretty lady deserves a dance. Would her boyfriend like to meet her on the dance floor?" He beckoned for Eddie to step forward.

Eddie could see that Grace didn't have a clue what had been said, but then the band leader turned and said something to her. Her eyes immediately found him across the room. He remained seated; his gaze transfixed to her.

Liliana chuckled. "Go on, you should never leave a girl standing alone on a dance floor."

"You're right." He stood and headed toward the front of the room and the beautiful blonde who awaited him. He kept his eyes on her, as she hopped down from the stage, and they met in the middle of the floor, amid a half dozen other dance couples.

Eddie smiled and extended a hand. "Would you like to dance?"

"*Boyfriend*?"

He bit his bottom lip in paused embarrassment. "Sorry, I had to tell the guy something so no one would hit on you."

She took his hand when the music started and followed his lead to the slow, love song. "You don't want anyone hitting on me?"

"Not anyone here, that's for sure."

"Not anyone *here*. So, if we were somewhere else, then it would be okay for someone to hit on me?" He noted her sly grin and wasn't sure how to respond. Of course he didn't want anyone else hitting on her, but he couldn't very well tell her that, either.

"Dance with me." He grabbed her hand and spun her around, to avoid the question. He was suddenly thankful that she couldn't read his thoughts. The last thing he wanted was for her to know just how much he enjoyed holding her in his arms.

*****

Sleep was hard to come by, that night. When his thoughts didn't dwell on Grace, he thought about Sarah, and when he finally managed to get her out of his mind, he couldn't stop thinking about his impending meeting with the Federales. From the intermittent sounds of cheap crinkly sheets and squeaky springs, he guessed that both girls tossed and turned all night, as well, their thoughts no doubt disturbed by their uncertain futures.

They showered and dressed before the sun was up, and after a quick breakfast, in the restaurant, they followed the directions provided by the waitress and located the nearest police station. Eddie didn't stop, but instead, drove around the corner and up a few blocks.

He parked along a side street and then turned to the girls. "Alright, Grace, you have the directions to get back to the compound?"

"Yep, they're in my purse."

"Okay, I'm going to get out and walk back to the police station. As soon as I leave, I want you to get out of here. Get back to the woods and hide, before I get there with the police."

Liliana frowned. "But, what if the police don't believe you?"

"If they believe that Americans have been kidnapped, to smuggle drugs across the border, they'll be interested. They won't take a rumor like that lightly."

"Are you sure you don't want us to stay close by?" Grace asked. "I hate to leave you without a car."

"I'll be fine. I don't want to take a chance that they might see you. They might ask too many questions. We don't want to have to explain what you're doing here. Once we reach the compound, I'll sneak away and come find you."

Grace frowned, and he placed a reassuring hand on her arm. "Don't worry. I'll see you soon."

"You're right. I'm sure everything will work out. You'd better get going."

They got out of the car, and Eddie hugged each girl, in turn. He was aware of the fact that he hugged Grace slightly longer, than he did Liliana, and hoped that she hadn't noticed, as well. Then, with a final goodbye, the girls climbed into the car, and he watched them drive down the street until they were out of sight.

*****

When Eddie entered the police station, the officer at the front desk greeted him, in Spanish. "Good morning. How may I help you?"

Eddie glanced toward the old man and two young women who sat in black, plastic chairs, in the lobby, and then replied, in Spanish, "I need to speak with someone in charge. I'd rather not discuss it out here."

"I need to know what the matter is concerning, before I disturb the chief. He will not be happy with me if it is only a trivial matter, you understand."

Eddie leaned in close, over the desk, and whispered, "Fine. You may tell him that I have knowledge of kidnapped Americans and a drug cartel."

The clerk's eyes grew wide. "I'll be right back." He rose from his chair and quickly departed into a back room.

A few moments later, he returned and motioned for Eddie to follow. "Please, the chief would like to speak with you." He ushered Eddie into the back room and closed the door.

The chief leaned back in a large, plush, leather chair; his feet were propped on his desk while he smoked a cigar. "Please, have a seat." He motioned to a chair on the opposite side of his desk.

Eddie accepted the invitation and hoped that his nerves weren't obvious.

"Now then, my assistant tells me that you have information we might be interested in. Please, tell me what you know and how you came about this knowledge."

"I work on a farm, near the mountains," Eddie began. "Sometimes, there is no one that goes up the road, and the past few days we have seen a lot of traffic coming and going, many expensive cars, you know? My friend said that his cousin was working for them. His cousin told him that they were going to use Americans to run drugs across the border.

"We were curious, you see, so yesterday we followed them to see where they were going. They have a hideout up there. We saw them take some teenagers out of a car, they looked to be Americans, and their hands were tied behind their backs. Then, we overheard the men say that they were going to make their move, later today."

"Thank you for this information. If you will give me the directions, I will look into the matter."

"I don't think I'd be able to. Their hideout was so well concealed; I think I'd have to actually show you where it is."

"Hmm...just a moment." The chief picked up his phone. From what Eddie could gather from the one-sided conversation, on his end, arrangements were made for the Federales to gather and meet in an hour. Then, he hung up the phone and turned to Eddie.

"It is not custom for us to bring a civilian on a raid; it could be dangerous, but it seems that we have no other choice. Please know that you place yourself at risk by coming with us."

"I understand. It's a risk I'm willing to take if it means helping those kids." When the chief raised an eyebrow, in question, Eddie wondered if he had sounded too eager. He decided he should try to seem more like a poor, farm worker who was looking for self-gain. "Will there be a reward in it for me, if I lead you to them?"

"Ah, let's just take one step at a time. I must go now to speak with my men. You may wait in the lobby."

*****

They drove, now, down the familiar dirt road. Eddie rode with the chief. They were followed by three vehicles, each filled with well-armed Federales, dressed in their black and blue fatigues.

Liliana and Grace would be concealed in the woods, near the compound. They would have a clear view of the road, so that once the vehicles were spotted, Liliana could let Tyler know that they were on their way.

As they neared the compound, the chief's phone rang.

"U.S. Government?" he asked. "Are you sure?" He was silent for a moment while he listened and then said, "I understand, yes, but if they are running drugs...Yes, Sir, we will stop."

The truck pulled over, on the side of the mountain road. Eddie glanced in the rear view mirror to see the black vehicles pull in behind. Eddie's pulse began to race. Had they decided to pull back and stop the operation?

"We're stopping?"

"Yes. It looks like there might be a slight problem. I need to go speak with my men, for just a moment."

The chief stepped out of the truck and strode to stand beside the black vehicle parked behind them. He leaned into the driver's side window and talked for a good five minutes. Eddie strummed his fingers nervously on the dash. He wished he could hear what the men were saying and wondered what the final result would be. Would they continue on or turn back to town?

A few raindrops hit the windshield, and then the skies opened, and it began to downpour. The windows were soon blurred with water, and he could no longer see the men.

A minute later, the chief hopped into the truck and hurriedly closed the door. Without a word, he put the truck into motion and continued down the road, toward the compound.

Eddie couldn't hide his curiosity. "Are we still going to the hideout?"

The chief glanced at him. "Yes. It appears that the hideout doesn't belong to a drug cartel, after all. But, if there are reports of kidnapped Americans, we have a duty to check it out and ask questions later."

Eddie relaxed, slightly. At least for the moment, the plan still held.

The heavy rain continued to pelt the truck and the wilderness around them. Eddie directed them to stop about a quarter mile from the entrance. They would continue the rest of the way on foot, so their arrival would remain covert for as long as possible.

He planned to lead them as far as the bottom of the hill; from there they would be able to find the rock entrance that Tyler had described. As soon as their attention was drawn off of him, he would escape to the trees and hike back to find the girls.

Once outside and on foot, it wasn't long before he was drenched from the cold rain. He continued on beside the chief. The Federales fell in behind and around them, their guns armed and ready. Then he looked up the hill and saw the rock formation, just as Tyler had described.

"The entrance is just up there, behind that big rock, on the left," Eddie said.

The chief motioned for the troops to fall into position. Some stayed back and hid behind trees, while others zigzagged their way up the hill. Just as he had hoped, his presence was quickly forgotten.

By now, the surveillance cameras would have picked up movement from the intruders, and the guards would be alarmed and on high alert. He hoped that Tyler and Toby were ready.

21 RESCUE

Anxious with anticipation, for the events of the day to come, and in shock that he had seen his father, sleep eluded Tyler. He lay on his bed, eyes fixed on the ceiling, but in his mind's eye he saw the man who he had long ago assumed was gone, forever. He closed his eyes, and their conversation played back in his head.

"Dad? Is that you?" he called out, to the man who had just stepped out of another office, down the hall. He hadn't seen him since he was four, but the image of his father was still freshly engraved in his memory. Tall, fit and muscular, with thick brown hair, he and his brother were the spitting image of their father.

"It is him," Toby whispered.

Rebecka leaned in to join their huddle. "Your father is here? What is he doing here?"

Their father turned toward them. "Boys? It is you! Hurry!" He beckoned them forward. "Come down here before anyone sees you."

They dashed down the hall and stopped when they reached him. He opened the door and ushered them into the office. "Come on, we can talk inside."

Rebecka followed, and they stood, gathered close, while their father locked the door. Then he turned to them. "I have missed you more than words could ever say." He stepped forward, pulled them into a group hug, and then stood back and looked at each, in turn. "My boys, look at you two, you're practically adults. I can't believe you're really here. I didn't know that I would ever see you again."

"You can't believe that *we're* here?" Tyler asked, incredulously. "What are you doing here?"

Before he could reply, Toby answered for him. "He's one of them."

Tyler turned to his brother. "What? He's I.I.A.? He can't be." Then he turned to his father. "Is it true? Are you really with them?"

"It's complicated. Not everything is always as it seems."

"But, you *are* with them?"

"I am, but please, give me a chance to explain, before you judge."

With a note of disdain, Toby asked, "Did you know that they've been keeping me here?"

"I just found out. That's why I'm here."

"So, you didn't help to plan my capture?"

"God no! That's why I left you boys in the first place. I knew that if I stayed with you, the agency would pick you up in no time. I didn't want you to grow up under a microscope and get dragged into all of this."

Tyler frowned. "You knew that we were...different?"

Their father nodded. "Yes. I knew from the time you were babies. Please, have a seat and allow me to explain."

Two sofas faced each other, with a coffee table in between. Tyler, Toby, and Rebecka sat on one, facing the door; their father sat on the other.

"I know that you must have a thousand questions. I'll try my best to answer them. To start with, I left you with your grandmother, after your mother passed away, because I knew she would take good care of you. I got hired on with the agency when you were babies. As time went on, I was required to travel more often. My job was to look after trackers, keep tabs on them, and follow up on potential students that they located.

"Once I knew, without a doubt, that your gifts far exceeded the guidelines of the I.I.A., I knew I had to leave you, for good. If I had kept you in my life they would have snagged you up, and I wouldn't have been able to stop them.

"When I found out that you were placed into the foster system, I wanted to come and get you, but I knew that you were better off without me. I thought that by leaving you, I was keeping you safe, but obviously I was wrong.

"I hope that one day you can find a way to forgive me and understand. I did what I thought was best for you, at the time."

Tyler looked at his brother and silently asked, *What do you think?*

He's telling the truth, Toby thought. *Everything he said is true.* Then he looked at their father. "So, you found out that they captured me. What are you doing here, though? Did you think that they would just let me go if you showed up?"

"I hadn't thought it through. I know you're much too valuable to them, to just let you go, but I had to see you. I thought I might be able to at least convince them to release you to my care. But Tyler, I never expected to find you here. I had heard that they were looking for you, but I hadn't heard that they found you."

"They didn't exactly find me. I found them."

"You came here on your own?"

"Yeah, I wasn't about to leave Toby here, by himself."

Tyler wondered if he should tell their father about their rescue plan, but before he could, Toby thought, *Wait, don't tell him. He sounds honest, and I can't see him doing us wrong, but he still works for them. I don't entirely trust him. We're so close; we can't risk blowing our plan, now.*

But, what if the police get here tomorrow and arrest him? We've just found our father; if he ends up in jail, who knows the next time we'll see him? Shouldn't we at least warn him?

Not yet. Let me sleep on it and see if I can get a vision of what's going to happen. There will still be time, in the morning, if we decide to warn him.

I hope you're right.

I think Toby's right, Rebecka thought. *It's not just our freedom that's at stake. We have to consider everyone else who is held captive here, as well. We need to do what's best for everyone involved.*

Agreed, Tyler thought. *You're both right.*

"Well, I'm glad that I have you both here," their father said. "We'll talk to Henry, tomorrow, and try to figure something out. In the meantime, may I ask what the three of you are doing out of your rooms? What are you up to? And how did you get out? I'm surprised security hasn't picked you up, by now."

Tyler glanced at Toby and Rebecka and smiled. "We were just out exploring."

"Somehow I suspect there's more to your story, but I won't ask. You need to get back to your rooms before anyone discovers that you're gone. I can escort you downstairs."

"No," Tyler quickly cut in, "that won't be necessary. We wouldn't want you to get in trouble, in case anyone sees you with us. We managed to get out of our rooms without being seen. We can get back in." The last thing he wanted was for their father to discover that they had an access card. That would require questions that they weren't prepared to answer.

"Okay then...if you're sure."

"Don't worry about us," Toby said. "Where will you go? You'll be here in the morning?"

"Don't worry; I'll be right here. I'm not going to leave you."

They stood and followed their father to the door. He hugged them again, and they quickly made their way back to their rooms. Uncertain how long the guard would be asleep, they didn't want their night time escapade to be discovered. Within a few hours, if all went as planned, the Mexican police would find them, and they didn't want their plan to be hampered in any way.

Now, as Tyler lay in bed, he pondered their new dilemma. Should they take the risk and forewarn their father or allow him to be arrested? Rebecka had been right; it wasn't just their freedom at stake. There were other residents at the compound who might want the opportunity to return home, as well.

You still awake? Toby silently asked, from his room.

Yeah, I can't stop thinking about him. All these years, I thought that he had just left, that he didn't care about us.

I know. I keep asking myself why I couldn't see the truth about him.

Probably because you didn't try. We both just accepted the fact that he was gone. We were so young when he left. I don't think it ever occurred to either of us to find out where he was. Tyler's thoughts were silent, for a moment, and then he asked, *What do you think we should do? Should we tell him?*

I want to. I want to believe that we can trust him. I'll sleep on it and see if I can come up with an answer. Try to get some rest;

it's going to be a long day.

*****

"How's the ankle?" Jesse asked, in the morning.

"Feels a hundred percent better," Tyler replied. He stood slowly, rotated his ankle a couple of times for good show, and then said, "Must have just been a temporary strain."

"Well, that's good. Glad to hear it. Henry wants to see you and your brother, first thing this morning. I told him that I'd bring you guys up to his office."

"He wants to see us both?" This was good news. With Toby by his side, they could visit their father before they saw Henry. He immediately began to communicate with Toby to form a plan.

"You ready?" Jesse asked.

"Sure, lead the way."

They followed Henry's second in command down the hall, and by the time they reached the security room, the plan was in place.

The Federales just passed by, on the road, Liliana thought. *They should reach the compound soon.*

Perfect timing, Tyler thought, in return. They were about thirty feet from the security room. *We're getting ready to do something.*

You're getting ready to do something? You're not going to do anything stupid are you? What are you up to?

I'll let you know if it all goes as planned.

And what if it doesn't all go as planned? When he didn't respond, she thought, *Tyler? Please be careful.*

No worries. I'll talk to you later.

Toby grinned and thought, *I think your girlfriend's worried about you.*

She has nothing to be worried about. Are you ready to do this? They were ten feet from the security room.

Jesse reached the first step and then stopped and turned when he realized that Tyler and Toby no longer followed. They had stopped in front of the security room. "What's up, guys? Let's go."

Toby pointed toward the door. "What's in here?"

"That's where Security monitors all of the surveillance cameras. Come on guys, Henry's waiting."

"That sounds cool, can we see?" Before Jesse had a chance to respond, Toby knocked on the door.

Jesse's eyes narrowed with suspicion. "What are you up to?" He stepped off of the stairs and walked toward them.

"We're not up to anything," Tyler said. "Don't mind my brother. He's always too curious for his own good."

When the door opened, the security guard emerged with his hand held to his forehead. "Oh, hey there, Jesse. Man I have the worst headache. I must be getting sick; I think I might have fallen asleep. Don't tell the boss-man; he'll have my head."

"Let me drop these two off upstairs, and I'll send someone down to relieve you," Jesse told him.

Tyler glanced at his brother. *Are you ready?*

Let's do it.

Tyler leaned casually against the wall and focused on the security system, within. A moment later, an alarm from inside the room began to blare. The guard glanced at Jesse and then hurried inside to see what had triggered it.

Toby took a step toward Jesse. "Don't you want to go see what the problem is?"

"Yeah, but I shouldn't—"

"Don't worry about us. Go ahead. You should check it out."

Tyler could feel his brother's influential energy take ahold of Jesse and defy the agent's knowledge that he shouldn't leave the boys alone.

"You're right," Jesse said. "I should check it out. Stay right here, okay?"

"We won't go anywhere," Toby assured him.

The moment that Jesse stepped inside of the room, Tyler grabbed the access card from his pocket, and with a quick swipe, the door closed.

"Now!" Tyler said. They would have to act fast before Jesse or the guard had time to notify anyone to come to their rescue. Together, they placed their hands on the door and focused.

The goal was to scramble and confuse all electromagnetic waves within the room. They would fry the batteries in the cell phones and walkie-talkies, and put the surveillance monitors, computers, landline telephone, and most importantly, the access pad for the door, out of commission.

"I think we did it," Tyler said, a minute later.

"Are you sure?"

He paused to listen to the thoughts of the men, inside the room. "Yeah, they're totally confused. Listen."

Toby closed his eyes, in concentration, and then opened them a few moments later and smiled. "Good. Hopefully no one will find them for a while."

"Well, even if they do, it will take some fixing before they'll be able to get the door open. By then, the Federales should be here. Ready to go find Dad?"

"Let's go."

By the time they reached the first step, hollers from within the security room called out to them. Jesse and the guard must have realized their unlucky predicament. Tyler glanced back and then turned to Toby and smiled. Then, they bounded up the steps in search of their father.

*****

Toby had a vision that their father would help them, and that cinched the decision to let him in on their plan. When the door opened, he peered into the hall and then raised his eyebrows in question. "You're on your own again? What are you two up to this morning?"

Tyler smiled. "Can we come in?"

"Of course." He ushered them inside. "I've been trying to think what I can say to Henry so that he'll let me take you boys out of here.

"Um...we kind of have another plan," Tyler said.

"You do?"

"Yeah, I didn't just come to Mexico to join Toby. I came here to break him out and shut this place down."

"You plan to shut it down? How?"

"With a little help from the Federales."

Their father shook his head. "The Federales have specific orders to stay away."

"I know, but they've been given some information that they can't ignore. They'll be here in a few minutes to check it out. And once they find a bunch of kidnapped, American kids, they'll have to help us."

"You're sure?" He frowned and narrowed his eyes in concern.

"Yep, our friends are out in the woods and just reported that the police passed by, on the road, a few minutes ago. That's why we came to see you. You need to get out of here."

"You know the compound won't shut down, for good. They'll just relocate somewhere else, in a few months. Most of the kids who are here willingly work for them."

"We know," Toby said. "But, there are a few who don't want to be here, who were taken completely against their will, like I was. They deserve to return home, to their families."

"The agency will retaliate," their father warned. "They aren't going to let you wander free, without a fight. You know too much, and you are much too valuable to them."

"They'll let us go." Tyler pulled the flash drive out of his pocket and held it up. "We have enough evidence on here to prove everything they've ever done wrong and pinpoint everyone who's ever been involved. If anything ever happens, to any of us, all of this information will be sent public. They can't afford to let that happen."

"Wow, it looks like they underestimated you boys. Okay then, let's get out of here before the Federales arrive."

"We can't go with you," Tyler said.

"What do you mean you *can't* go with me? I can't leave you here."

"We have to make sure that Henry knows we have this information."

"Yeah? And what if he decides that he's not going to let you go? I know him well. He's not one who easily gives in, without a fight. I can't take the risk that he'll hurt you."

"He won't hurt us," Toby said. "I've seen the future. If we time it just right, the Federales will show up and take him."

"And what if you don't time it just right?"

"Well then, I guess we better not mess up," Tyler said.

"You need to get going," Toby said. "There's not much time left."

Their father sighed and with obvious reluctance said, "Okay, but I *will* find you boys, again. Please, trust that I will. I won't let you go back to that foster family." He turned and started for the door.

"Wait," Tyler called out.

He took his hand off of the door and turned. "Yes?"

"Our friends are hiding in the woods, up the road. They came here to help me find Toby, but they don't have passports or a way to get back into the states. Can you help them?"

"Of course. I know of a border tunnel that we can use."

Toby raised his eyebrows in question. "A border tunnel?"

"Sure, border patrol agents discover tunnels all of the time. They're used for smuggling drugs and illegal immigrants. Sometimes the tunnels get closed up, but other times the government takes them over for their own purposes. The I.I.A. has a few tunnels here and there. It shouldn't be too difficult to get your friends home safe."

"Thank you," Tyler said. "I'll let Liliana know that you're coming. Will you be able to get out of here, though? I imagine the Federales are close."

"Don't worry. There are a few tunnels that lead out, to other exits, in the woods. I'll be long gone before the police arrive."

After a goodbye hug, the boys parted ways with their father and strode down the hall to Henry's office.

When he opened the door, Henry frowned and narrowed his eyes with suspicion. "Where's Jesse?"

Tyler shrugged. "I don't know. He told us to come see you."

"Did he? I'll have to have a talk with him later, I see. Well, you're here at least. Come on in and have a seat. Let's talk."

Tyler took the chair that he had sat in the previous evening, and Toby sat beside him.

"So, boys, have you given any thought to working with me? You have a lot to offer the agency."

"We've thought about it," Tyler said, "and it comes down to this. What if we decide that we don't want to work for you? Can we just go home? Or, what if we decide that we do want to work for you but then decide in a year that it's not for us. Can we just get out whenever we want?"

Henry leaned back in his chair, folded his hands, and smiled. "Those are complicated questions."

"No, really...they're not. Either we can get out or we can't. It's a fairly simple answer."

"I hear that you boys have some concerns; that's understandable. Let me get a cup of coffee, and then I'll try to explain the situation, the best I can, okay?"

"Go ahead." Tyler glanced at Toby and smiled.

Henry strode to a side counter and grabbed a mug. "Would you boys like a cup?"

Tyler shook his head. "No, thanks."

"I'm good," Toby replied.

He resumed his seat, swiveled his chair so that he faced them, and took a sip of coffee.

"I'm guessing that you aren't prepared to just let us walk," Tyler said. "This is just a little insurance to make sure that you leave us alone." He held the flash drive up for Henry to see.

The next sip of coffee missed his mouth and spilt onto his pristine, white, collared shirt. "What's on that?" he sputtered.

"Oh, just about any and all information on the I.I.A. that you'd never want the public or any other government agency to find out about."

"It's a bluff. There's nothing on that disc. You don't have access to get into the main system."

"Why? Because we would need an access card, like this one?"

He held up the small, plastic card.

"Where did you get that?"

"It doesn't matter. What does matter is that we have all of the proof we need. So, you *will* let us go, and you'll make sure that the agency leaves us and all of our friends alone, because if anything should happen to any of us, all of the information on this little disc will be sent to the media."

"So, what's stopping you? Why not just take it straight to the public?"

"We're under no illusion that the agency is just going to fold under and close up shop. If we went to the media, now, it might cause a hiccup or two in operations, but you'll just reopen, somewhere else, and continue on with your work. Once that happens, you'll come after us, again.

"We're better off this way," he continued. "You let us go, the compound closes down, and we go on with our lives like we never met you. As long as we never hear from the agency again, we stay quiet."

"And I'm supposed to believe that? I'm supposed to just close the compound and let you walk? You can't really think I'm going to let that happen, do you?"

"No," Tyler said. "We didn't really think you would just let us go. That's why the Federales are on their way. We figured, once they find us, *they'll* let us go."

"You aren't serious? We have an agreement with the Mexican government. They won't touch us."

"Never say never," Toby said. "Just wait. They should be here soon."

Just then, the phone on the desk rang. Henry picked up the receiver and snapped at the recipient on the other end. "What is it?" He was silent for a moment and then said, "Right, and you've tried to call?" He listened again and then said, "Okay, I'll go check myself."

He hung up the phone and looked at the boys. "Apparently the police are outside, and my guard in the security room didn't notify anyone. Do you know anything about that?"

INDIGO INCITE

The boys smiled and shrugged.

"We need to go for a little walk."

"Where?" Toby asked. "The police are already here."

"There are a few exits that they don't know about. We should still have time. Let's go." He pulled a gun out from under his desk and aimed it at them.

Tyler sucked in his breath. *Do you still see a way out of this?* He silently asked his brother.

Toby was silent for a moment and then thought, *Um...yeah. Just a few more seconds and we'll be good.*

"Come on, boys." Henry waved the gun toward the door. "Let's walk. First, I'll take that disc off your hands." He walked around the desk, aimed the gun at Tyler, and held out his other hand for the flash drive.

Any second, huh? Tyler thought. *Are you sure about that?*

Um, yeah. Right about n— Toby's thought was interrupted by a knock at the door, and before Henry had a chance to put his gun away, an I.I.A. security guard entered, followed by three members of the Federales.

"I am Chief Morales with the Mexican Police. What is going on here?"

"What are you doing here?" Henry demanded. "This is my private office and property of the United States Government."

"The United States Government does not own property in Mexico," the chief corrected. "They simply lease the land. We have every right to be here."

"That may be, but we have an agreement with your government that you won't disturb us. Our business here is private."

"That is true," the chief said. "Unless we hear that you are breaking one of our laws, then we have the responsibility to check it out. We have word that there are kidnapped American children."

Henry must have realized that he still held his gun, because he hastily tucked it into his back waistband.

The chief turned to Toby. "Have you been kidnapped?"

255

"They weren't kidnapped," Henry interrupted. "They are criminals. Our agency has arrested them under suspicion of a threat to national security."

The chief eyed Toby with curiosity. "Really? Is this true?"

Toby shook his head. "No, Sir. My brother and I were both kidnapped. They've kept us here and we don't know why. You can check it out for yourselves. There are other kids who are locked up, downstairs, too."

"Secure him until we can find out what's going on," the chief said.

The other two uniformed men marched toward Henry. One of the men aimed a gun at him while the other removed the gun from Henry's waistband and handcuffed him.

With his hands secured behind his back, Henry glared at the boys. "You know once the agency hears about this, they'll have me out and back home, in no time. We'll just relocate somewhere else."

"You're probably right," Tyler said. "And we trust that once you do make it home, you'll make sure that the agency leaves us alone...Liliana, Grace, Eddie, Sarah...all of us. You might go on with your work, but we're going to go on with our lives."

"Would you kids like to come with me?" the chief asked.

"Absolutely," Tyler said. "We're ready to go home."

EPILOGUE

"Boys, go ahead and grab your bags. If you'll just follow me, your room will be on the second floor."

Tyler and Toby each grabbed their two large duffel bags, which contained all of their personal belongings. They followed the guidance counselor out of her office and down the hall to the stairs, which would lead to their new room.

The Portland, Oregon boarding school housed students from around the world, and the twins were thrilled to be able to call it home. For some, the school meant confinement and rigidness, a residence filled with rules and proper etiquette. To the twins, it represented freedom, a place of independence.

The counselor glanced over her shoulder, to ensure that they followed, and then continued down the hall. "I have to say, it is unusual for students to transfer to our school, mid-year. We do make special exceptions, on occasion, but usually only for students whose parents are, what you might call, influential. Now don't get me wrong, we pride ourselves upon the confidentiality of our students. We understand that many come to us because they desire privacy. So, please understand, if you ever want to share anything with me about where you come from or who your parents are, the information would be kept strictly confidential."

She stopped and turned to the boys with an inquisitive gaze. Tyler knew that she wanted information. Their arrival, almost at the end of the school year, along with a very generous donation to the school, from an anonymous donor, had left the guidance counselor more than a little curious. The boys simply smiled.

"Ah, I see you'd rather not talk about it. I understand. Just know that I'm here anytime you need someone to talk to." They reached the second floor and arrived to the room that they would call home, for the next two years. It wasn't large, but it was comfortable and would suit their needs. "So, here we are. I'll let you get settled in. Dinner is at six, downstairs, in the dining hall. I've given you your class schedules. You'll find them in your folders. School starts at eight, tomorrow morning. Do you have any questions before I go?"

"Um, yeah," Tyler began, "just one. What's the policy about weekend travel?"

"Well, we offer a variety of weekend getaways for our students. We do backpacking trips into the mountains and excursions into the city to visit museums. They are all voluntary, of course, but we like to encourage our students to participate as much as possible."

"That sounds like fun. What I was curious about though was if we are allowed to go off on our own, for the weekend."

"Oh, well, weekend travel on your own isn't encouraged, but it certainly isn't prohibited, either. If you did leave for the weekend, you would need signed, parental consent, and you would have to be back to school on Sunday evening, by seven. If your parents don't live around here, they may fax a written consent. You would have to provide your own transportation."

"That's not a problem. Our dad left us a car to use."

The counselor smiled. "Well, great then. Do you plan to visit friends in the area?"

"Seattle," Tyler told her. "I have a friend, in Seattle."

✶✶✶✶✶

Toby sat in the window seat and gazed out of the rain speckled, dorm room window. The tall, lush, green trees were a welcome change from the brown desert of Arizona that he had always known. It seemed appropriate that he would start out his new life in a new state. A future, filled with endless possibilities, welcomed him with open arms.

He thought about Rebecka and the future. Though their time together had been short, they had definitely shared an undeniable connection, which he would like to further explore. He would be a junior next year. Two more years of school and after that, well, who knew? Perhaps he would go to college, in California.

When his cell phone rang, he didn't have to look to know who it was. He answered with a smile in his voice. "Hi there, I was just thinking about you."

"I know," Rebecka said and then laughed. "I heard your thoughts, but I figured I would call, like a regular friend. We've never really just talked on the phone before. It's kinda fun, huh?"

Toby smiled. "Yeah, it's good to hear your voice. How are things going?"

"I'm back to school. My guidance counselor worked things out so that I can take some summer classes and get caught up. I'll be able to start out next school year as a Senior. Isn't that great?"

"That is great. Just one more year of school, huh?"

"And then college, I guess. So, did I hear that you were thinking about coming down here, to go to college with me?"

Toby laughed. "You really were listening to my thoughts. Yeah, the idea crossed my mind. What do you think?"

"I would be more than thrilled. Of course, I don't know what my parents would think. My last dating experience left me kidnapped; I don't think they're going to allow me to see any boys until I'm thirty. But, don't worry, I'm sure once they meet you, they'll like you as much as I do."

"You like me?"

"You know I do. You're a wonderful friend."

"A friend." It was a simple statement to test the waters.

"You're more than just a friend."

"Oh yeah? More than a friend?" Toby closed his eyes and envisioned Rebecka. She lay against a giant stack of pillows, on her bed, and grinned.

She laughed. "Why do I feel like that's a trick question? Alright, I'll say it. I like you. I like you a lot...more than just a friend. I miss you already and can't wait to see you, again."

"I like the sound of that. I'd like to see you again, too. Of course, I can see you right now. You're lying on your bed and you're wearing huge, fuzzy, pink slippers."

"You *can* see me! That's not fair. I wish I could see you, too."

"Can you? I mean, do you think you could do your thing and transport yourself here?"

"I don't know. I've never tried to travel over such a long

distance. I'm not sure what would happen. That's why I never tried to escape the compound; I was scared I might end up in limbo or something. Maybe I could practice. I could try to teleport a little bit further each time. In the meantime, take a picture of yourself and send it to my phone, so I can see you. Okay?"

"I will," Toby promised.

"Thanks. I'd better go. Dinner's ready. You take care, okay? I miss you."

"I miss you, too."

*****

"Grace, Honey! Come downstairs. Derek is here," her mother bellowed.

"Coming!" Grace called back. She had hoped that she wouldn't have to face her boyfriend until school on Monday, but that apparently would not be the case. She took a quick survey of herself in the mirror. She wore no make-up, her hair was pulled back in a messy ponytail, and she wore a baggy sweatshirt and athletic pants. It occurred to her that she didn't care what she looked like. She no longer felt the need or desire to impress Derek.

Then, she suddenly realized that Derek was downstairs, alone with her parents. After she had been so careful to cover her tracks, to make her parents believe she had gone to Florida on the band trip, it would take only one conversation with Derek to ruin everything.

She darted out of her bedroom and practically flew down the stairs. She came to a sudden stop in the entryway, out of breath, and faced her mother and Derek.

At her abrupt entrance, her mother turned to her with raised eyebrows. "Well hi, Grace. I didn't exactly mean for you to come downstairs quite so quickly. You only saw Derek yesterday. Do you miss him that much already?"

"Oh," Derek began, "well actually, Grace and I haven't seen each other since—"

Grace quickly cut him off, "We haven't seen each other in what seems like forever. Come on, Derek. Let's go out to the front

260

porch. We can talk there."

"Oh...uh...okay." He reluctantly followed her outside. Grace knew that he wanted to go up to her bedroom, where they would have more privacy. She decided that the front porch would be a better location for what she was about to say.

He sat close beside her on the swinging bench. She scooted a few inches away and turned to face him.

"So, how have you been?" he asked. "I really missed you on the trip. I wish you could have come."

"Yeah, I think it was good that I stayed behind. It gave me time to think and reflect on life. You know? I realized what's important and what I want my future to be like."

"Um, how come I get the feeling I don't like where this conversation is going? When you say future, am I included in that future of yours?"

"Derek, you know I like you. I always have. You're a wonderful friend."

"Oh...this is the part where you say you just want to be friends, isn't it?"

"Sort of...I'm sorry, Derek. I've tried. I just feel like you're more of a brother to me than anything else. You're a great friend, and I don't want to lose your friendship. I understand if you don't want to ever see me again, but if we can still be friends I'd really like it."

"Is there someone else? Did you meet someone else, while I was in Florida?"

"No." Grace realized it was a lie when an image of Eddie immediately popped into her mind. "I've felt this way for a while. It's just...I meant what I said. I don't want to lose your friendship."

"Is there anything I can say to make you reconsider?"

She shook her head. "No, I'm sorry."

He stood then.

"Are you leaving?"

"Yeah, I need some time alone. I don't want to lose your friendship either, Grace. I need to think right now, but I'll see you on Monday. Okay?"

"Absolutely. I'll see you at school."

She walked back into the house, slowly closed the door, and leaned against it. She hated to break Derek's heart, but at the same time, she felt a huge sense of relief.

Her mother poked her head out of the kitchen. "Where's Derek? Is he staying for dinner?"

"Uh, no, Mom. We kind of broke up."

"You did what? Why?"

"It just didn't feel right, you know? I tried, but I knew that it would never work out between us. I figured it was best to just end things now before it went on any longer."

"Oh, Honey, I'm sorry."

"It's fine, Mom. I'm happy. Derek will be happy, too, once he realizes it's for the best. He'll find someone who's just right for him before he knows it. I want to be alone for a little bit. I'm going up to my room until dinner's ready. Okay?"

She dashed upstairs and closed her bedroom door before her mother had a chance for further comment. She sat on her bed and picked up her phone. Should she call Eddie? What would she say to him, if she did? She knew that he had felt something for her when they had shared a dance, in Mexico. The look in his eyes and his aura had been undeniable proof that he had feelings for her.

She found his name under her contacts but then second guessed herself and tossed the phone onto the bed. What was she thinking? She had just broken up with her boyfriend. Shouldn't she at least wait a day until she called him? Then again, who ever said there was a certain protocol to follow after you broke up with someone? She picked up her phone, again, found Eddie's number, and before she had a chance to think twice, she called.

*****

"Welcome back. How was your little excursion with your friends?"

Eddie set his notebook on the lab counter and turned to see Jenna's familiar smile. He had known that he would see her soon;

he had just hoped that it wouldn't be today. He wanted to dive headfirst into his homework and not have to dwell on any thoughts of girls for a day or two.

"Hi there, yourself," he said. "How have you been?"

"Not bad. Class has been dreadfully boring without you there to keep me company. I can't believe you missed more than a week of school. I don't think I'd ever be able to get caught up on my work if I missed that much."

"Yeah, it'll be rough, but I figure a couple of late night study sessions, and I should be back on track."

"Well, I'd be happy to help. You could come over to my place, we could order a pizza, and I could help you make some flash cards or something." Her tone was flirtatiously sweet, and she wore a playful grin.

Any guy that he knew would jump at the chance to have a private study session at Jenna's place, and yet he couldn't help but think about Grace and Sarah. *What I need*, he thought, *is to swear off all girls completely, for a while.* He didn't want to drive Jenna completely away, but he needed time to figure out his life before it became complicated with a girl, any girl.

"I appreciate the offer, but I think I should do this on my own. I want to just sit down and get it done. If I studied with you, I would be too tempted to talk and get sidetracked."

The disappointment was apparent in her expression. "Oh, okay. Well, if you change your mind, I'm just a phone call away. Do you mind if I join you, now? I just came to the lab to finish up a little bit of work."

"Sure, I don't mind. Pull up a stool." In truth, he really did want to be alone, but he wasn't about to throw her off twice in one day.

"So, did your friends go home, already?"

"Yeah, they all had to get back to school, too."

"Oh, well that's too bad. Maybe next time they're in town we can all hang out and I can meet them."

"Sure, they'd like to meet you."

He turned back to his project. He just wanted to work, but a moment later she asked, "Where did you guys go? You said you were going to show them the sights."

"Oh, um, we went to the Grand Canyon and spent a couple of days there, and then we toured Sedona."

"Sounds like fun."

"Yep, we had a good time." He kept his response brief and to the point. He hoped that she would get the hint.

With his back to her, he was thankful she couldn't see his face. He rolled his eyes and sighed. Obviously, he wouldn't find peace and quiet in the lab today. Before she had time to ask another question, his phone rang. *Saved by the bell*, he thought. Maybe she would get lost in her work and forget about him by the time he got off the phone.

He took his phone out of his pocket and looked to see who called. It was Grace. *From one girl to the next*, he thought with a sigh, and yet he realized that he was excited at the idea that he would hear her voice, again.

"I've got to take this," he told Jenna, then he stood and walked to the window. "Hey, Grace. How are things back home?"

"Everything's great, more than great actually. How are you?"

"Ugh, well, you know, it's good to be home, but I'm now faced with enough homework to last a week. But I'm sure you know; you probably have a ton of homework too, huh?"

"Yeah, I've got quite a bit. I've been working on it all weekend. I just wanted to take a quick study break and call to say, hi. After spending all day, every day, with you and everybody else, it seems strange to suddenly be so far apart, you know?"

"Yeah, I know." He realized that as much as he had tried not to admit it, to himself, he missed her.

"Liliana invited all of us to come see her, this summer. Do you think you might go?"

He wanted to see her; and yet, he also wanted to see Sarah. *Okay, maybe I don't know what I want*, he told himself. Perhaps a few months would help to clear his head.

He didn't want to get her hopes up, so he said, "Yeah, we'll see. I don't know for sure yet what I'll have going on, but if nothing else comes up I might be able to go." It was a vague answer, but for now it was the best he could do. Grace was an incredibly beautiful, sweet, and caring girl, and the last thing he wanted to do was get her hopes up and then break her heart.

The disappointment in her voice was clear. "Okay, well you know we would all love for you to come. It wouldn't be the same without you, so at least promise you'll think about it."

"I will," he said. Then he added, "You know you can call me, anytime."

"Thanks. I appreciate that."

He knew that Jenna undoubtedly had one ear focused on his conversation, so he said simply, "And please, call me if you ever hear from any of our friends from Mexico. I'm always here for you."

"You're a good friend, Eddie. The same goes with you, call me anytime, okay?"

"I will. I'll talk to you soon. Bye, Grace."

"Bye, Eddie."

He looked out the window and sighed. He would like nothing better than to tell Grace that he liked her, but she was in high school. The last thing she needed was a long distance relationship with a college student in another state. Time was what he needed, he told himself. Hopefully, in time, everything would figure itself out.

*****

"Hi, Tyler!" Liliana answered the phone, on the first ring. "How are you? Did your dad finally find a school for you to attend?"

"Yep, it's great. I can't tell you how wonderful it feels to not be under the watchful eye of my foster family. The only thing that would make it better is if you were here, with me."

"I wish we were closer. Where are you anyway?"

"Hey, before I forget," Tyler interrupted, "there was a reason that I called."

"You mean, other than the fact that we haven't talked in three days? I was starting to worry about you."

"I know. I'm sorry. With the move and transfer to new schools and everything, I was busy. Forgive me?"

"Of course. So, you were saying? There was a reason that you called?"

"Oh yeah, right. Do you remember that beach that you were telling me about? The one that you wanted to take me to?"

"Yeah. What about it?"

"Well, I was thinking, if you're not busy today, maybe you could go there and I could chat with you, in your mind, like we used to. You could describe the beach and what you see, and it would be like I was there with you. I know it wouldn't be the same, but it would be the next best thing. What do you think?"

Liliana smiled. "I'd like that. I can be there in an hour. I'll contact you when I get there, okay?"

"Sounds good. I'll be waiting."

After she told her mother where she was headed, Liliana rode the bus the short distance to the beach. It was a cloudy, drizzly day, and the beach was nearly deserted. Except for an older, white haired, couple who walked hand in hand along the shore, and two other people further down the sand, she was alone.

I'm here, she thought to Tyler.

I wish we were walking hand in hand right now, like that older couple you just passed, he thought. *Can you describe what you see, so I feel like I'm there with you?*

She continued to walk toward the water's edge, and once she reached it, she began to slowly walk the shoreline. *It's a cold, drizzly day. The water is gray and the waves are rough. There are a couple of seagulls floating on the water, and I can hear a sea lion hollering somewhere, nearby.* She paused her thought and considered about what he had said. Something didn't seem right.

Wait a minute! I never told you that there was an old couple walking hand in hand. How did you know that?

Are you sure? You must have thought it and weren't aware of it.

Hmmm...I guess. She continued her walk. *One day, I'd like to bring you here. If you were here right now, we could walk up to*

266

this little restaurant, go inside and warm up, and get something hot to drink.

That sounds nice. Tell me something else; if I was there with you, right now, would you kiss me?

Liliana smiled at the thought. *Oh, you know I would.*

Kiss me.

Excuse me?

Look up the beach. Tell me what you see.

She looked up, then, and saw a guy walking alone, toward her. He was about thirty yards away and he looked like...*It can't be...It isn't...Is that you?*

You said that one day you wanted to bring me here. One day seemed too far away. I couldn't wait that long.

"Tyler?" she called out. She started to walk faster and then broke into a run. He ran toward her, and the moment they met, she was spun off of her feet and greeted with a passionate kiss. By the time her feet rested on the sand, she felt dizzy with emotion.

"I can't believe you're really here!" she said, breathlessly. "You are here right? I'm not dreaming?"

"I'm here."

"But...how?"

My new boarding school is in Portland. It's just a few hours away. I can drive up here on weekends.

"You're kidding! That's wonderful! Why didn't you tell me?"

"There was no guarantee that we'd get into the school. I didn't want to disappoint you; and then, I decided that I would wait to tell you, because I wanted to surprise you. Are you surprised?" He grinned and kissed her again.

"Yeah, I'm surprised. I'm...beyond words."

"Good, that's what I was going for."

"You're sure this isn't a dream?"

"If it is, then I'm dreaming right along with you."

"You know, this reminds me of a Chinese Proverb that my grandma taught me. It goes, 'If I am dreaming, let me never awake. If I am awake, let me never sleep'. It seems kind of fitting, don't you think?

"Absolutely," he said and kissed her again.

*****

Sarah gazed down at the newborn who slept peacefully in her arms. She smiled and gently kissed the top of his full head of curly, red hair. He had communicated with her so much when she had been pregnant, she hadn't known what to expect from him once he was born, but so far, he seemed like a typical newborn.

Ian had explained that her baby seemed normal because he was overwhelmed with the new sensations of life. Birth for any baby was traumatic. Within the womb, babies never feel cold, or hungry, or tired. After they're born, the world is an overwhelming place to be. He assured her that once the baby got used to things, she would begin to notice his uniqueness.

The door opened, then, and a nurse walked in. "Good morning. How are the two of you doing, today? Were you able to get any sleep?"

"Not much," Sarah admitted.

"Welcome to the world of motherhood. You'll find you won't get much sleep for the next year or so. Amazing what we sacrifice for our children, isn't it? It's all worth it, though."

"Yes, it is." Sarah looked down at him, again. She was aware of the dangers that lurked outside of the hospital walls. Even though the compound, in Mexico, had been disbanded, she was fully aware that the agency still existed, and there were plenty of people who would do just about anything to find her child. And she knew that she would sacrifice her safety in a heartbeat in order to protect him.

In order to protect Trevor and the sanctuary of Roswell, she had returned, to Granite Falls, a week before her due date. She had been aware that waiting so long had been pushing her luck, and it had been a fine balance in the timing. Too long away from Roswell would put herself and the baby at risk, but it would have been a greater risk if he had been born in Roswell. The moment he was born, a paper trail would be created. The announcement of his birth would be public record, and he would need to be issued a social security card and birth certificate. Even though Roswell was a sanctuary, a paper trail would immediately draw the attention of the I.I.A. So, the plan had been formed to return to Granite Falls, only long enough for the birth of the baby and to recover. Then, she would gather the remainder of her belongings, and once again, disappear.

Ian had insisted that he escort her back to Washington and remain by her side. Sarah had tried to refute his offer, but he had been stubborn and wouldn't take no for an answer.

"He'll need my protection," Ian had insisted. "If any trackers come for him, I'm the only one who will be able to sense their presence and get the two of you to safety."

"But once you're away from Roswell, they'll sense your presence, too. You can't risk being captured."

"That's a risk I'm prepared to take. Your baby will be helpless. His safety is more important than my own."

Sarah couldn't argue with that and so had hesitantly agreed that he should join her.

Sympathetic to their cause, Patricia had hired two private security guards to stand outside of her hospital room, around the clock.

There was another knock at the door and the nurse opened it. Sarah smiled and waved at the security guard who hovered behind Ian and her aunt, in the hall. At her wave, the guard nodded and returned to his post.

"With that red hair of yours, I'm guessing that you must be the husband," the nurse said, to Ian, when he and her aunt entered the room.

"Uh, no." Ian looked embarrassed. "I'm a cousin."

"Oh, I'm sorry."

"It's alright," Sarah said. "My husband is overseas, in the military, right now."

"Oh, you poor dear. I'm so sorry. I hope you have some help, at home."

Sarah looked from Ian to her aunt and smiled. She had known that her arrival home, with a man other than her husband, would seem odd, and so she had explained that Ian was her husband's cousin. The red hair made the lie seem plausible. Aunt Mae had welcomed him into her home with open arms.

"Ian and I will help take care of them," her aunt said. She walked to the side of the hospital bed to admire the baby. "He's beautiful, Sarah."

"Thank you." Sarah kissed the top of his head, again, and he opened his eyes.

"What's his name?" the nurse asked.

"Tristan," Sarah replied. "Tristan Daniel. Daniel is my husband's first name."

Aunt Mae smiled. "It's a good name. I'm sure his daddy is very proud. Have you talked to him?"

"Yeah, I was able to get ahold of him last night. He is very happy. He's excited to come home."

"When does he get to come home?" the nurse asked.

"If all goes as planned, it should be in two months. Ian has offered Daniel a job with his business, once he gets out of the military, so we plan to move with him.

She looked into Tristan's eyes and he looked into hers. He was only a day old, and he already looked wise.

Daddy won't be home in two months. The voice in her head was unexpected, and she wondered for a moment if she had heard correctly. She looked up and met Ian's gaze. Her voice faltered when she asked, "Did you hear that?"

His silent nod was answer enough. Tristan had communicated with her. It had begun. *Daddy won't be home in two months*, he had thought. *She didn't want to know what that meant.*

ABOUT THE AUTHOR

Jacinda Buchmann lives in Arizona with her husband and three children. She graduated from Carroll College, in Helena, Montana, with a B.A. in elementary education and later received a Master's degree from Northern Arizona University, in school counseling. After spending several years as a teacher and later a school counselor, she now spends her time writing, any free chance she can get, that is, when she's not spending time with her family or creating a new concoction in the kitchen.

Did you enjoy **Indigo Incite**?

Look for **Indigo Instinct, Book 2 of the Indigo Trilogy**
coming 2014!

Connect with me at:

Facebook: https://www.facebook.com/IndigoIncite
Twitter: https://twitter.com/JacindaBuchmann
Webpage: jacindabuchmann.wordpress.com